3      1st 10$^{y}$

*The Mask of Memory*

BOOKS BY

# VICTOR CANNING

*Mr. Finchley Discovers His England*
*Mr. Finchley Goes to Paris*
*Mr. Finchley Takes the Road*
*Polycarp's Progress*
*Fly Away Paul*
*Matthew Silverman*
*Fountain Inn*
*Everyman's England (travel)*
*Green Battlefield*
*Panthers' Moon*
*The Chasm*
*The Golden Salamander*
*A Forest of Eyes*
*The House of the Seven Flies*
*Venetian Bird*
*The Man from the "Turkish Slave"*
*Castle Minerva*
*His Bones are Coral*
*The Hidden Face*
*The Manasco Road*
*The Dragon Tree*
*Young Man on a Bicycle (and other stories)*
*The Burning Eye*
*A Delivery of Furies*
*Black Flamingo*
*Delay on Turtle (and other stories)*
*The Limbo Line*
*The Scorpio Letters*
*The Whip Hand*
*Doubled in Diamonds*
*The Python Project*
*The Melting Man*
*Queen's Pawn*
*The Great Affair*
*Firecrest*
*The Rainbird Pattern*
*The Finger of Saturn*
*The Runaways*
*Flight of the Grey Goose*
*The Painted Tent*
*The Mask of Memory*

# The Mask of Memory

VICTOR CANNING

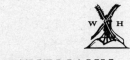

HEINEMANN : LONDON

William Heinemann Ltd
15 Queen Street, Mayfair, London W1X 8BE

LONDON   MELBOURNE   TORONTO
JOHANNESBURG   AUCKLAND

First published 1974
© Victor Canning 1974
SBN 434 10785 9

MADE AND PRINTED IN GREAT BRITAIN BY
MORRISON AND GIBB LTD, LONDON AND EDINBURGH

CHAPTER ONE

WITHOUT ANY AWARENESS of what she was doing Margaret Tucker picked up a packet of brightly coloured, cellophane-wrapped boiled sweets and dropped them into the pocket of her light overcoat. Against her forehead was a warm pressure as though a large, familiar hand had been placed there, a hand she welcomed for the slow spasm of comfort it gave her. The store was a long, brilliantly lit cave of delights, the people moving about it suddenly silent, remote figures in an innocent dream. Nowhere was there any threat, any ache, any loneliness.

She added a slab of chocolate to the sweets in her pocket. On the wrapper a brown and white cow stood in deep meadow grass. She moved slowly down the filled racks and took three more packets of sweets, waiting once patiently for another buyer to move on so that she could take a particular brand which had caught her eye. Armoured against thought and reality by the soothing, obliterating hand on her forehead, she drifted between the stalls, stopping once to finger the material of a blouse hanging from a floor stand. Then, unhurried, untouched by guilt or shame, she went out of the place without paying.

She walked down the main street, turned off through the walk that cut through the yard of St Peter's Church and so to the car park. She unlocked the door of her small car. With a little awkwardness, for she was a tall woman, she slid into the driving seat and fidgeted for a second or two disposing her loose coat comfortably around her. As she did so her right hand palmed the bulk of her pocket and she heard the sharp protest of cellophane.

In that moment the comforting pressure against her forehead was withdrawn, awareness returned and with it the birth of a swift, familiar agony. She sat in the driving seat, staring straight ahead of her as the rare but recognisable panic symptoms hit her. Her body trembled with a sudden violence. She shut her eyes against it and felt the warmth of tears escape and touch the length of her cheeks as she said to herself, "Oh, dear God . . . dear God."

A man walked across the front of the car and glanced her way. She quickly dropped her head to hide her tears, pretending to be occupied with fitting the car key into the ignition lock. Her hand shook, trembling with a violent life of its own.

The man passed on, moving up the row of parked cars towards his own. He sucked at a short pipe, the stem of which had been cracked and mended with a twist of black insulating tape. He had seen Mrs Bernard Tucker in the store and had followed her, without haste or fear of losing her, to the car park. It was not the first time he had witnessed one of her occasional shoplifting activities. He knew, too, that she had no financial need to steal. So far some benign guardian angel had protected her from discovery. As he was cynical about guardian angels he knew that some time or other hers would let her down. He got into his own car and pulled a notebook from the dash pocket. He flipped it open to a section which was headed in capitals, MARGARET TUCKER, turned over two or three pages filled with notes and then began to add more notes. As he wrote he saw Margaret Tucker's car drive out of the park. For a few moments he wondered if he would follow her. He decided against it. He knew exactly where she was going. Her routine on the afternoons of Monday, Wednesday and Friday was always the same. Billy Ankers did not believe in wasting time confirming regular routines. In his opinion Mr Bernard Tucker was wasting his money.

By the time she was through the town and out on the

2

estuary road Margaret Tucker had recovered. Brief though her shame was on these occasions when she became aware of what she had done, aware that for a few minutes she had acted, without realising it, like a common thief, the swift passage to composure left her drained and lazily exhausted in mind and body. There was something almost drowsily voluptuous in the aftermath . . . as if, though she always tried to push the comparison from her mind, she had just been loved, deeply and physically and satisfyingly by a man. She pushed the thought from her now, a puritan spurt of self-censure shivering through her body.

She drove the six miles of road along the estuary through an urban sprawl of housing estates, motels and caravan parks. The October sun burned high in a clear sky and two jet fighters from the R.A.F. station drew wind-shredded trails across it in fast fraying ribbons. The tide was half in, sweeping rapidly over the last sand banks in mid-stream. Where the two rivers met and the tide fronted their outflowing waters a cloud of gulls wheeled noisily in the air. Beyond the golf course which occupied the first footings of the long westward stretch of dunes and marshes, she turned down to the beach and left her car in the park. The holiday season was over now and there was only a handful of vehicles in the place.

She climbed the dune above the beach and dropped down to the summer-filthy stretch of sand that awaited the winter gales to cleanse it. The beach stretched westwards three miles to the estuary mouth, the far waters lost in a low, russet haze. A few people, some with dogs, studded the wet hard sand at the tide's edge in pygmy perspective. They would mostly be residents like herself, glad to have the long vistas and lonely sweeps of dune, marsh and burrows restored to them. She pulled off her woollen tam o'shanter and stuffed it into her pocket, the left one, still well aware of the sweets in the right-hand one.

The steady on-shore wind lifted her fair hair and blew loose sand into the corners of her pale blue eyes and made them

3

water. She walked with long, easy strides over the hard fringe of sand. A straggling crocodile of a dozen small children came down the sands towards her. A nun in a billowing black habit headed them and another brought up the rear.

Margaret Tucker altered her course and moved up the sands to meet the leading nun. She stopped in front of her. The crocodile came to a halt. The children, wrapped up in an assortment of short coats, large-eyed, faces bright and wind-polished, fanned out raggedly between the two nuns.

Margaret Tucker took the sweet packets from her pocket. The nun watched her. This was not the first time it had happened. She blinked her eyes behind steel-rimmed glasses. A small boy who was now sitting down and beginning to dig in the sand with his bare hands looked up at Margaret and grinned cheekily, wrinkling his nose at her.

Margaret Tucker said, "For the children, Sister." She handed over the sweets. The nun took them and they disappeared swiftly somewhere within the voluminous folds of her robe.

"Thank you, madam."

Margaret Tucker moved on. The nuns called to the children, the crocodile came to untidy formation and straggled on. Margaret Tucker held a picture in her mind of the children. Over a dozen of them. All orphans. She could afford easily to adopt one . . . Even Bernard wouldn't object . . . But that was not what she wanted. Suddenly, and it was the first time the thought had ever come to her, she said, "Maybe I steal for the child I want."

The moment of self-pity faded, leaving her amused at her own mawkishness. She walked on with the wind pulsing at her side, sweeping her light coat skirts clear of her legs like untidy, powerless wings.

A mile up the beach she turned away from the shore. She followed a familiar path through the dunes, twisting and turning between patches of yellow-berried buckthorn, dwarf

4

bramble and thorn growths. After a while she came to a shallow hollow, backed by two high dunes whose sides had been worked into sandy, dropping-marked moraines by rabbits. She took off her coat, spread it on the short turf and lay back on it, looking up into the pale blue sky.

From a quarter of a mile away where he lay on the fringe of the dunes above the beach Maxie Dougall saw Margaret Tucker as she stopped briefly to talk to the nun. He sharpened the focus of her image in his fieldglasses, saw the coloured flash of the sweet packets as she handed them over, the pale hand movements of a small girl who stood behind the leading nun, scratching at her ribs through her overcoat, and the bright movement of Margaret's fair hair, caught by the wind, sharp and golden against the slate-grey sweep of wet sands. He swung the glasses from the group and picked up the tide-fringed strip of sand a hundred yards away.

A flock of sanderlings, little white and grey ghosts of birds, worked the water's edge, running and feeding ceaselessly as the returning sea brought life to the beach fringe, stirring shrimp and sandhoppers to activity. Now and again the birds took to the air, wheeling and curving low over the water in a remarkable precision of black and white-barred wing beats. They were here for the winter now, to join the moorland curlews and the oyster catchers working the tide flows. Other migrants were beginning to pass through. There had been dozens of golden plover on the marsh pasture this morning with the lapwings and he had seen knots, dunlin and whimbrels each day for two weeks.

He pushed the glasses into the pocket of his worn pilot jacket and turned to watch Margaret Tucker. He liked the way she walked, a firm, easy stride as though she knew exactly where she was going. He had watched her now for over two years, noting her at first with less interest than he gave to the birds and animals of the dunes and beach, with less interest than he had for a lot of people who came into his view. It was only when the summer crowds went that she fell into her

5

weekly routine. In the summer she might appear at any time. But as the sands and the dunes lost their visitors she came back to a familiar routine. Mondays, Wednesdays and Fridays. Only the worst weather broke that ritual. He knew who she was, and where she lived, he knew her car and its number. To know such things was second nature. He had lived in these parts far longer than she had done.

As she swung to her left from the beach and entered the dunes he knew what her movements would be, just as he knew that when the tide was almost full the sanderlings would rise and stream in a thin, precise echelon across the water to roost on the rocks at the cliff foot on the eastern arm of the bay, and that at midnight a fox vixen would lope a mile across the marshes to work the litter bins in the beach car park, her pickings thinning as the holiday season wore away. Knowing was a passion with him.

He turned over on his back and narrowed his eyes against the sun. He began to think of the three holiday girls he had made love to on these dunes during the summer. He remembered their names, their faces and their bodies, and he knew they were trash and there was no warmth in his memory of them. Suddenly there was a picture in his mind of a recent morning when, lit by the rising of a red sun, he had seen a salmon jump as it came from the sea, running the estuary, hitting the first of the brown-tinged spate water of the East river, and leaping high; a silver mark suspended against the morning like an exclamation from God. No woman could shock and stir his senses with the same bowel-slashing pulse of delight.

After a while he rolled over and got to his feet. He walked the length of the beach to the car park. In passing Margaret's small car he paused for a moment or two and looked inside. It was neat and clean, no signs of the family rubbish and disorder that marked so many of the cars. There was a paper-back on the dashboard shelf. It was an historical romance. The cover showed a Highland clansman standing on a windswept rock,

6

the wind tearing at his kilt and mantle, in his right hand a sword raised in defiance to a blue and grey bruised sky, his left arm holding to him a slim girl, fair-haired, bare-footed, and wearing a ragged shift that revealed most of her breasts. Blazing across the cover ran the title—BOLD BE MY LOVE.

Smiling to himself he turned away, back along his path. He wondered if that was how Margaret Tucker saw herself? A fair-haired waif from the glens, royal blood unacknowledged in her veins . . . a mess of soothing fantasies, an escape from a too familiar, unexciting morning, noon and night? Probably. He didn't know anyone who wasn't looking for an escape from something, living on the hope or the dream of a richer tomorrow. He did it himself, but it never troubled his sleep. In his dreams he travelled no wild glens in search of plunder, a lost heritage and a bedding with the dispossessed daughter of a chieftain in whose veins ran the blood of kings. He had come from a well organised limbo. Dumped in an orphanage at the age of two, unnamed, unmarked, charity his nurse, but when he had reached the age of twenty-one, the possessor of a monthly remittance whose source was a London solicitor tied to professional secrecy. From pride and contempt—although he accepted the money which lifted him just out of reach of poverty and far from easy comfort—he never once tried to trace the donor. An Irish nun, long dead, who had led him in crocodile line up and down this beach, had named him Maximilian Dougall. Maybe she had felt that the grandness of his name would offset the pettiness of his birth. She was a little mad anyway in her own affectionate fashion, and he had given her all his childish love.

Walking back up the beach, the whistle of sandpipers on the tide edge to his left, he decided—knowing that the decision must have been coiling and uncoiling in his mind for a long time—that he had waited long enough for opportunity to rattle the door latch for entry. He had to make his own opportunity. From all he knew, Margaret Tucker was as good a

7

person to fit his future as any others he had considered. Yet he knew, too, that if he hadn't seen her today he could as easily have picked someone else, some other woman who walked this beach, the dunes, the cliff paths, the moor slopes to the east. Any woman with a reasonably acceptable body and the right background would have suited him.

He turned off the beach and into the dunes where three or four hundred yards away he knew that Margaret Tucker would be sitting or sleeping in her sun-filled, windless hollow.

\*     \*     \*     \*

Billy Ankers had an office over a baker's shop in Allpart Street. The entrance was through a narrow door at the side of the shop. At the back of the office was a long, narrow bedroom with a small kitchen recess which held a gas stove and a yellow-stone sink which served him for all his cooking and washing purposes. At the bottom of the stairs leading up to the office was a small toilet belonging to the bakery, the use of which was granted to Billy in his rent agreement.

Billy was a clean, scrupulously neat and tidy man. In his rooms everything had its place and was kept clean and polished. Billy loved all the things he possessed. When they were broken or damaged he repaired them and went on using them—he did this less from economy, though he was always tight for money, than from an almost physical ache he experienced when something old and well-tried finally outlived its function and he had to throw it away. A smashed cup dropped into the dustbin was some small part of his life gone for ever and he knew it would take him weeks to break in a new one and come to love it. Love for his meagre possessions was a gentle passion with Billy. He was a pleasant man, affable, companionable and quite unscrupulous where money was concerned. Apart from his one-man enquiry agency which was unmarked by any name plate on his entry door, though advertised in the local

8

and county papers as—*William Ankers. Confidential Enquiries. Tel: 083–65397*—he did an intermittent business as a middle dealer, no questions 'asked on either side. Watches, radio sets, poached salmon and venison, silk underclothes, motor parts and tyres—Billy could find a discreet market for them and his commission was reasonable.

He tapped away at an old Royal portable typewriter, composing his monthly report to Mr Bernard Tucker, a man whom he had met only once in his life. He typed meticulously but with no great speed. He did not over-concern himself with the effort of correct spelling because on the whole he was unaware of his mistakes. A little fleur-de-lys of wrinkled concentration marked his brow, a brow that ran sharply back to thinning, sandy-coloured hair laid close to his head without parting. His face was thin, wedge-shaped, the skin a pale olive colour and, for all his thirty-five years, smooth and unmarked as though it were fashioned from polished plastic. His eyes under the faintest smear of sandy brows were large, dark, and bright like sloes which had lost their bloom-haze. His long legs thrust under the table were almost touching a small electric fire on the far side of the table. He loved to keep his feet warm no matter what the season. The feeling now of the fire's heat beating against the leather of his shoes' soles gave him a mild, sensuous pleasure.

There were steps on the stairs and Nancy Barcott came into the room, pushing the door open with a slow swing of her thigh, holding a tray in her hands. On it were a jug of coffee, cup and saucer, and a plate with a large slice of Dundee cake.

Billy stopped typing and pulled the loose top of the paper in his machine over on to the keys so that she could not read what he had written.

"Hullo, Nance."

She put the tray on the desk at the side of the typewriter. "Your bliddy feet'll drop right off one of these days. You can smell the leather burnin' down in the shop."

9

Billy chuckled. "Long as it's only my feet, eh? Warm feet, warm heart, and a warm heart, Nance, is what a lot of people I know could do with."

As he spoke he put his hand under her skirt, running it up her inner thigh over her tights until it was in a position to massage her ample bottom. Nancy took no notice of the caress. She was a short, dark-haired, plump woman in her middle thirties with a pleasant but plain face. She lived with a widowed old mother who was a tyrant but from whom out of an incomprehensible—at least to Billy—loyalty she would not be parted to live on her own. Billy and Nancy loved one another without letting it disturb their lives much. They slept together three nights a week from half-past nine until half-past eleven (if Billy's business commitments allowed). Then Billy drove her back to her mother. Sometimes, if commitments were too frequent, she would come up for half an hour after the shop closed. Both of them knew that when her mother died they would get married, but it was a prospect so remote that they seldom considered it. Mrs Barcott at sixty was as hard and durable as well-seasoned oak.

As Nancy poured his coffee, Billy said, "Got a good price for that load of paint on Thursday. Treat you to a few gins at the pub tonight if you like."

"Can't. Got to take Ma to bingo. It's her night. You'll get a good price from the police one of these days."

"Not me." He moved his hand to an untouched area of her bottom. "You're putting it on, old girl. Too many doughnuts between serving customers."

"If you don't like the goods, stop messin' them about."

She pulled his ear and moved to the door. From a safe distance—because you never knew with Billy—she lifted the front of her skirts, made an obscene gesture and was out of the door, laughing.

Billy chuckled. Then, ignoring his coffee, for he liked it lukewarm, he went on with his typing.

The finished letter read:

*Dear Mr Tucker,*

*Four weeks report on subject up to October 21st. Have carried out random checks as per instructions given 1st August last. All observed routines are normal, except for incident of todays date which is replicker of three others already noted for your kind attention.*

*Subject entered Marks and Spencers Stores, Allpart Street, 1420hrs, spent a few minutes wandering round store and then proceded to confectionary and sweet section at back of shop. Without any attempt to conceal, subject then took four or five items of sale and pocketed same, and then walked back through store without paying. Subject proceded up Allpart Street, through St Peter's churchyard to car park and got into car. Yours truly followed and passing subjects car noticed—without drawing attention to self—that subject seemed temporily upset. Could have been crying. Subject then drove off. Subject followed to North Lobb Burrows and took her usual walk up the sands and then proceded to place of domocile.*

*Again no indication of special aspects as notified by you to watch out for. Random surveys to continue as per your honoured instructions.*

*Yours truly,*

*William Ankers*

*Yours truly.* Well, mostly, Billy told himself. And why not? He couldn't waste too much of his time half-assing off after a woman who clearly had an almost set routine for every day of the week. It was damn funny about the shoplifting, though. About once—sometimes twice—a month. Not always Marks and Sparks. Other stores, too. Walks in, bold as brass, just lifts the stuff and out again. God must look after His own or something because it was a miracle she hadn't been spotted. Not a woman you would overlook, either. Tall, good-looking, all that fair hair and those dreamy, faraway eyes. Must be pushing forty but she still had it all. Though, if he knew his onions, she didn't get much or any chance to use it, but clearly that was what Mr Trusting-I-Don't-Think Tucker was after with his special aspects.

He poured himself coffee, sipped it, and then addressed an

11

envelope for Mr Tucker's letter. Euston Road, London. Graingers Tobacconist. Accommodation address for sure . . .

*    *    *    *

Margaret Tucker came half-awake, her eyes still closed. She lay for a moment or two, hearing the near sound of the sea as the tide ate its way up the beach, and the buzz of a few late bees working the last of the thyme and gorse blooms. She rolled from her side on to her back and stretched her arms, enjoying the aftermath of sleep and the relaxation of her body. The movement drew her skirt well above her knees and she felt a faint current eddy against her legs and touch with idle, light caress the bare flesh above one of her stockings. The flexing of her arms brought her breasts hard against her brassiere, straining against her blouse buttons.

She sat up, opening her eyes. Shaking her head, she ran her hands across her hair to settle it away from her face. As her head came up from the movement she saw the man. He was sitting on a small grass mound on the other side of the hollow, his knees drawn up, his elbows resting on them and his large hands cupping the sides of his face. For a moment a touch of alarm moved through her. The burrows had a bad reputation locally.

As though there were already a settled yet distant relationship between them, the man smiled and gave a little shake of his head.

He said, "It's all right, Mrs Tucker . . ."

Margaret stood up, pulled her skirt straight and brushed loose sand from it. She was embarrassed and a little angry. How dare anyone sit there and watch her while she was sleeping? She realised now that she had seen the man about before . . . indeed vaguely from local talk knew something about him.

Before she could control herself, she said, "Your name's Dougall, isn't it?"

She dropped her eyes and shook her light coat, brushing

12

dried grass from the sleeves. She was wondering how long he had been there, watching her, his eyes on her legs. With a strange certainty she knew exactly the limits of intimacy his eyes had covered.

"That's right. Maxie Dougall. Maximilian, that is. Blame an Irish nun for that." He laughed gently, and the sound brought her eyes to him. It was a slow laugh, marking the swift passage of memories. He jerked his head backwards to indicate the beach. "I used to walk in that orphanage crocodile. I've been around here for quite a few years." He spoke well, not crippling or undervaluing any words, but they all carried the firm touch of the local West Country accent. He grinned. "I see you give them sweets sometimes . . ."

"Only now and then . . ." And having said it, she wondered whether in the times he had seen her before, must have seen her before, he had sat on some dune-top watching her, waiting for some small movement of sleep to expose. . . . A faint shiver made her tauten her shoulder blades to contain it.

Although she was on her feet, he sat still on his mound, his hands now clasped between his legs, his elbows still supported by his widespread knees. She had a swift feeling that his lack of courtesy was maintained as part of some deliberate calculation to rouse her to some emotion which would mark him among other men. She began to move, discarding the nonsense of her thoughts.

From a buckthorn a small bird flirted across the path, a brief exhibition of black head and patches of whiteness before it was gone over the crest of the dunes.

From her right he said something which she could not catch. She halted and had the impression that some stranger inhabiting her body had overridden her own will. She looked at him, poised for movement. In that moment a gulf opened in her mind into which flooded a presentiment that she must go . . . go quickly. It was the same sensation she always got before the comforting hand spread over her forehead and the great peace of confidence and immunity possessed and controlled her.

She stood there, poised, and waited for the warm caress of the hand. But the hand was withheld.

He said, "Stonechat." He was standing now, and a loose, friendly smile spread over his large, sun-tanned face. "The bird. *Saxicola torquata*. His cousins, the whinchats, were here until the beginning of the month, but they're well on their way to Africa by now." Then with a shrug of his shoulders, he went on, "I'm sorry I disturbed you, Mrs Tucker."

She nodded and then moved on. Maxie Dougall watched her go down the dune path and then disappear over the slight crest to the beach. Watching her in the few moments before she had awakened, he had known the swift desire for possession which had marked the beginning of affairs with summer girls . . . the small nakedness, asking for the touch of a hand, above a stocking, the thinnest edge of lace filigreed across a thigh. She was a handsome woman, well-built . . . a fine woman, almost as tall as himself, a woman to measure himself against. But, even so, she wasn't what he had seen. She was married. Maybe he should forget the whole thing and look for the obvious, the easier type, a widow with money. There were plenty about among the retired residents of this place, and plenty that any man would welcome in bed. Then, remembering the rise of her breasts against her blouse as she had roused herself, the swift tangle of fair hair flung back from the pink and white handsome face, he knew that he was committed.

He turned away and began to walk the burrows westwards to his small cottage on the estuary marsh where the two rivers parted.

Margaret Tucker sat in her car without attempting to start it. There was a deep reluctance in her to begin the journey home. Nothing waited for her at home except the monotony of an all too familiar, uncompanionable routine.

Without any strong emotion, she thought, why do you stand it? Who would miss you? Certainly not Bernard. Apart from all else he was seldom at home and when he was . . .

For three years now, and infrequently for long before that, he had not touched her. A housekeeper with a splendid post— the master seldom at home and when he was his demands were minimal, his awareness of her mildly affectionate but never intimate. All that there had been between them of man and woman had died long ago. Not from her wish. But it had gone. Not suddenly but dying away, like a photograph fading. . . . They had never discussed it. She never discussed certain things with Bernard. If she tried he looked at her with a mild stare, and if she persisted—which she had once or twice in the beginning—he would get up and leave the room. Long ago she had once forced him to listen, and he had ended by getting up and walking out of the house. Sometimes, now—when they had settled to their detached, personal existences—she thought that he had gone gently, permanently mad or something. Or that he was impotent and there was a masculine pride in him so twisted that he could not bring himself even to frame the word in his thoughts let alone discuss it with her. Whatever it was, the man she had married long years ago had gone, his place taken by this new Bernard, living his own business life in London and coming home for a weekend which might be gapped by a month, two months . . . there was never any knowing.

As she leaned forward to turn the ignition switch, her eye was caught by the cover of the paper-back which she was reading. She smiled wryly to herself. There had been a time when it was the last kind of book she would have read, a time when love—at least in her reading—needed no specifics. Now she knew, acknowledged with a rueful, even slightly amused eagerness, that she enjoyed the frankness, lingered over it, drawing out with pleasure her physical response to the words, substituting herself with such detailed, awakening fidelity that there had been times when, in a fit of prudish anger, she had thrown a book from her—yet knowing even in the act of rejection that she would come back to it.

For God's sake, she thought angrily as she twisted the key

and the engine fired, what kind of life is this? She drove off with a fierce skidding of rear wheels on the loose grit of the park. She saw the Highland chieftain's left hand, large and firm, cupped vigorously over the girl's bare breast. Big, firm brown hands like the hands of the man who had sat and watched her sleeping. She shivered suddenly, the whole skin of her body electric with the feeling of a man's hands running over her.

\*     \*     \*     \*

He had known the house at Lopcommon for years, from the time when he had been a scholarship grammar school boy, boarded out with foster parents who were kindness itself to him. Yet they had never established any real contact with him because he would take nothing from anyone except of his own choosing. An artificial family life was the last thing he had wanted. He had come up here at night ferreting for rabbits, waiting for the subterranean thud of feet, seeing the burrow mouth net bulge in the dark, then slipping the rabbit free to break its neck with a quick twist of the hands. In summer the heat-lazy adders would sun themselves on the granite outcrops and he would take those, too, with a forked stick jabbed lightning fast to pin them down behind their heads. He killed them and tossed them away, remembering the only dog he had ever owned which had died from one of their bites.

There was mist lying still and heavy over the low ground, but up here the air was clear under the bright starlight of a windless night. He lay on the flat top of a boulder, resting on his elbows, his fieldglasses to his eyes. The house was on the far bank of the narrow combe through which ran a small stream. A low stone wall, broken by a wicket gate, edged the bottom slope of the house lawn with its flanking shrubberies and rockeries. It was a long low white farmhouse, slate-roofed, which had been converted into a country residence many years ago. The main entrance was on the far side by a driveway that ran down from the road which followed the combe crest.

Since talking to Margaret Tucker over a week ago on the burrows, he had watched the house most nights and had walked around it during the day when she was away in the town shopping.

The glasses held the long windows of the lounge. The curtains were carefully drawn but the inner light showed round the vertical edges of the frame in a soft glow. She would be sitting in there reading or watching television. On a night recently, when one of the curtains had been badly adjusted, he had gone down and looked in to see her in an angle of limited vision sitting in her chair reading. When he wanted to he could drift through the night and the darkness with the ease of a fox, with the deliberate, silent naturalness of any night creature. No dog was kept at the house, there were no children and no servants—except a daily who came two or three times a week and was gone by midday. In the summer a jobbing gardener came three times a week for the day. Now in late autumn the man came once a week on a Saturday. Margaret Tucker was clearly not a woman who was worried by loneliness or frightened by being alone at night. It was general knowledge that Mr Tucker, who worked in London—though it was not known clearly at what—was often away for weeks at a time.

The light in the lounge went out. A moment or two later a light was switched on in the bedroom at the far righthand side of the house. The curtains were undrawn. He held the room in focus as Margaret Tucker crossed it and drew the curtains. One day—he knew this with a certainty that held no arrogance —he would know that room.

He lowered the glasses and watched the palely limned cracks of light at the curtain edges. She would be undressing, stripping the clothes from her tall, boldly formed body, shaking out, combing and brushing that fair hair, the mild blue eyes perhaps watching herself in the mirror. The thought triggered a contraction of muscle in him, a fractional response to the sexual tones of his imagery . . . but there was no lust. The time would come when he would take her and know her body and

17

she would know his and tell herself that she loved him. He would wrap her in the web of her own illusions as surely and with as deadly intent as any spider slowly and expertly cocooning some trapped, struggling moth in its web, draping it with silken filaments, adorning and destroying it.

He rolled slowly from his boulder, drew his jacket collar about his neck and walked away. From the far side of the combe a lone curlew called. Far away, above the low mist, the red aircraft warning lights on the power station stacks across the Two Rivers estuary were steady marks for his line across country to the dunes. He saw Margaret Tucker lying asleep in her hollow. Because he planned to use her there was already growing in him a love for her. All possession was a form of love and he saw no contradiction in the fact that he could love the thing which in the end he would have to discard. For a moment she was recreated in the lens of his glasses, fair hair blowing in the wind as she gave sweets to the nun at the head of the crocodile chain of children. He remembered the Irish nun who had him named Maximilian Dougall. When she had died he had wept. He had never known such tears for anyone else, would never know them, if the moment came, for Margaret. Once you had walked in the crocodile chain you were marked apart. All such children know instinctively that charity is a form of conscience money or—though it came later—an offering to the gods for continuing good fortune. When you came into the world unloved, unwanted, was there any wonder that you brought a new and personal form of morality with you?

\*    \*    \*    \*

Propped against her pillows, wearing a silk quilted bed jacket, Margaret was writing in her diary. It was something she did two or three times a week. Generally the entries were brief, little more than an aide memoire to the even flow of weeks and months. Nothing much happened in her life of note or of such personal intimacy that she could confide only in the diary. Nevertheless she kept it locked away in one of the side drawers of the bedroom bureau—to which she alone had a key. Innocuous though the entries were, she would not have liked Bernard to read them . . . could not imagine even that he would be remotely interested in them. A long time ago Bernard had withdrawn into his own world.

She wrote:

*It happened again. There I was sitting in the car and my pocket was full of sweets. At the time it always frightens me so much—but then the feeling soon goes and I really feel quite calm about it and soon I've forgotten all about it.*

*I ought to go to a doctor, I suppose. Surely it couldn't be the c. of l. How could it be yet? Sometimes I feel quite angry that I can't talk to Bernard about it. He phoned this evening—he may be home next weekend or the following. He's got to go abroad for some conference and can't be sure. If I had any courage he'd come back and find me gone . . . but where would I go? And where would I find the courage? I'm hopeless and useless in doing things. Sometimes I get the feeling that Bernard would like to come back and find me gone. . . .*

*Mrs Panton broke the smallest of the set of silver lustre jugs doing the dining-room. She made a great fuss about it, so I made all the right noises. I think, though, I was a little upset. The set was quite expensive and was one of the last things Bernard bought me when he used to bring things like that unexpectedly. . . . Ten years ago. Now it's just formal Christmas and anniversary stuff. Nice to have a man again who just brings you things because he's seen them and thought of you.*

*Gave the sweets to the Sacred Heart children on the beach. Thank God the visitors have gone and we have the beach and the dunes to ourselves.*

CHAPTER TWO

QUINT WAS WORKING steadily through the pile of files
which had accumulated on his desk during the three days he
had been away. There were the usual intelligence reports,
inter-department minutes and the propaganda analyses based
on the European weekend press. The same dreary routine stuff.
His head still nourished a fine ache from last night's whisky.
All in the cause of duty . . . though he had taken time out
at the end for his own purely personal pleasures. He didn't
imagine it would have gone unnoted. The woman herself
could already have passed it on. Well, Warboys and Tucker
were tolerant men. After four years with them he was beginning
to read them nicely. Tolerant men—who would wipe you off
the map if you broke a known code, stepped over the clearly
drawn line. He had no desire to be wiped out. One day he
wanted to sit where Tucker sat, and later—why not?—where
Warboys sat.

The yellow light over the door flicked on and off in rhythm
with Warboys' buzzer. Tucker pushed his chair back and
stood up. He glanced across at Quint and caught his eye.

"I gather, Roger, you slightly extended your professional
brief last night?"

Quint smiled. There was no reproof in the tones. News
travelled fast—but only because somewhere the woman fitted
into the pattern of which he was a small piece.

He said easily, "My brief was physical and personal
characteristics. You have to get under a blanket to do a good
job in those areas—sometimes."

"You're a cheeky young sod."

21

Tucker smoothed a large hand over his thinning dark hair, fastened the buttons of his open blazer and twitched his tie straight. His moving right hand flicked and adjusted the set of the silk handkerchief in his breast pocket.

A big man, a finnicky, amiable man with a heart like a lump of ice. But if he wanted it, you had to like him. Quint liked him anyway. In twenty years' time he would happily settle for being where Tucker was now, for being what he was—more his own master than anyone else in the department except Warboys. Nearing sixty, ex-Navy—long ago—a large, loosely built man with a brain and a memory that could have brought him to the top in any line he had chosen. Quint had an idea that, like himself, somewhere in the past the choosing had been done for him, leaving him no room to maneuver. It was not an unusual recruiting drill and, surprisingly, seldom left hard feelings.

"When you do your report keep the details clinical. Warboys likes to imagine his own romantic touches. And don't see her again. We've got all the photographs we want."

"Photographs?" Quint's surprise was genuine. The bastards. Of course, he should have known.

Tucker chuckled, moving to the door. "Now, I presume, you're only pretending to be naïve."

"Of course."

With Tucker gone, Quint scratched absently at his leg. Though he knew it was without reason, he was suddenly angry. Not because of the way it had been done, or that it had been done, but because even after his few years here he should have known that it would be done, just as in the future other things would be done to surprise and prepare him, to test and assess him. There might be a genuine motive behind it, probably was, but the chief one had been to go on training him, to show him how much he was controlled and manipulated when they had a mind to assess him periodically. His moment of surprise was a mistake. He should have covered it, been unemotional. That was what was expected of him.

22

The bastards. He smiled suddenly. He loved them both. They were what he wanted now to become. Thirty years ago it would have been Tucker sitting in this seat, facing some similar moment. Had he shown surprise? He doubted it. Tucker, for all that big loose-limbed amiability, was an ice-cold solitary. No wonder he had never married.

Warboys sat at a large, highly-polished, kidney-shaped desk. A vase of tawny red and yellow chrysanthemums stood on one side of it. The vase was Georgian cut glass. There were two scallop-shaped silver ashtrays on small ball legs. The walls of the room were covered with a pearl pink damask paper. There were no pictures, and no windows. A lustre chandelier of Bavarian glass hung from the centre of the ceiling. It was the only light in the room. The floor was covered with hand-crafted Norfolk rush matting. Facing the desk was a shield-backed Hepplewhite armchair.

From behind the desk, where he sat in another Hepplewhite chair, Warboys said, "Morning, Bernard."

Bernard Tucker sat down in the spare chair.

"Morning, Percy."

"Quint in?"

"Yes, he's back."

"You told him about the photographs?"

"Yes, I did."

"Well?"

Warboys reached across the desk and nipped off a leaf from one of the chrysanthemums. Its surface was marked with the workings of some leaf-tunnelling insect. A strand of his loose white hair fell in a curved line over his right eye. He pushed it back with an almost feminine gesture. His eyes were polished, worn hazel, the skin over his thin, drawn face a moonscape of chalky white. His morning coat was humped up at the back of his neck like a horse collar. He had had the same tailor since he was sixteen and the man had never mastered the long, emaciated vagaries of his bony, spindly body. Tucker some-times played with the conceit that if someone set off a fire-

23

cracker behind him without warning he would jump clear of his clothes in one bound.

"He said that he imagined something of the sort had gone on."

"Did he now? What a kindly old gent you are this morning, Bernard."

Tucker grinned, pulled at his fleshy nose, and said, "Well, it's probably exactly what you said to old Milverton when it happened to me and you sat here."

Warboys chuckled. "It was indeed. Ganging up against our masters. Working class solidarity. Which is exactly what I want to talk to you about. I was summoned to lunch at Chequers on Sunday. Socially that will never happen until I retire and get my K. Not that I care—the food is mediocre. Present were the P.M., one newspaper proprietor who shall remain nameless, and one of our premier dukes. A chatty little bunch of buggers . . ."

Tucker smiled. Warboys had a fine range of messdeck language when he needed it. He had served under him more years ago than he cared to remember—not because of the time element but because of the loss of a sweet, carefree innocence which now, in rare moments, he recalled as a nostalgic balm. In this life he doubted whether there was any man or woman who did not have similar moments. They were unimportant, they carried no weight, but they were worth turning over for a moment or two like curiously marbled pebbles treasure-plucked from some childhood beach.

"The P.M. disappeared when coffee was served. He said he wanted to put in a little time—seldom available to him—working on a monograph of British shrews. It could have been his idea of a joke. You never know with him. Bloodthirsty little buggers, shrews. A short life and a productive one. I gather that the female while suckling one litter can be pregnant with another and already have conceived the third. Stoats, if you remember the simile, are hopelessly outgunned by them. . . ."

Tucker, the movement a symbol of his standing here, pulled one of the ashtrays close to him and lit a cigarette.

He recognised the preamble. It was unusual and deliberate, and it meant that Warboys didn't like the brief he had been given and preferred to keep it at arm's length for a while.

"The Duke, not over neglecting his havana and brandy, held the floor. Stripped to not too bare details his monologue went something like this. In all the major trade unions the Left Wing elements for some years now have been keeping up a growing and relentless pressure for militancy. They see themselves as a Third Force. Control the Labour Party or to hell with it. This you might say is a traditional and publicly accepted role. Something which is part of the normal pattern of trade unionism, an element which all governments are well used to and which they can more or less confidently anticipate in political terms. How am I sounding?"

"Like a T.V. political pundit. But you're warming up, Percy."

"Thank you, Bernard. The essential policy behind this solid Left Wing union section is not, of course, aimed against economic ills—real or imagined—but it is a political strategy. If they don't like a law—democratically imposed on the country—they feel they have the right to ignore it, disobey it, kick it overboard and to hell with whoever gets hurt. I'm trying to make this sordid little account simple so I'm sure it's not necessary for me to go into a detailed review—which the good Duke did—of the present situation in this country; a lust for economic growth, a fear of the inflation bogy, regular and crippling strikes every winter—the miners, the dockers, the postmen, the electricity power boys and all the rest of the merry clan. The main point is that some time next year, sooner or later, there must be a General Election. It was made discreetly clear, too, that for all the sounding out of the experts, the opinion polls and the various other sacrificial gut examinations the high priests of the media and politics have made, there is a large element of doubt about the confidently predicted outcome. The good old common sense of the man in the street is not to be relied on—if it ever was. What is wanted is an overwhelming victory, when the citizenry stand up in unbroken ranks and are counted, all bloody good men and true. Is the picture taking shape?"

Tucker blew his cigarette smoke idly towards the chrysanthemums. The action reminded him of Margaret and the first years of his marriage when he had been a keen gardener. Smoking a pipe which he hated he had gone round puffing great clouds at aphis-smothered blooms. A fruitless exercise but one which pleased Margaret. Pleasure now was dead. He and Warboys and time with its attendant dirty acts had killed it. He should never have left the sea, never have allowed himself to be ensnared. . . .

Quietly, holding easily the imagery of nights at sea as officer of the watch, the slow wheeling of the stars marking time and its small happinesses as he spoke, he said, "They want—or they think they've got—a powder keg. They want to blow the power—particularly of the Left—of the unions skyhigh for years. You touch the keg off a week or so before the election and up she goes."

Warboys nodded. Tucker had his rare faults, but he was his star pupil. He was a creditable achievement, a near perfect creation—the best, anyway, in the whole place, and—out of affection and unreturned love—he had made him so. He said, "So let's go to the heart of the matter."

Tucker stubbed out his cigarette in the dead centre of the silver ashtray to avoid tipping it, a neat, precise movement of his big fingers. Good sailors, like good fishermen, have good hands. He said, "There's a big payment involved?"

"Yes. A hundred thousand pounds."

"Officially funded?"

"No."

"That's why the newspaper proprietor was there—he's buying publication rights?"

Warboys nodded. "Came from some Overseas tin shack. He'd run full frontals of his wife and daughters to up circulation another bloody twenty thousand. The P.M.

probably has the same feeling about him as I have. He needs him, but prefers the company of his shrews."

"And the Duke?"

"He keeps a very old and dog-eared Almanach de Gotha with the bible at his bedside."

Tucker lit another cigarette and tilted his chair back slightly to stare at the chandelier.

Warboys said, "That chair cost me a hundred guineas years ago. If you break the back I'll put it on your wardroom tally."

Ignoring this, Tucker said, "If we touch this and it gets out you'll never get a K. and we shall both have a dishonourable little footnote in the history books. We shouldn't play private games with dukes and newspaper proprietors. The Duke knows that, so does the newspaper proprietor, so do you and so does the P.M."

Warboys chuckled. "All the right noises. But the P.M. knows nothing. He left us for his shrews after lunch. We had a chat. Warboys felt that there was a fair chance that the project could be well within the scope of his Department. Warboys didn't think so—but a quiet hint from the P.M. before he left made it clear that this was no time for niceness over scruples. So—you're sitting there now, Bernard, because it's your baby. Some time within the next month you'll be given a rendezvous. You've all the qualifications for vetting whatever is handed to you. Naturally that will come from the Duke's side, though in the event of an upset nobody would ever be able to prove it. You go through this stuff. You say genuine or fake. If it's genuine you bring it back here. No payment will be made unless you give the word."

"Opposition?"

"None in the sense you mean. I gather only one man from the other side knows this stuff is for sale—and he's the one selling it. Nobody's going to jump you but—"

"But, of course, I presume someone might."

"You would anyway. You've got to check the stuff on the spot before you approve the sale. Then I want you to go to ground for a couple of days, put the material in order and cover it with a report and analysis of the political implications and project the possible lines of refutation from the other side. That mustn't be done here on our paper or our machines. Do it somewhere clean so that if trouble comes we can look innocent. Naturally we will hold all the stuff. Even though they will have paid for it the newspaper won't get it until the P.M. decides that it is going to be used."

"They could be a hundred thousand pounds up the spout."

Warboys nodded. "So what? They'll get it into their book-keeping somewhere as a tax loss."

"One man's providing this stuff?"

"Yes."

Tucker dibbled with the end of his fresh cigarette into the ashes of the old one, making a little silver lagoon surrounded by lava coloured dunes. They'd done this kind of thing before. Neither of them liked it.

"Union man?"

"A fair bet."

"They're tough boys. Sooner or later he'll get the chop. The money won't protect him."

"His problem. We don't play nursemaid. He must have gone into all this."

There was a little silence between them, the beginning of a familiar ritual. They faced one another across the desk, holding each other's eyes. There was a dark, drainlike autumnal smell from the chrysanthemums. The smoke from Tucker's cigarette curled like a disappearing signal between them. Slowly they both smiled.

Tucker said, knowing nothing could alter his brief, "Why me? It all seems very simple. Something that Quint could cut a few more teeth on."

"The Duke wouldn't wear him. Or the P.M. I gather, too, there is a language problem about some of the stuff. That puts it in your field not his. . . ."

Momentarily Tucker lost the few following words as dirty,

grey water sheared over the bows of a destroyer, icing shrouds and rails, and the gale flattened the smoke from the stacks into a racing ribbon low over the white wake. God, he thought, endows some of us with rare talents which lead us into strange places. Why should a youth of seventeen have suddenly wanted to read Tolstoy, Gorki and Lermontov in the original? Only God knew without, it seemed, being accountable for what followed.

". . . besides, if it all turns out well, then—at some distant, not too distant, date the P.M. will show his gratitude. In five years' time you could be retired—Sir Bernard Tucker. A fat pension, a nice seat on the board of some government agency. . . ." Warboys grinned. "You might decide to stop being a bachelor . . . marry some nice widow or divorcee ten years younger. Anyway, it's now your baby."

Tucker stood up and flicked ash from the front of his blazer.

"Will the word come from you?"

"No. You'll get an invitation to spend a country weekend somewhere."

Quint looked up as Tucker came back into the room. Visits to Warboys were seldom on routine matters. When Tucker came back from a chat with the old man he always knew at once whether he was involved too. Tucker would give him a little nod and a wink, sit at his desk and say with a deliberate heartiness, "Sailing orders, me lad. Draw up a chair."

There was nothing for him this morning. Tucker went straight to his desk and sat down. He put a hand to the outside telephone and began to dial a number. Quint dropped his eyes to the papers on his desk. He had watched Tucker dialling outside numbers many times. From the movement of his finger he knew the regular ones. He knew, too, that Tucker must know he knew them and didn't care. If Tucker had cared, wanted any secrecy, he would never have got within a mile of knowing.

Tucker spoke briefly, but the flexion and timbre of his voice

—as always on this number—made it clear to Quint that there was a woman on the other end. A simple curiosity made Quint wish that he could speak the Slav languages as well as most of the Latin ones. For all he knew Tucker could have been giving instructions for his laundry or being amorous and affectionate—though affection was not something Quint readily associated with the man.

Tucker put the telephone down. Collecting his hat and coat, he said, "From lunchtime on I'll be at my flat."

Tucker spent two hours in the library on the first floor overlooking St James's Park. He collected the latest confidential cassettes on the trades unions, and the reports and summaries on the present higher membership from Presidents down through Executive Committee men and General Secretaries to Regional secretaries and committees with biographical notes, and a cassette which contained secret biographical and other notes on a wide selection of noted shop stewards in key industries. He sat in a booth listening to them until half-past twelve. When he came out there was little of what he had heard which he did not have at instant recall.

He walked through to Whitehall and got a taxi. He paid the cab off a hundred yards short of Graingers' tobacconist shop in the Euston Road. He walked to the shop, paid a collection due, and received the letter from William Ankers. A hundred yards above the shop he flagged another cab. He gave the driver a direction, and then sat back and read the letter. He read it without interest. It contained nothing which he wanted to know. From a professional point of view he had a low opinion of Ankers. But, for his purposes, he was the right man. Ankers had been born and bred in the town and knew the district, its people and its gossip as well as anyone. The whole business with Margaret had been a mistake. All he wanted now was a sign, the signalling of one hard fact which would give him a shabby but reasonably honourable reason for ending the miserable business. There had been times when he had considered throwing the whole thing into Warboys' lap, but lingering prudence—for he was still ambitious—cautioned him not to do it. The sin, a deliberate breach of their professional code, was an old one, condoned now by time and his own changed rank, but like the old man's albatross it was still around his neck. He wanted to be rid of it quietly and without its ever leaving a mark on his record. His record, his ambition, his professional pride were obsessional and not to be marred.

He sat back, stuffed the letter into his pocket, and blew out his breath. Jesus Christ . . . how time could change things . . . people. . . . Once Warboys had found him—even though he recognised the provenance of his regard for him without ever encouraging or acknowledging it—the man had never let go.

He stopped the cab a few yards past the main gate to Lord's cricket ground, and then walked to his flat. On the way he tore the letter and envelope into tiny, ragged squares and dropped them down through the grating of a road gutter. The thought struck him that Ankers and Commander Bernard Tucker, R.N., Retired, were brothers under the skin.

He unlocked the door of his flat, hung his coat and hat in the hall and went through to the large sitting-room whose windows looked down to the autumn-thin crests of plane trees in the square and the oval of thin, spiritless grass. He fixed himself a small pink gin, flicked the switch of the electric fire with his toe and stood in front of the growing heat and drank the gin slowly. Although there was no noise from the kitchen at the end of the corridor past the bedrooms and bathroom he knew that she would be there.

He put the empty glass on the mantelshelf and walked down to the kitchen. As he opened the door she turned to him, smiled, and then came towards him, one hand still holding a wooden ladle, its wet face shining under the electric light. She wore a pale blue woollen dress with a tiny square of apron tied across its front. She dropped the ladle on the table, put her arms around his neck and her mouth to his lips. He slid his arms around her shoulders, held her for a while, and then let

31

his hands travel down her body. They stood together in a long embrace and then he gently freed himself, smiled into her smiling eyes, and slowly dropped to his knees. He pushed the dress high above her waist and then kissed the smooth, brown skin of her belly while her fingers curled into the hair at the nape of his neck.

She said, "There was fresh whitebait. So I brought some to have before the chicken."

*    *    *    *

At a safe distance Billy Ankers followed Margaret Tucker into the car park. As he walked past the back of her car she was already sitting in the driving seat. He moved further down the rank of parked cars and got into his own car. He meticulously packed himself a fresh pipe and lit it with care. For a moment or two he contemplated taking out his notebook and making notes . . . not just for the morning which had passed but for the afternoon and the evening to come. At eleven she had gone to the Town Library as usual on a Wednesday and changed her books. Over lunch at the Two Rivers café she had begun to read one of the books. Billy had gone into a pub across the road, timing his two beers and a plate of ham sandwiches to pick her up as she came out of the café. She had walked up Allpart Street, looking at the shop windows, had gone into W. H. Smith's and come out with a paper-wrapped magazine under her arm with the library books. On the way to the car park she had stopped at a delicatessen called The Nutmeg Tree. Through the window he had seen her buy camembert cheese, a jar of ginger, a bottle of white wine, and half of a cold roast duck. He had seen the routine so many times on a Wednesday. There was nothing unusual about it—except perhaps the white wine. He couldn't remember her buying wines or spirits ever before, though he was pretty sure—even from one meeting with Mr Tucker—that he would keep his house fairly well stocked.

Mrs Tucker's car moved away, out of the park. An unexpected twinge of something resembling conscience stayed Billy's hand from his notebook. It was some time now since he had followed her out to the beach. It wasn't a bad day and he could think of nothing that claimed his attention elsewhere that afternoon. Billy drove after Margaret Tucker. He made no attempt to keep her in sight. He turned the radio on low and the heater on full so that the hot draught comforted his feet. It was an easy way to earn a monthly remittance. . . . Funny bloke Tucker. Only met him once. Half an hour, if that, in his office over the baker's shop. Never at home much. Some job in London. Nobody knew what, though there were a lot of guesses none of which, he would lay odds, came anywhere near the truth. One thing he was sure of though—Mr Bernard Tucker didn't care a damn what his wife did. Stuck out a mile. When they were jealous and wanted to know who it was they generally screwed themselves up into a tangle pretending to be casual. When they didn't care but just wanted to know so that they could kiss the whole thing farewell . . . well, they could have been giving a builder instructions for laying new drains. Clear out the old muck and let's have a fresh start. Funny, though. Looking at them both you'd think they were a good match. Damned good looking woman, all the goods still first class and in their right compartments. And don't think that Mr Tucker still didn't get it somewhere. He looked the kind that would go on wanting it even when they pushed him about in a wheelchair. No, Mr Tucker wanted there to be another man somewhere. Well, for his money, Mr Tucker was going to be disappointed.

When he reached the car park, Margaret's car was parked facing the beach near the closed seafood stall. Billy parked a hundred yards away from it. He climbed the dune bank overlooking the beach.

Margaret Tucker was a hundred yards away, moving easily up the fringe of sand, narrowed now to a thin strip by the tide which was full in. Billy climbed down from the dune and walked

33

over to her car. Her library books and shopping—in a decorated Nutmeg Tree bag—lay on the back seat. The magazine she had bought had half-slipped from its paper bag. *Homes and Gardens.* The house beautiful, thought Billy. A damn fine house, plenty of money, and nobody to keep her warm at nights. Shame. Still. . . .

He went back to his car, wrapped a rug around his legs and stared at the sea and the sky letting his mind go comfortingly blank. Billy had the great gift of being able to sit and do nothing, think nothing, content with the bliss of nothingness, a state far more refreshing than the deepest sleep and granted to only a few.

The orphanage crocodile came down the slender strip of sand between dunes and sea. Margaret smiled to herself. They were a few days into November now and the children were wearing their winter scarves. Winter coats at the beginning of October. The scarves when November came. Never gloves. Maybe the nuns had some health fad about gloves. Maybe they just didn't have gloves, or the children too soon lost them to make them worth bothering with.

The tall, leading sister inclined her head as she passed, a stiff, storklike gesture. A little boy behind her, trudging heavily through the sand, turned his face towards Margaret, cheeks fired with the sharp wind. He sniffed and beamed at her. She wished she had sweets in her pocket. . . . The thought, not knowingly bidden by her, came into her mind that the man Dougall had once walked as these children walked, sniffing at a running nose. She wondered if he had ever beamed innocently at some passing stranger or occasional benefactor. It was hard to imagine him so young. . . .

She walked the full length of the beach in a mild reverie. The narrow strip of sand slowly broadened as the tide began to run out. In the gut of the estuary mouth a timber boat was moving upstream and a little way behind it were two fishing boats each with a separate cloud of gulls over its stern. She turned southwards, away from the sea and kept to the dune

34

edge along the run of the estuary channel. It was farther than she usually came, but there was still plenty of daylight left and there was nothing at home to draw her there. With each week that passed a growing idleness seemed to have taken her whenever she was in the house. It needed little care; she gave it less. She kept her one main meal simple, for there was small heart in her to cook. She ought, she knew, to have more outside interests. Bernard had long urged that. There were women's organisations, voluntary and charity works . . . no excuse, with all the time she had on her hands, to accept boredom. Gardening she still liked, but there was little she could do outside at this time of year. She could have a greenhouse. There was room for it and money was no object, but somehow she could picture no pleasure in it. She played bridge once a fortnight with three other women, visiting each other's home in turn. When it was her turn her house came alive, recognisable, meaning something, but when the women went it lost its significance, became a shell about her which she took for granted. Curiously she felt no anger, no frustration; she just remained untouched. The only times her heart raced, when she felt vividly alive, were the moments when she suddenly realised that she had stolen something . . . sweets, a paper-back book, cellophane-wrapped tights, once three packets of useless screws . . . and then, over her anguish, came a strange sense of fulfilment and physical relief swamping quickly her guilt and shame.

Tiring, she turned away from the estuary shore into the burrows, selecting a small path. For all the years she had lived in the district and walked the North Lobb burrows she knew there were parts of them she had never seen. Over their six square miles were areas she had never explored. The initiative which she lacked about her house and her daily affairs kept her to a familiar pattern in her afternoon walks. Today because she had come farther than she usually did and was steering a guessing course back to the sands she soon found herself confused. She followed a path, caught a glimpse of the sea at

35

the crest of a dune and then descended into a thorn and furze banked hollow to find that the path died away into a drift of sand. Two or three times she had to take a line across rough ground until she picked up another path. There was an occasional irritation in her at the way she kept being balked by dying paths and forced to the rough dune slopes and over-grown hollows, and then it slowly began to amuse her, became a game which she played with some unseen joker who magically opened a path for her and a few moments later teasingly made it vanish.

When she was half a mile into the dunes with the sea as far away again on her left, she clambered up the sandy side of a steep pathless slope and found that from its ridge a path, clearer and broader than any she had met before ran down into a little valley below.

Sitting beside the path at the foot of the slope on a length of dead tree trunk was Maximilian Dougall. He had seen her when she had first come on to the beach by the car park. Unseen by her, keeping to the shelter of the flanking dunes, he had followed her progress. With some amusement he had watched her zig-zagging movements as she lost and found paths and had now placed himself where she must pass him.

When she was a few yards from him he stood up. He was wearing his navy blue short coat and a seaman's cap with a black, shiny peak. A red bandana handkerchief was wrapped about her throat under the almost closed coat collar. He put his hand to the peak of his cap in polite greeting, nodded, and gave her a half smile.

"Good afternoon, Mrs Tucker."

"Good afternoon. . . ."

She stood there, her face flushed from the sea wind and her exercise, her hair escaping untidily from the small woollen hat she wore. Without knowing she did it, she put up a hand and touched it to some order, waiting for him to move from her path, caught for a moment in the confusion of surprise.

His smile broadened across the hard, sun-tanned face and

she had a glimpse of even, white teeth. Strong, biting teeth.

He said, "You're a bit off your beaten track, aren't you?"

Surprise and the shadow of distant, stupid panic went from her at the sound of the words. His voice was friendly, easy, almost gentling as though he had immediately sensed her mild resentment at meeting him.

"I went farther than usual. I was trying a short cut back to the beach."

He half-turned and began to move down the path and she found herself moving slightly behind him.

"I'll show you, Mrs Tucker. Some of the summer people get lost around here. They're pretty daft some of them."

The West Country burr was in his voice, a slow, almost lazy voice but one that fitted him she felt . . . a strong voice yet gentle. She followed a fraction behind him, suddenly wanting and not wanting him there. On these dunes she liked her own company. She sensed that there must have been something deliberate in his being there on the path. But then as he walked ahead and said no more, made no move to turn and mark whether she followed him, she felt a little ashamed of herself. She was making up fancies, quite unjustified, about a man who by sheer chance was being kind enough to help her even though she didn't need to be.

She said, "Why do you spend so much time here? Is it the birds?"

Over his shoulder he answered, "Aye, that's so partly, Mrs Tucker."

Something about the way he called her 'Mrs Tucker' made her feel matronly, old.

"You see they bring me a little money." Level with her now that the path had broadened, he went on, "I watch them all over the place. Here, along the estuary, up on the moor. Then I paint them and sell them to the summer visitors . . . that and other stuff. . . . But I'm here mostly because I live here." He stopped, standing close to her, looking at her, his eyes steady on hers. He nodded away to the south, his eyes still on her.

37

"Over there on the edge of the dunes and the marsh. Just a little old broken-down cottage. Two quid a week. Well water. Nothing found. The summer people know it. They come and buy. A man must eat."

Out of politeness though awkward because of his easiness she said, hearing and hating the stuffiness in her voice, "Really? How very interesting."

He shrugged his shoulders. "It's something to do. I've never been able to stick any regular job. When the nets are on in the season I work with the salmon fishermen sometimes. Harvest time I help out. But it's the summer folk that pay best. We could go by the cottage if you like. You could see the paintings." He looked at her briefly, giving her a smile now that skirted the borders of an almost boyish impudence. "I give a twenty-five per cent discount to locals."

She said quickly, "I'm sorry. I'm afraid I'm late as it is, Mr Dougall."

As she spoke she saw the red-faced smile of the boy in the orphanage crocodile of that afternoon, but the face had changed to his.

He laughed and said, "That sounds funny. Mr Dougall. Everyone calls me Maxie. But I like it. Mr Dougall. As for the paintings, well, you can see them anytime. In the summer I have a little stall in the garden. Mostly I lay the stuff out, mark the prices and people can leave the money in a box if I'm not there. I've found that it's a sight more honest world than most people think. Or, perhaps it's being on holiday and folk feel a bit different than usual."

They came out on to the edge of a steep dune. The path ran clearly down its ridge to the beach a hundred yards away.

He stopped and nodded to the beach. "There you are, Mrs Tucker. Careful how you go down. The path edge is all loose sand. You could take a tumble." He stood aside for her to pass.

As she did so the wind flicked up the skirts of her coat and for a moment they flapped against his legs like wings. She was so close to him that they were almost touching.

38

She said, "Thank you, Mr Dougall."

She went down the path and out to the beach without looking back.

Maxie watched her go. She was going to change. Not Mrs Tucker. But Margaret. He was going to make the change. He looked forward to it, but wasted no imagination on future details. He was going to take her. There was no point in over-anticipating future pleasures.

Billy Ankers was on the point of leaving when Mrs Tucker came back to the car park. He had had to switch his motor on three times for the heater but even so his feet were far colder than he considered good for them. He was very susceptible to sudden colds. And where the hell had she been all this time? Whenever he had watched her before she had kept a fairly strict routine. He could have given the time of her return before she left. A good three-quarters of an hour over the limit she was today.

He packed a fresh pipe as he watched her get into her car and drive off. Bloody woman. He might just as well have stayed back in town. There wouldn't be any coffee and Dundee cake from Nancy. She'd be away home by the time he got back. And no Nancy this evening. It was old Ma Barcott's bingo evening. Life was hard and it took a man of character to deal with it.

# CHAPTER THREE

ON THE FOLLOWING Friday Billy Ankers followed Margaret to the beach car park. He watched her go over the dune ridge and down to the beach. Any temptation to follow her was shrivelled by the blast of a strong northwesterly wind that was sending long, cresting rollers sweeping into the bay and blowing spinning dervishes of dry sand from the ridges of the dunes. Billy had no desire to be frozen by the wind or blinded by the sand. He merely wanted to check whether or not she would revert to her usual timing. If she didn't . . . well, then the next time, no matter what the weather, he would have to follow her and find out the cause of her altered routine. Billy got back into his car, switched on the engine and turned the heater full up. Then, staring happily ahead of him, slid away into a blissful state of nothingness.

Margaret walked briskly up the beach, her coat buttoned fully around her against the wind. There was no orphanage crocodile today. The weather was much too bad. For a moment she smiled at the thought of the whole skein of children being whisked up by the wind, sucked up into the low-clouded sky to disappear, shrieking and shouting with laughter, to some magical land where they would live happily ever after.

Three hundred yards up the beach, she turned away from the sea and on to a path through the burrows. Half an hour later she was sitting on the leeward side of one of the most southerly dunes, sheltered from the wind, though wraiths of gale-blown sand occasionally hissed above her head, and watching the small cottage. She watched through a pair of old Carl Zeiss binoculars which Bernard kept in the house.

The cottage was served by the spur of an old military road which ran between dunes and marsh out to the headland which marked the meeting point of the two rivers where there was a military training area. The cottage garden was small, enclosed by stone walls which were banked on two sides by wind-twisted growths of thorn and alder bushes. The roof was thatched with one chimney in the centre. Its face, like a child's drawing, held a central doorway, flanked by two windows and three windows across the top of its façade. The thatch was old but in good repair, the walls white plastered and the paint and woodwork of the door and windows in good condition. To one side of the cottage was a large pond, edged with cotton grass and rushes and on this moved two white geese and some ducks.

Maxie Dougall was working in the garden. He wore a thick, navy blue seaman's jersey, the sleeves pushed up over his elbows, and the peaked, dark cap on his head. He was so close through the glasses that Margaret felt she could put out a hand and touch him, touch the glints of light on his face, which was marked with sweat from his work. He was turning over a small vegetable patch with a spade, his movements unhurried, rhythmical and easy with the deliberate strength and grace of a man who does a long familiar job.

Margaret watched with interest. Although the man meant nothing to her, her curiosity was strong. She was not a fool. She sensed clearly that this man had gone out of his way to make himself known to her, that—detached though her curiosity was—his interest in her was personal. She could resent this—had at times when she had sat thinking about it at home—but she clearly accepted her curiosity. If it were nothing else, it was something different with which to concern herself, a break in the routine of the predictable days she lived.

She watched him now, aware of the strength in the shoulders and arms, the almost lazy control of power which was realised in the growing length of the dark marsh soil which lay, mahogany-fresh, in spade silvered slabs under the pale light of the cloud-filtered sunshine.

She saw him reach and pick something from the ground. He pushed his cap back so that a frond of sweat-lacquered, dark hair streaked his brow. For a moment or two he examined something in his hand. Then he tossed it away over the garden wall into the pond where ducks and geese raced across the water to it. Clear, vivid and unnaturally near to her in the lenses she saw him laugh, his teeth marking the brown face, his lips red wet, the colour of ripe hawthorn berries. Then, his face was hidden as he half turned and the spade began to rise and fall again.

She dropped the glasses, letting them hang around her neck by their strap. Without warning her whole body was swamped with a sense of utter misery, a sensation of sadness that she had never known before . . . an emotion which went swiftly beyond misery and desolation to a nameless possession of her body . . . neither loneliness nor longing, but a living nothingness which for a moment or two completely immobilised her. Her whole nature called out its want in terms which she could not understand.

She got up and went down at an oblique angle to the old military road. She began to walk back to the car park along the road, the whole width of the burrows now between her and the beach. There were tears in her eyes but whether they came from the wind which whipped across her face or from her own feeling she did not know because she walked now like an automaton, beyond knowing, just walking, just being without feeling or awareness.

Maxie watched her go. He had been unaware of her until, pausing in his digging and looking round, he had seen her come down the dune side to the old road, the sloping path setting the binoculars round her neck swinging against her coat front. For a moment or two he had thought she was coming to the cottage. Then she had turned away down the road to the east and he knew that she was going back to her car. Unmoved, not even touched by a moment's egotism, he knew that she had been up on one of the dunes watching him. Why

43

not? This woman wanted him. He would take her want and satisfy it, and then take her and satisfy himself. There would be no retreat from this courtship. He turned back to his digging, loving the richness of the fresh-turned soil, relishing the mirror-bright face of the spade which cut like a knife into winter-bare ground.

Margaret passed within two yards of Billy Ankers, coming from behind him and across the park to her car. She walked with her hands in her pockets, the fieldglasses swinging still around her neck. Her head was bowed a little against the thrust of the wind. For a moment Billy saw her face, wind-rouged, and her eyes glistening and tear-bright.

Watching her get into her car he wondered whether the tears were from the wind, and wondered, too, about the field-glasses. There had been no sign of them when she had left. And now, here she was, back from another direction, one he had never known before, coming back up the old military road along the marsh edge, fifteen minutes over her time.

He watched her as she turned her car and drove out of the park. The fifteen minutes meant little, not in this wind. But the new direction was interesting and so were the field-glasses. He had never seen those before. Perhaps she had taken up bird watching. A lot of people did it about here. She drove by, thirty yards away, and he saw that she was still wearing the fieldglasses about her neck. She had the look, he thought, of a woman in a trance, oblivious of the glasses. Either that or she was overproud of her new toy and, like a child, wanted everyone to see it. No, that wasn't her style. Not from what he knew of her. For his money, something was happening, and that something was out there in the dunes. . . . Well, next time he would follow her, though that would be no picnic unless the weather turned milder.

He drove back to lukewarm coffee and Dundee cake with Nancy and, for the first time, admitted her to his confidence over Margaret Tucker.

He said, "Nance, you know that Mrs Tucker woman . . .

44

you know, tall, well-built blonde number what lives out at Lopcommon?"

"Yes. Comes to the shop sometimes. Not regular. She one of yours?"

"In a way. Ever hear anything about her?"

"No."

"Well, if you do, let me know."

"You do your own bliddy snooping. You know I don't like it, anyway. And now if you've finished doing what you're doing I'll have me leg back and go down to work. You ought to tire yourself out with more exercise. Take a bit of the Old Nick out of you."

*  *  *  *

The letter was addressed to Bernard Tucker at his London flat. It read:

Dear Commander Tucker,

I wonder if you might find it amusing to come down here for the first weekend in December? My brother was a contemporary of yours at Dartmouth and I think you served together later. Come on the Friday. If you are not travelling by road you can be met at the station—Salisbury. My father and a few friends of his will be here.

Nothing formal. We live very simply.

Yours sincerely,
Cynthia Melincourt

An hour later he passed it across the desk to Warboys. The man read it, fiddling with the point of his chin, then flicked it back, saying, "Lady Cynthia Melincourt. Woodford's daughter, spinster in her late thirties, mad as a coot. Two or three dubious phases in her life. A very minor English eccentric and, if she's in the mood, a praying mantis."

Tucker picked up the thick, green, deckle-edged paper

45

with its black engraved address—Vigo Hall, Horsfell, Wiltshire. He knew as much about Lady Cynthia as Warboys. She was in their files somewhere. He asked, "Vigo Hall?"

"Bloody great place on a hill over the upper Avon. Tudor origins overlaid with a mess of additions since then. Nice collection of Dutch sea paintings. No central heating. Cold as charity, but the food and drink are excellent. You knew the brother?"

"Paul. Yes. Nice, quiet chap. Killed in submarines off Taranto in forty-four. Would Lady Cynthia know the object behind the exercise?"

"No. Woodford probably dictated what she should write." Warboys leaned back and raised his peaked face to the ceiling chandelier. "I'd give odds there's no need for the precaution, but don't go by car. There isn't an official one existing that hasn't been marked by someone or the other. Use the rail and take a roundabout route. Pop down a hole like Alice and come up in Wonderland. . . ." His voice trailed off as his eyes came back to Tucker. "Sorry, Bernard. I must be getting old. Teaching my grandmother to suck eggs. I'll be telling you to wear a false moustache next."

Tucker smiled automatically. He had hardly listened to the directions because he was thinking that Warboys didn't like this job. That made him garrulous and fussy, a shield that concealed a professional anger. Both of them knew the limits of the Department's brief. Both of them could move easily through the underworld of politics nationally and internationally, but there was a long-standing official reluctance to become involved in party politics. Labour, Liberal and Conservative were newspaper terms, interchangeable labels almost. The present Prime Minister like all others before him understood the veto against using the service purely for party ends. He had to be a frightened man, or a far more powerful and persuasive one than any of the others to have involved Warboys and the men who ranked above Warboys in this.

Back in his own office Tucker said to Quint, "I want a train timing for December the fifth to Salisbury. Arrive late

46

afternoon. I don't want to go direct. Give me a roundabout route with two changes."

"Return route?"

"I'll arrange that." Tucker palmed his watch from the pocket of his double-breasted waistcoat. "I'm going over now to the Navy division. I'd like it when I come back." He dropped the watch back into his pocket and moved to take his hat and coat from the office stand.

Quint took a time-table from his lower drawer and began to look up trains. He had no curiosity about the request. He had been in the service long enough now to sense at once when a new job was being prepared. Tucker was as remote as an iceberg, the bulk of his real personality submerged—which meant that he did not like the job. And Warboys whenever he had had reason recently to be with him even on routine matters was quietly fussing, openly woolly in his talk—which meant that there was something around which he did not like. All this rarity of behaviour from two men who were seldom touched by professional scruples, who had lived with well-disciplined deceits and the smooth—deadly, sometimes—stratagems of power beyond and above the common run of the laws which the man-in-the-street recognised meant that someone had set the wrong dish before them. The smell was getting up their noses.

\*     \*     \*     \*

It was nine o'clock. Margaret had had, for her, a late dinner, taking it on a tray before the television set in the sitting-room. Before eating she had changed from her tweed dress into a long, blue, velvet housecoat. As the news came on the screen she leaned forward and switched it off. She had already seen or heard the news twice that day, and tomorrow morning there would be the papers. There was too much news. It had become an obsession with the human race, she thought. In Scotland, as a girl, there had been a weekly paper only. . . . She leaned back, ignoring the book which already rested in her lap. The

47

intermittent shake of a strong westerly wind against the window panes took her back to the same wind noises coming up the loch, full of sea vigour. As a girl her father and the ghillies and the keepers had taught her every inch of the lochside and the surrounding country, but she had never been able to take any special interest in their particular passions . . . shooting, fishing, and stalking. Her father, since she was an only child and not the boy he wanted, had tried to interest her with kindness and no sign of disappointment. She had wanted to respond, knowing his feeling, but there was no answering passion in her. To walk the loch shore and the hills, she loved. To shoot and fish gave her no pleasure. Her father was dead now and it was sad to think that he had carried his big disappointment to the grave with him. Her mother had soon followed him because she had always been his shadow, drawing a large draught of her spirit and contentment direct from him. That was when Bernard had come; five years after the war, from the experimental station run by the Navy at the loch mouth, an establishment that filled the neighbourhood with wild rumours of the things which went on there. Not the Bernard she knew now. The Bernard of then. Much older than she was, for she was hardly nineteen. She lived—chaperoned by an old aunt—the wealthy young heiress of the estate and the family fortune. It was like one of the books she now read. The young Highland girl, sheltered, untouched by the rough buffets of life, and the virile, swashbuckling stranger from the sea. She smiled. Not that even in those days, or any days, Bernard could have been described as swashbuckling. But he had swept her off her feet, captivated her half-senile aunt, and they had been married in the local kirk with only a handful of witnesses from the estate. He had been the first and only man she had known. Halcyon days followed—though even then he would be away from her for days, sometimes weeks. But even in his absence his flesh was part of her flesh . . . their lovemaking a wonder which even in his absence fired her body with sudden torments of bliss which would often force her to get up and leave the room and the company of her aunt because the vividness of his presence even in her thoughts was something only to be supported in the solitude of her own room.

Then, over the years, the whole thing had gradually died, like some tropic growth succumbing year by year as the natural climate of its life changed, the seasons turning through cycles that brought a slow death.

Anger touched her suddenly, and she picked up the book from her lap and forced herself to read, the fingers of her right hand playing nervously with a loose strand of her fair hair.

A stronger squall of wind pulsed against the windows. As it died away she heard the front door bell ring. It was after nine and no time for callers.

The bell rang again insistently, a finger pressed long on the button. The length of the ring gave her a sudden assurance. Now and again her daily woman would find that she could not come on a promised day—and it was her day tomorrow—and would send up her small son with a message. He was a boy who thought that when you rang a bell you kept your finger on it until someone answered.

Margaret got up, smiling to herself, and went out into the hall. She switched on the outside light and freed the door lock.

As she drew the door open, the wind rushed into the house, forcing the door back against her restraining hand, setting the ceiling hall light swinging on its pendant and rippling like some living thing under a loose rug on the polished floor boards.

A man stood on the doorstep, full under the portico light. It was Maximilian Dougall, cap on head, the coat collar of his pilot jacket turned up against the wind, and a large brown paper parcel under his arm. He smiled at her and made a half gesture of touching the peak of his cap with his free hand.

"Good evening, Mrs Tucker. Hope I haven't disturbed you?"

As he spoke her first instinct was to close the door quickly against him. How dare he come up here at this time of night? As her lips framed to give him some curt dismissal, a balm for

49

the outrage his smiling insolence presented, the wind gusted
again with even greater force. It smashed into the hallway as
though it were in league with this man, powering him, adding
its strength to his to bear her down. A picture slid at an angle
on the wall with the slew of racing wind, the ceiling light
swung in an erratic orbit and the loose rug raced to the foot
of the stairs to collapse in an untidy heap. Then the wind was
sucked back by the gale outside. The open door, caught in the
retreating vortex, was jerked from Margaret's hand and swung
away from her. She gave a small cry of alarm, fearing, even
in her anger with him, that the door would smash outwards
into the man's face.

Maxie reached out a hand, caught the door knob and
halted the violent swing with a thrust of his shoulder. He moved
round the door and shut it. He turned to her, taking off his
cap, the smile still on his lips and—the West Country accent
fuller than Margaret had ever heard it before—said, "Well,
what a night, Mrs Tucker. A full scale westerly that'll make a
lot of craft run for shelter. It's not so bad down here. You're in
a bit of a hollow, but coming over the cliff path . . . well, I
thought I was going to take wing and join up with the sea-
gulls——"

Margaret broke in stiffly, "Mr Dougall, it's very late and
I . . . I . . . Well, I was not expecting anyone to call." She was
angry still, but through her anger she knew that she sounded
like some stammering idiot.

"Oh. . . ." Maxie sounded genuinely surprised. He looked at
his wrist watch and then went on, "Well, yes, I suppose it is,
Mrs Tucker. Trouble is I don't pay much attention to time.
Only you see—" he patted the parcel under his arm, "—I've
just been over to Lobhill to show some of my paintings to a
client of mine." He grinned. "Client is a nice word. He's a
dealer, has a couple of secondhand shops and buys now and
then. Coming back, I suddenly remembered I'd promised to
let you have a look at them sometime. But I see what you mean.
I'm sorry if I've upset you." He grinned ruefully. "I'm not

much of a hand at . . . well, at thinking about what other people consider proper times and things like that. I'll come back some other day." He put his cap on and reached for the door with his free hand.

For a moment or two Margaret was content to know he was going, the flurry and surprise of his coming calmed in her now. Then, as his hand touched the door knob, she heard herself say, as though some other Margaret Tucker spoke from within and through her, "You don't have to go. Since you've taken the trouble, and on a night like this, I'd like to see your paintings." Having spoken, she felt a quick sense of relief. The man was polite. He might be unusual in a social sense, but to take the trouble to come up here . . . to think about her . . . and, anyway, it would only take a few minutes to look at his stuff.

As though echoing her thoughts, Maxie said, "It won't take more than a few minutes. If Mr Tucker's here, perhaps he would like to see them?"

Margaret said, "Bring them into the sitting-room. The light's better there. My husband's not here at the moment. . . ." She was tempted to say that he was out at a meeting, would be back soon, and then dismissed the idea as stupid. There was nothing to fear from this man.

Maxie followed Margaret into the sitting-room. He looked around, knowing some of the room already, completing the picture and then watched Margaret as she cleared magazines from a table so that he could lay out his pictures. The movements of her arms and her body under the velvet housecoat told him that she had little on underneath. He pictured her body naked without excitement, as though she were a rare bird species flown into the field of his glasses.

Maxie put the parcel on the table and undid the rough cord which bound it. He said, "I've got about a dozen. They're all done on that hardboard stuff. Sometimes, if people want it, I frame them. Mostly they're content to take them as they are. Framing's extra." He half-turned and smiled at her.

Feeling easier in herself now, Margaret watched him as he

51

began to set the pictures out. They had been done in water colours.

As he placed each one on display on the table he gave a running commentary.

". . . That's a dipper. You get those farther up the Two Rivers and on the moor streams . . . Redshank, plenty of those on the estuary. . . . That's a little ringed plover. They're quite rare down here in the West, but we get some in the autumn on migration. . . . That's a pair of knots. They come in the winter. You can mix them up with sanderlings at a distance. . . . Common tern. We get those late summerish. They breed up north and in the autumn they take off and go thousands of miles down to the Antarctic. Unbelievable. Just a handful of feathers, skin and bone and they were doing it long before the first sailing ships rounded the Horn or the Cape. . . ."

Margaret watched the pictures come out one by one and found it hard to believe her eyes. Maxie talked with complete absorption. She had the impression that he had forgotten all about her. She was glad because as he dropped the pictures one by one on the table she did not know what to say, felt that words were demanded of her but could find none. The paintings were completely unexpected.

Maxie said, "That's a red-throated diver and then these last two . . . an osprey and a golden eagle. . . ."

Without thinking, finding relief in words of any kind, Margaret said, "But you can't possibly get those down here, Mr Dougall. I used to see them as a girl in Scotland."

Maxie straightened up and turned to her and a brief, conspiratorial grin creased his brown face. "No, you don't. I've never seen them—did them from a book. But we get a lot of people from Scotland on holiday down here. They go for them. I have to meet the demand of the market." He chuckled, the sound marking his complete ease in this strange room. The slight shrug of his shoulders as he stepped back to allow Margaret to see the paintings better carried a gentle familiarity as though they had long known one another.

From behind her—and she was glad that it was so because she would not have wanted her face to be seen by him at this moment—Maxie went on. "What do you think of them?"

The question she had dreaded from her first sight of the painting of the dipper had come. She did not know what to say. The paintings were awful. As far as the colouring of the birds' plumage was concerned she had a feeling that each feather had been faithfully copied. But the birds themselves were stiff and wooden without even the primitive grace or appeal of an untutored skill or an original eye. They were just very bad. They were so bad that they were almost laughable.

"Well, Mrs Tucker, what do you think?"

As he spoke Maxie moved round the end of the table. Margaret, stepping back from the paintings, could no longer avoid his eyes. She searched desperately for words, for some kindness of phrase which would relieve her embarrassment and not wound him.

Almost stammering, she said, "I think . . . well, I think . . . the colouring is very . . . very exact. . . ."

In that moment Maxie liked her, his liking an emotion isolated from all the others which she evoked. She had good manners, and a gentleness and kindness which made her slow to hurt. That he liked, that too he could use—but the character note at that moment was marginal. He just liked her, standing there finely set up, the lines of her housecoat draping her body, a firm, boldly shaped woman's body, her fair hair still unsettled by the wind in the hall, and little creases of embarrassment puckered in the corners of her eyes.

He said easily, "Frankly, I think they're bliddy awful. But they're the best I can do. I can shut my eyes and see the birds, every detail, every movement, and I want to put it all down on paper . . . recreate it. But the moment my hand touches a brush or pencil I just become a clumsy ape." He laughed, drawing the sound out as though enjoying his own self-criticism. "I've got the soul of a painter and the hands of a five-year-old child." He grinned. "You must have had a nasty

53

moment when I laid them out. I apologise for that—but, you know, I really do sell a lot of them and for a long time I couldn't understand it. But I do now. People on holiday go a little mad. They'll buy anything that takes their eye. Like magpies, they are. Anything bright or unusual . . . so that in the winter or years later they can look at it and remember a summer, a place, a whole bagful of memories with a golden frame round them." He paused, and then added, "Sorry . . . talking too much."

Margaret said, "What you've said is interesting, Mr Dougall. But what I can't understand is why you brought them for me to see. I'm not a summer visitor." She felt no asperity. She was calm now. The stupid fears which had rushed in when she had opened the hall door were gone. She had no resentment, no concealed disapproval of the way he had almost taken over the room, talking with complete self-confidence. She was her own mistress now, not a disturbed woman, and in her own house she had—and was compelled to exercise—a right to ask him for an explanation.

For a moment or two Maxie hesitated. This was the moment when his own confidence and his reading of this woman were to be put to the test. It was a measure of a slight waning of his own arrogance, a misting of the vision of the future which he had nourished for so long, that he said almost in an apologetic mumble, "I don't know. . . ."

Quite sharply, sensing her own triumph, Margaret said, "Of course you must know. I'm not a child, Mr Dougall. You didn't go over to Lobhill, did you? There's no dealer over there. You just came straight up here."

Maxie smiled. The challenge from her restored him.

"That's true."

"Why?"

It was easy now. She was helping him without knowing it.

He said, "I wanted to be in this house. To know what it was like so that when I went away and was thinking about you I could picture you here. It's as simple as that. I've got a hundred pictures of you in my imagination. Some of them I know from life, from seeing you walk along the sands and in the dunes. Others are just made up. I wanted to make them true as well. . . ." He paused. She was standing with her body tensed, her lips pressed tight and her arms were crossed, hugged close below the fall of her breasts, armouring her body against him while her eyes, touched with brilliant points of anger, watched him steadily. He went on, "Do you know why a man would want that?"

She said coldly, "Take your paintings, Mr Dougall, and don't come near me or this house again."

Maxie shook his head. Her anger was expected and now it worked for him, gave no armour to her against his frankness. "It won't do, Mrs Tucker. Some things you can't properly fight. You've got to go with them. And there's things some people know right away in their bones if only so much as a look passes between them. You can call it just wanting or love. But call it something you must and there's no power will lay the pain of the wanting except to give in to it. We've got it between us." He gave a small shrug of his shoulders, and then a quick, boyish smile, a smile which brought back to Margaret the innocent, mischievous face of the orphanage boy in the beach crocodile. "I knew you wouldn't do anything about it. It's the man's part. So I came up here."

Margaret said sharply, "Take your paintings and go, Mr Dougall." She turned her back to him and began to move to the door.

Maxie went quickly to her. He put one arm round her shoulders and the other about her waist. He kissed her, following her lips with his as she pulled her head back and tried to twist away from him. His body was pressed hard against hers. His hand around her waist moved with a gentling, steady stroke up the small of her back and then slowly down again as she began to struggle. But the struggle, the beginning of her body's protest, was barely half-formed when he took his lips from hers and stepped back.

55

She faced him, breathing heavily, and said, "Get out of here!"

He nodded, pulled his cap from his pocket and moved across the room. With his hand on the door knob, he said, "It's all right, Mrs Tucker. I wouldn't ever hurt you. But it's no good for some people for things to be in the air—they've got to be done. From then on there's either wanting all the way or an end to it. . . . Don't worry about the paintings. Put 'em on the boiler fire."

She said angrily, "Don't ever dare to come near me again."

Maxie gave a little shrug of his shoulders and then left the room. Margaret heard the thud of the hall door pulled sharply against the wind.

She ran her tongue over her outraged lips. There was the faint tang of salt on them from his kiss, the salt which had filled the air on the roaring westerly wind coming in from the sea on his night walk up here. Down the small of her back the sensation of his roving hand ran still. But now there seemed no velvet cloth to mute the caress. The hand was warm and masterly over her bare skin.

\* \* \* \*

Bernard Tucker came home that weekend. He arrived at half-past three on the Friday afternoon, coming up from the station in a taxi. He went up to his bedroom and changed from his London clothes to a tweed jacket and comfortable corduroy trousers. Margaret was out.

He went across to his wife's room and left the door open so that if he missed the noise of her car returning he would hear the front door opening. He liked to arrive when she was out of the house. He liked to walk around, his professional eye checking and observing the household pieces and arrangements. Margaret was a creature of habit. Things were seldom moved. There had been a time, long before he knew Warboys and the work he did now, when he would have been appalled at even

56

the impulse to violate the privacy of another person's room. Now he did it automatically and without any prick of conscience. Her bedtime book was a volume of Sir Winston Churchill's memoirs. For the last three months it had rested on the bedside table. He went into her bathroom, his eyes moving around briefly, checking with a scrupulous professional accuracy. He picked up the soap from the bath holder and passed it under his nose. *Floris*. Stephanotis. Stephanotis or Geranium, always one or the other. There was a new bath mat of blue-dyed sheepskin.

Back in the bedroom he pulled out his key ring and opened her bureau top drawer—the only one which was ever locked. He took out her diary and read the new entries since his last examination. There was nothing new. He was used to her comments about himself and the references to her queer spells when she took things from shops.

> . . . *If I had any courage he would come back and find me gone . . . but where would I go? And where would I find the courage? I'm so hopeless and useless in doing things. Sometimes I get the feeling that Bernard would like to come back and find me gone. . . .*

He would. There was no question of that. He wanted to be freed from her, but he knew that she was right when she said she had no courage to find. The only hope was that someone else would find it for her.

He put the diary back, and picked up two paper-back books which lay in the drawer. They were always of the same type. It was more often these than Sir Winston Churchill she read. Trash. But he knew why she read them. A twinge of distant conscience touched him. Once he had loved her and her body. If he had never known her and were to meet her now he knew that there would be a response in him. His appetites were alive, demanded satisfaction, but on the few and distant occasions when he had tried to recapture what there once had been between them the flesh had refused to be driven. He could find plenty of explanations but knew that he could never discuss them with her. The betrayal had not been of her but of himself.

Through her he had once tried to escape from Warboys' world, had deliberately put himself in jeopardy hoping to be discovered—and nothing had happened. Fate had played its own game with him. There had in those days been the strictest embargo on marriage for trainees and junior ranks. Anyone who broke it was dropped from the service. In Scotland, with self-revulsion growing in him against all he did and represented, he had met Margaret, years younger than himself, more a girl than a woman. He had made her a woman and later when she had told him she was pregnant, he had married her, quickly and quietly. He had been sure the Department would find out. But it never had. Margaret's pregnancy had turned out to be a myth, a semi-hysterical, emotional irregularity. He had been caught in the aftermath of sudden regret for his impetuosity and the equally sudden knowledge that he *was* the man whom Warboys had always known he was. The life offered him was the only one he wanted. There was a sadistic ambition in him, and a fulfilling excitement in the conceits and dark maneuvers which would enrich his existence. From then on he had concealed his marriage, and with each month, every year, was more and more concerned that it should not be discovered, that he should not be cast out of the peculiar paradise which he had found. Years later when he had reached the status—and time, too, had changed the injunctions and vetoes against marriage—when he could have revealed his distant lapse he had still concealed it. To reveal it—no matter how distant the transgression—would have been a black mark against him. Forgiveness because of his worth could not have erased it. Carrying the mark he could never have hoped to sit where Warboys sat, never be allowed to take that seat and hope to rise even higher. . . .

He dropped the books back into the drawer and locked it. Margaret then. Margaret now. A stupid woman from whom he wanted to be discreetly freed, wanted to have her off his hands so much that there were even times when he contemplated the fantasy of taking some direct action himself.

So far have I come, he thought, as he went down the stairs to the front door, having heard the sound of her car moving down the drive, from the young officer reporting to his first ship, to the cold bridge nights and Warboys beside him, moving from stranger to companion, to a friend who longed for more than friendship.

He opened the door, greeted Margaret, took parcels from her arms, and putting them down on the hall chest turned and kissed her, laying his cheek against hers with a sudden, unexpected tenderness from which he withdrew quickly.

The gesture was not so quick that it had been unnoticed by her for as they sat in front of the fire having their drinks before dinner, Margaret said, "Bernard, what has happened to our marriage?"

For a moment he showed his surprise. Then, not wanting to waste himself in the futility of analysis, said, "Nothing."

"You regard it as normal?"

The tone of cynicism was clear, and surprised him. He stirred uncomfortably.

"No marriage is normal. They're all different. They all have something missing if that's what you mean."

"Do they?"

"Of course they do." He knew what was coming and he tried, loyally for a moment, to hold down an irritation which he could not escape.

"Oh, they all have something wrong, yes. But I'm not really talking about whether you can't or don't want to sleep with me. That can be common enough, I suppose, in a lot of marriages. But they could still have something, even without that . . . a sort of, well, platonic happiness. Or don't you think so?"

"Happiness? What the hell's that anyway?" Her mood increased his irritation and he showed it now, hoping thereby to end this line of talk.

Quietly she persisted. "It's the relationship where two people don't—whatever else has gone—have to live in the same house in two different worlds."

"I'm not here much. This is all your world." He paused and then, going farther than he had ever done before, added, "If you wish I'll leave you here with it if it won't cause you embarrassment. You can reshape it any way you like."

He stood up and crossed to the sideboard to pour himself another drink. His back to her he waited for her reaction. When it came it was unexpected, following a line he had not anticipated.

"And what is your world, Bernard? Sometimes I wonder about it. You've never been very . . . categorical about it."

The pause before the word categorical irritated him more. Whenever she used a word outside of her normal vocabulary there was always this pause, not made for emphasis but as though she were some slow learner, anxious to get an unfamiliar word right.

He said, "You know what my world is. A damn hard slog, particularly these days. Here there and everywhere, chasing even the ghost of a chance of business."

"You make a lot of money."

There was no question in the phrase. It was a clear refutation of all he had said. He had a comfortable flat in London, she was saying. He liked his life there and kept her from it. He had friends who were kept from her; women, too, no doubt. He travelled, had a good time and was unburdened by her presence, but he came back now and then to go unenthusiastically through the limited motions of being her husband.

"You're in a funny mood tonight," he said, turning with his drink and forcing the wraith of a smile.

Looking at him, her face calm, her self-possession very clear, she said, "Perhaps I am. I know you don't like this kind of talk, but I think there is something you should know. I think it has something to do with our relationship in a . . . psychological way. I go into shops and when I come out I find sometimes that I have things in my pocket. Things, Bernard, which I have stolen and can't remember stealing."

"I can't believe it!" His disbelief sounded genuine, his surprise unfeigned. He had known that there might come a moment when she would tell him this. He was well prepared for it.

He sat down, elbows on his spread knees, fingering his glass in his cupped hands.

Margaret said, "I would have told you before. But I hoped it would go, that it was something . . . well, something to do with my age and, frankly, the way our marriage is. But it doesn't go. Once or twice a month I just steal. Small things. And I don't remember doing it."

"Then we must do something about it. You'll have to see someone. Perhaps it would be better to start with your own doctor. I'll go and ring him now and make an appointment for you. You can see what he says. He'll probably put you on to a specialist who'll clear the whole thing up. Good Lord, we can't have this kind of thing. Think of all the fuss if you were caught."

He stood up, touched her for a moment on the shoulder, and then went to his study to telephone the doctor, carrying his glass with him. As he sat and sipped his drink before dialling, a small agony passed through him. Now that she had told him about it, he had to do something for her. Jesus Christ, how people changed and were changed. All he had had to offer was a touch on her shoulder and the cold logic of telephoning a doctor when he should have taken her in his arms and shielded her from her worry with his love. But how could you take a stranger into your arms? Even for him there were some deceits which could not be stomached.

Margaret sat in the lounge, possessed by a cold calmness which was curiously comforting. One thing was certain, one hope now absolutely dead, their life together was finished. There could be nothing between them even if they lived together for another hundred years. His hand briefly touching

61

her shoulder had meant nothing because he had nothing to give her. She sat there, remembering the touch of another hand recently on her body and for the first time since that had happened she made no effort to push the memory from her mind.

CHAPTER FOUR

BERNARD WENT BACK to London on the Monday. It did
not surprise Margaret that Bernard could or would not wait
over until she had seen her doctor on the Tuesday afternoon.

Her doctor, Harrison, an elderly, overworked man who had
known her for some years, and who had a shrewd idea of the
lines along which her marriage ran, was sympathetic but
deliberately evasive in committing himself to any specific
judgment or recommending any particular treatment.

After a few general questions when she had outlined her
problem, he asked, "How do you and Bernard get on . . . I
mean as man and woman?"

Margaret said, "We don't sleep together. We haven't for
years. Is that what you mean?"

"Yes. What about children?"

"We wanted them when we were first married. Nothing
happened . . . then, after a time, well we just accepted that
there would be none. Secretly, I think Bernard was relieved."

"Lots of marriages are childless. But, apart from that, are
quite normal. We'll have a look at you in a moment and see
how you are physically. Just give me a general idea of your
routine during the week. You know, the friends you see, the
things you do. Social activities and so on."

She told him. The account was brief.

He said, "You keep yourself pretty much to yourself, don't
you? It could help if you had more interests and contacts.
There are plenty of things you could find to do. Social work,
recreational stuff. Why don't you join a golf or a tennis club?

63

See more of your friends. If you don't absorb yourself in outside things, with other people, you turn in on yourself and that upsets the balance of a lot of things." He smiled. "Would you be annoyed if I suggested that this impulse to steal is merely a desire to escape, or a wish to draw attention to yourself—forced on you subconsciously—because you are dissatisfied with what you are and what you do to fill your days?"

"I'm a frustrated woman?"

"In a sense." He looked at her over his glasses, twisted his mouth wryly and said, "The only thing is you've been landed with a rather awkward form of compensation. However, since you've been to see me if you do have any trouble I'm sure it can be handled discreetly. So don't worry about that side of it. This is a small town and we know how to look after our own. Right, well now let's have a look at you."

She went away with a prescription for pills which she was to take three times a day and an injunction to report to Harrison any further incidents in shops. He was confident, however, that now she had talked to someone about her trouble it would go. If it did not, he would make an appointment for her to see a specialist.

Margaret went home, relieved to have talked to him and to have had his reassurance, but quietly convinced that in some way neither of them had really gone to the heart of the matter. She did not blame Harrison for his friendly dismissal almost of her problem. He had too many real problems of other people to keep him busy. Perhaps, she felt now, she had known all along what her trouble was. She had wanted in marriage what every woman wanted, a man to love her and to give her children. Bernard had denied her this. Not deliberately, maybe, but effectively. And to be fair, she could now ask herself whether part of the trouble had not been her own fault. He had been the first—the only—man to know her. And with her rapture had gone fear. She had genuinely thought in their early unmarried days that she had been pregnant. Now, she could consider quite clinically whether he would ever have

64

married her otherwise. Without meaning to she had trapped him. And without knowing it, she had found herself the only true prisoner in the trap.

When he rang that evening from London, she said that Harrison felt there was nothing to worry about, that she was run down, that the bad patches would pass, and that already she felt much more confident herself that all would be well. She was content to dismiss the whole affair as of no importance because she knew that it was now quite clear that she was of no importance to him.

When he rang off, she replaced the receiver and went back to her chair and her book. She knew now that without any true point of crisis—unless that brief moment of his hand touching her shoulder before he went to call the doctor had been it— the break between them was final. From now on there was nothing he could do which could touch her with even the slightest shadow of distress. She was her own mistress. From now on she was accountable only to herself. What she would do with her freedom—and she was determined to do something with it—she had at the moment no idea. There would be plenty of time to make a decision. Until then she was content with the knowledge that she was free and the options open to her many.

Two days later on an afternoon of November mist which hung like still wood smoke over the town and river, shrouding from sight the gulls who called through it, she stole three pairs of grey socks, children's size, and only discovered them in her pocket when she got out of her car at the beach park. She gave them to the leading nun at the head of the orphanage crocodile and continued her walk up the misty beach without any distress.

Billy Ankers sat in his car and waited for her to return. She was away half an hour and came back across the dunes to the car park. She was carrying a long ribbon of dark green seaweed and two small pieces of drift wood which she put in the boot of her car. Billy saw nothing unusual in this. The beach walkers often took pieces of drift wood home to brighten their fires with salt blue flame and many took seaweed ribbons to hang outside their doors as weather gauges. He went back to Nancy and his coffee and Dundee cake. Mr Bernard Tucker was wasting his money. It would be nice, he thought, to have money to waste.

\* \* \* \*

In the next two weeks Maxie went up to Lopcommon at night and watched the house for an hour or two. Without any arrogance, he had no doubt now of what must happen. Sitting in the darkness there were long periods when, although his eyes watched the lighted house, his thoughts were far from her directly. He looked ahead, seeing his future, not settling for any definite shape to it, planning and altering it as the fancy took him. He wanted money and he wanted freedom of a different nature from the one he already enjoyed. He had been brought into this life with a debt owing to him and, with each day, without any self-pity, he knew the debt had grown. Somebody had to pay it. That somebody was going to be Margaret Tucker. The details of payment could be decided when she belonged to him.

During those two weeks, too, he showed himself to Margaret on the beach and among the burrows. He never went near her, but as she walked the sands he would sit sometimes on a dune and watch her and know that she had seen him though no recognition passed between them. Once or twice he hid himself as his glasses picked her up coming on to the sands by the beach park. Unseen by her he watched her as she came up the strand. The turn of her head opposite the places from which he usually watched her told him that she was looking for him. Usually he would let her pass without revealing himself. But now and then he would suddenly stand up in full sight of her. Always she would turn her head away and walk on. But her walk from the moment of sighting him betrayed her. It lost its natural rhythm, became for a while awkward and self-conscious, and he was content to see that it was so.

66

When Margaret did come, it was in no way as he had imagined it. In hiding he watched her come along the sands. The tide was low, baring the mud flats and sea-wrack-covered rocks at the estuary mouth. The wading birds moved and flighted restlessly at their feeding. A handful of shelduck took to the air and winged in a black and white skein up river. He saw Margaret pause and watch them. It was a mild day for November and the westering sun streaked the wet sands with a silver lustre. The southerly breeze down the estuary took the skirts of her light coat and flared them away from her body as though she had suddenly grown wings and was awkwardly trying them. She stood facing the sea, leaning back a little into the strengthening breeze. Then she turned and began to walk diagonally across the sands towards the dunes. For a moment or two Maxie watched her, wondering where she was going.

She came to the highwater mark and picked her way through the drift and tide rubbish and then into the dunes. For a moment or two he had her in sight, and then she vanished behind the shoulder of a grassy slope. For a while he watched the dunes for some sight of her, but she did not come into view. He rolled over from his lying position and sat up. She knew the burrows fairly well and he guessed that she was taking one of the many paths that led back to the car park. For a moment or two he was tempted to cut across the burrows and find some spot where he could, in full view, sit and watch her pass. Then he decided against it and began to walk slowly back to his cottage.

\*     \*     \*     \*

There were many things which told her exactly where she was, although she had no memory of coming here. She had stood on the sands, feeling the wind against her back, watching the birds feeding on the mud flats and rocks. Five or six had taken off, black and white ducks, rising into the wind and going

67

inland and she had half-turned, seeing them through the moving web of her hair blown across her face. Then, as they moved up the estuary, heading for the junction of the two rivers, she had turned further to hold them in sight and had found herself moving too.

There was no thought in her then because a warm, assuring peace, so sure that it was almost a physical presence near her, had drawn her into movement, compelling her, making her laugh a little to herself as the odd notion took her that she had to follow the birds, wanted to follow them, to rise and join them. And then, as her feet moved splashing through the water-rilled sand, the warm pressure of familiar hands had cradled her brow and she had been drawn forward, letting herself go wherever the calmness and certainty in her should lead, abandoning herself without any fear, her consciousness taken in trust by some power outside her.

Sitting now, she knew what had happened. For a moment she half-started to move her hands to her coat pockets, wondering what she would find, and then stopped the impulse, knowing without alarm or the brief, familiar agony of other times, that there would be nothing there.

It was a large, low-ceilinged room, taking up most of the ground floor of the cottage. She sat on a wooden chair at a broad table whose top was covered with some flowered plastic cover. In its centre a small glass vase held a few sprigs of yellow gorse mixed with the blue faces of periwinkle that bloomed most of the year in the hedgerows here. A pile of stiff-backed exercise books sat on one corner of the table. Immediately before her was a half-finished water colour of a heron propped against a slanting drawing board supported by two bricks. Something about the heron's long beak and the wooden expression in its eye reminded her of a rather dour clerk at her bank, void of personality, shoulders hunched spiritlessly. She smiled at the memory. Whenever she saw him now she would think of the heron.

The curtains at the far window were cheap cotton, clumsily

68

hung and the sill below them was a mess of odds and ends. An open door to her left gave her a glimpse of a small kitchen with a white sink and a brass tap from which water drippped steadily. She had an impulse to get up and busy herself doing things for this place. She could turn off the tap, tidy the mess on the window sill. There was a fine lacing of old cobwebs above the entrance door, everywhere the small untidinesses in the general rough order and cleanliness of the place which were never registered by a man's eyes. On the mantel over the fireplace were two brass candlesticks and a row of hermit crab shells, two of them painted with silver and gold gilt. Perhaps he collected and decorated them and sold them with his crude paintings to the summer visitors. A corner cupboard, glass-fronted, held crockery and cups and saucers and on top of it lay a bunch of thistles, their dried heads faintly touched with a fine festoon of cobwebs. He had picked them and put them there and forgotten them. She could see him coming into this room, pausing and looking for a place to put them and forget them. To one side of the fireplace was a set of shelves, standing shoulder high, crammed with books which she would have liked to examine and from them learn so surely something of him to mark more of the man he was. But she sat where she was. The time for that would or would not come. She was content now to sit and wait for events to shape themselves around her.

She heard him coming up the garden path, half-turned and saw the inside movement of the door latch as he thumbed it from outside. He came into the room, his back to her as he shut the door, not seeing her until he turned.

As he faced her, there was more calmness in her than she had ever known. His pilot coat was unbuttoned. The top of his shirt was open, his skin brown, a few dark hairs showing above the loose white vee of his shirt. For a moment or two he said nothing. He stood there watching her and then slowly took off his peaked cap. Without looking, he reached behind him and hung it on the door hook.

Making no move, he looked at her and she knew that there

69

was surprise in him. He was flooded with it and needed time to rise clear of it. She watched him slowly surface, watched the expressionless face move to a smile and then to the deeper muscle movements of a chuckle which briefly flashed white teeth against the hickory tan of his face.

He said, "So you've come?"

"That was what you wanted. You told me there was either wanting all the way—or an end of it."

"And which do you want to happen?"

"I haven't asked myself that. I just want to know."

He nodded and then said, "Come on then, girl."

He moved past her, behind her. She turned her head and watched him. Across the last third of the room two red curtains, ceiling high, were strung on brass rings along a stretched wire to close off the end of the room. Raising his arms he slid the curtains aside and then stood at the entrance he had made and waited for her.

She rose and went to him, past him. The curtained space held a large old-fashioned brass-bedstead covered with a patchwork quilt, the pillows exposed. On a wooden chest by the wall at the head of the bed was a cheap alarm clock and a pile of magazines.

She heard him pull the curtains over, the bedroom space suddenly shadowed, lit only by a narrow window beyond the bed. He went past her and drew the cotton curtains over the window. He said, "I never use the upstairs rooms. The floors are bad."

As he turned back and looked through the gloom at her, the trance-like certainty and calm in her were ripped away as though in one magical sweep of a hand she had been stripped naked. Her body shivered and her shoulders shook and she felt all strength and acceptance ebb from her.

He came towards her, put a hand gently on her shoulder and said, "It's all right, girl. It's all right."

He moved her forward and turned her to him at the bedside. His face was close to hers. She knew that he could feel her

70

body shaking, and against the weakness of her flesh she wanted his arms around her to still her, to gentle her back to the calm and peace she had known until now.

He put up a hand and laid the back of it against her cheek and said, "It'll go. It's been a long time for both of us." His hands went to her shoulders and pressed her down gently so that she sat on the edge of the bed, sat like a child, obediently, the shaking in her body easing. He knelt down and began to untie the latches of her shoes. He took them off and slowly fondled her feet with his big hands, lowered his head and kissed the instep of her right foot through the stuff of stocking, the warmth of his lips lightly stirring against her cold flesh. Then he looked up and smiled, and the smile was the smile of the small boy she had seen in the orphanage crocodile, but grown now to the smile of a man, mischievous, pleased, acknowledging the gift and the giving to come.

His hands went up to the waistband of her skirt and began to deal awkwardly with the zip fastener, so awkwardly that without looking she knew now that they were trembling as her body had trembled. She smiled and shook her head at him, and dropped her own hand, brushing his away, and began to free the fastener herself.

\*     \*     \*     \*

Billy Ankers was worried. He was also cold. It was a combination which did not improve his temper. What could the bloody woman be doing? She had parked her car at half-past three and gone off down the beach. The tide had been dead low then. It was now half-past seven. When he lowered the window of his car he could hear the returning tide, noisy in the calm which had followed the sudden dropping of the southerly wind, as it ate its way up the beach. There were only two cars left in the park. His and Mrs Where-the-hell-was-she-Tucker?

At half-past six he had left his car and taken the old military

71

road at the back of the burrows. Something could have happened to her. Sprained ankle, couldn't walk? Perhaps some assault on her in the far burrows. God knows it happened occasionally. Or it was easy enough right up the far estuary end of the sands to go mooning along and be caught by the tide coming in around the back of you.

He came back through the darkness to his car at seven o'clock. It was useless to go stumbling around unable to see a yard in front of his face. But now, there was real concern in him unlinked to his professional curiosity. Something must have happened to her. He sat in his car and decided to give her until half-past seven—and then what would he do? Go to the police? Well, he supposed he could. They knew him. He could tell them that he had been watching her. They'd keep it quiet and arrange a search for her . . . but Mr Tucker wouldn't be pleased if it came to his ears. What man having his wife watched would be?

When half-past seven came, he still sat in his car, the engine running to give him some heat against the night cold. Ten minutes—and then he would really go and get the police. He kept looking at his wrist-watch anxiously. If he went to the police he wouldn't get away for hours. God Almighty, they would probably expect him to come out here again with them. And this was one of Nancy's nights. Goodbye to any warm cuddling up in bed between nine and eleven. Life, he thought, was full of disappointments for some. Mr Bloody Bernard Tucker was probably sitting down to a posh dinner somewhere in London right now, with some fancy tart who'd later keep him busy in bed half the night. Nice to be Mr Tucker, well-heeled, having his wife watched while he tom-catted about London boring the neat backsides off willing girls explaining the troubles he had with his wife.

His angry, rueful mood was suddenly broken by the flare of headlights from the car across the park. Margaret Tucker's car backed and then swept forward in a fast arc across the gravel. She passed within a few yards of Billy Ankers' car. In the

72

reflected glow of light from the headlamps he caught a glimpse of her face. Then she turned sideways and, for an instant, he could have sworn that she half raised an arm in a gesture of farewell towards the far side of the park.

He looked across the park but could see nothing except the dark swell of the rising dunes against the pale, starlit night sky.

*    *    *    *

Bernard Tucker was not 'tom-catting around London'. He was in his flat, a glass of whisky on the table at his side, reading a fat dossier on Sir Harry Parks, once the general secretary of one of the largest trade unions in the country, for many years a member of the Trades Union Congress and, for a year not long before his retirement, chairman of the Congress itself. He was a man who, in his time, had been a national figure, a man much respected and, though moderate in his views, one who had always known how to be iron-hard in negotiation when the circumstances called for it.

Earlier that day Warboys had come into his office and dropped the file on his desk. Quint had not been in the room.

Warboys, shrugging his collar up around his lean neck, said, "You might like to do some speculative homework. I'm only playing a hunch, Bernard—but it cheers up a dull day. The file comes from the darker side of the Department of Trade and Industry. You'll find it compendious but far from complete, but there's a chattiness about it which may be helpful."

Looking at the file cover Tucker asked, "You think he's the man?"

"Like to take a bet that he won't be dangling his feet under the ducal board?"

Tucker had smiled and shook his head.

Now, he lowered the file to his knees and reached for his glass. The material was chatty, true enough. Gossipy, too. But badly arranged and perfunctory and irritatingly disconnected at times. If Quint had made such a file and presented it to him, he would have blistered him. Even so, he could see why Warboys had given it to him. A picture of the man rather than the trade unionist came over clearly and—surprisingly from the official jargon and press cuttings—warmly. Sir Harry Parks had to be a likeable man.

He wondered what was leading him to Vigo Hall. He could have thought of a dozen trade union officials of rank who might have come higher in the betting odds as a likely traitor. But you never could tell, he thought. Some beetle was gnawing him. Nothing, nobody, was ever what the surface showed. Dig away, strip off the covers and there was always something underneath to surprise you.

The flat bell rang, three times, short and sharp and then, after a pause, with one long ring. Although she had a key she always obeyed his injunction and then waited. If he did not answer the door within five minutes she would let herself in. She knew little. What she might have guessed he had never asked her. And she herself was a woman who had a sure instinct for not asking the wrong questions.

He took the file and locked it in his desk. When he opened the door she stood there, holding in her hand the loose silk scarf she had taken from her dark hair, her small face framed in the high roll of her fur collar, eyes almost tear-bright from the cold outside. It had been three weeks since he had seen her but he had no need of absence to heighten his pleasure as he drew her into the hallway and kissed her. She possessed the miracle of always coming freshly and surprisingly to him, delight wrapped around her like a constantly changing aura.

She sat in an armchair and talked while he made her a drink. He listened, asking a question now and again. She had been to Paris and then down to Rome on a business trip. She had her own business in London, a small fashion house whose limits she rigorously and exclusively controlled. He knew more

74

about her than she would ever know of him. But they both understood exactly the boundaries of their liaison and shared intimacies. If he ever were free of Margaret she would not be the woman he would marry. She would stay in his life until the easy terms of their relationship lapsed without dispute. He was far from certain that, if freedom came, he would ever marry again. It was a question he was in no hurry to answer.

She drank, arching her eyebrows over the glass at him and said, "Now you. Tell me what you've been doing. Did you go down and see your mother in Dorset?"

"Yes, I did. A couple of weeks ago."

"How was she?"

"Old and able as usual. She's having the house redecorated and is fussing about new curtains." He sat down on a stool close to her and took one of her hands, gently massaging and warming it with his own. She knew his mother was a myth, but had never suggested her knowledge in more than a quiet teasing remark which carried her disbelief like a faint shadow. He loved her for that, just as he knew she loved him and knew that he, not even in the mildest way, would ever imply that her trips abroad might not all be on business. When she had first come to him he had soon known that she had two other lovers, and had known when they were her lovers no longer. If she slept with someone abroad he neither minded nor wanted to know.

She said, "I could get patterns for her. You could take them down. The material, too, if she wishes. There'd be a trade discount. If you like I could motor down with it. I'd love to meet her. She sounds such a marvellous old lady." Her eyes met his, the thrust put gently, knowing she could never embarrass him in this familiar deceit.

He said, "The wilds of Wiltshire are no place for you."

"You said Dorset."

"I know." He grinned, because there was no question of recovering from any mistake made by him since he relished the

75

intentional byplay, the mock, affectionate cut and thrust which delighted them both. "You see, it happens that the house stands on the Dorset–Wiltshire boundary and the drawing-room, where the curtains are needed, is in Wiltshire."

She laughed and then leant forward and kissed him on the forehead. As her lips rested there he reached and took her glass from her hand and placed it on a side table. Her mouth came down to his lips, brushing them lightly then withdrawing a little so that she looked close into his eyes and said quietly, "I believe everything you say. It is so much more interesting than the truth."

\*  \*  \*  \*

The wind which had been southerly all day had gone round to the west, strengthening and bringing rain with it. Now and again it gusted strongly against the bedroom windows, the blown rain noisy against the glass like the sharp assault of hailstones. Sometimes in a lull Margaret could hear the sound of the brook at the bottom of the garden beginning already to run in a fast, brown-coloured spate. Against her own warmth and contentment the wildness of the night outside made a wild contrast. She felt secure, safely cocooned against all fears, the short memory of the passing day a shield against the shadows of remorse or anxiety if they should ever come.

The telephone at the bedside rang. She picked it up and heard the brief pipping sound of a call-box mechanism.

She said, "Hullo?"

He said, "Hullo, girl. Were you asleep?"

She said, surprised by the evenness of her voice, "No, Maxie . . . I was just lying here. Where are you?"

He laughed. "Out in the wild night. The call box at Lopcommon Cross. Listen—it's no night for either of us to be alone. Slip down and unlock the door. I'll be with you in ten minutes, love."

Before she could say anything the connection was broken.

76

She slipped out of bed, put on her dressing gown and went down and unlocked the front door. There had never for a moment been any thought in her that she should say no, or even passingly pay some thought to caution. Already she knew that his wants were hers, that there could be no question of trying to school the force and frankness of his manner. Time might do it, would do it, she was sure, but for now she was happy to be, do and to think in his service. He was the small boy grown man, love his pleasure and gift to her, appetite his strength. That afternoon he had taken her awkwardly and greedily the first time. She had been hurt but the pain was lost in the pleasure of being wanted. He had taken her twice more before she had left with a greed little less than the first time. She had matched his greed with her own, both losing themselves in it, and then, talking with him as the darkness grew, she had been happy in her own knowledge that the first days of breaking their famine would bring the others. . . .

She heard the front door open and then his steps on the stairs. He came into the room, pausing at the door as she sat up. He was wearing his peaked cap and a large seaman's oilskin coat, its blackness sleeked to the shine of wet coal by the rain. He hesitated, smiling at her, and then slowly took off his oilskin and cap and dropped them at his side in a heap on the floor.

He came over and looked down at her.

"You look," he said, "like I've always known you would look when I've been out there and watched the windows. I take no shame from that . . ." the West Country burr thickened a little in his voice, ". . . a man in love knows no rules."

He bent, cupped her face in his cold, wet hands and kissed her gently on the lips and she felt the damp sweep of his loose dark hair fall against her forehead like another caress.

He stepped away from her and said, "Lie there. I'll be with you."

He went to the bathroom door and opened it, then paused and, looking back at her, said, "Have you ever seen the

77

washplaces at the orphanage? Bare as charity. To go to a tin tub full of hot water in my own kitchen was a luxury. I like luxuries, girl. The right kinds. You can talk to me through the door."

He went into the bathroom and began to run the bath and she called to him, "Use the big blue bathtowel."

He called to her now and then and she answered him, but what he said or she said meant nothing to her. She lay waiting for him, hearing him splashing and breathing, knowing that he was bringing not life to her alone, but to the house. Never once had she seen Bernard bath. He had his own bathroom off his own bedroom. Even in their early days he had maintained an almost prim convention about nakedness, coming to her in the dark as though to be seen defenceless was some shame, some weakening of his manhood.

He came out of the bathroom to her, naked and unhurried, and into the bed with her. He slipped her nightdress over her head and shoulders and took her in his arms and lay still with her for a long time, his lips against hers, his hands and arms marking the smooth contours of her body which stirred and abandoned itself to his caresses as she held herself to him. And then he took her, now gently, moulding and swinging her to the leisurely crests of bliss and then holding her sated in the long troughs of contentment, her mind freed of all thought.

When she woke in the morning and reached for him, he was gone, but on the pillow where his head had rested he had left a smooth, red sea pebble, wind- and wave-shaped so that it had roughly the form of a thin, flat heart with fine streakings of green and white veining through it. She took it and put it against her lips, tasted the salt from it, and shut her eyes against the slow beginning of tears of joy.

*       *       *       *

Maxie as he cooked his breakfast in his cottage kitchen was content. It had begun. Begun as he had wanted it. She had a

78

body that any man who was a man would want. And the hunger in her had been so strong that he had taken her with a rough hunger which had surprised him. She wanted no fancy wooing. Not to begin with. Later, last night, yes, and that he welcomed, preferred, because there was no true unthinking lust in him. He knew himself too well for that. The old Adam could send you forward, stir the flesh, but—even in the brief days of a holiday dunes encounter—he had always taken what was given and coloured it his way. Love was whatever it was. You could argue that from here to Land's End and get no answer. But a man was no more than a beast if with the taking and the giving he did not make some worship, paint the plainest idol in his own colours. A man had a tongue and a body and they should serve him well, leaving frank coupling to animals. When you were inside any woman you could only despise yourself if you did not offer more than the flesh. Although his eyes could tell him, and his hands confirm that the years had slackened and plumped some parts of her body, that there was a slight coarseness in the fair hair and the tiny wrinkles set about her eyes made her no girl, though he called her such, his delight in her dismissed all this. She was a woman with a strong, shapely body, no lean, unused girl; a woman who now belonged to him. He was her master, the mastery already begun with the smooth gentling of caresses and words. You thickened your accent a little, you put a slight old-fashioned touch to your words, you called her 'girl' and so wrapped the barely visible mantle of fatherly protection around her, and when you took her to the high pitch of her body's joy, you could coarsen your words and against her passion ride her hard into the exhaustion of the body's bliss. . . .

He turned the two eggs in the pan, closing their eyes with the hot fat. He could handle her, he could talk her through whatever days had to come. As a painter he was nothing, but with his body and his words he could do what he wanted with her. He smiled at the thought of the heart-shaped stone he had left on her pillow. Sentimental, romantic, a love token—and of love she would have awakened filled to the brim. He'd picked it up two years before and kept it, knowing then that it would have its use one day. Two years ago, and he had known then that one day he would place it on a pillow in some woman's bed, and not any woman, but the woman of his choice.

\*     \*     \*     \*

A week later Billy Ankers typed another report to Mr Bernard Tucker.

He began it at half-past two in the afternoon and was still at it when Nancy brought his coffee and cake at four. He was taking his time over the report. A man, after all, was entitled to all the pleasure he could wring from the few triumphs that came his way. As a concession, too, to the report's importance he occasionally looked up the spelling of a few tricky words in the pocket dictionary on his desk. On the whole, he thought, he'd done a damned fine job. Mr Tucker might not be exactly pleased, but at least he couldn't be disappointed with the service. Thank God, too, he'd earned the bonus for positive results. That had been bargained for and promised. No matter the different sorts of man Mr Tucker might be, he knew that he wasn't the kind to welsh on that. And thank God, too, he didn't have to sit half frozen in a car any longer, or snoop about the burrows getting sand all in his clothes and hair watching Maxie Dougall's place. Lord, you never knew, did you, what would take a woman's fancy? Margaret Tucker he'd have bet would have gone for fancier game. Like one of the toffee-nosed types at the golf club. He knew a thing or two about them. Or maybe some doctor, young and hot-blooded enough not to have got over the kicks yet of having it laid out without a stitch on, ready and waiting on a surgery blanket and else-where. Like that young Barwell last year who'd got the chop from the British Medical Council. God, you'd think they'd have more sense. But it had to be Maxie Dougall. Well, good luck to him. Nice chap, but a bit of a dark horse. Plenty of rumours, too, about him and holiday girls on the dunes. Though there was no blame in that. They came down here from a year in an office or a factory and, one sniff of the briny air, and they were romping away like a lot of fillies let out to spring grass. There was no knowing with woman, and that was God's truth. And, you had to face it, it might be a damned sight duller world if there was.

He flicked the three-quarter-filled sheet of paper down over the typewriter keys as Nancy put the tray by the side of the table.

Billy looked at the tray and said, "That's not Dundee."

"Madeira. We've run out of Dundee. What's so special about it anyway?"

Pleased with himself, ready to include her marginally in his euphoria, he said, "I'll tell you what's so special about it. A man has a fancy for something. He doesn't know where it comes from. But he has it and it means a lot to him. Same goes for a woman, too. You don't have to be able to explain it. You just know you like it."

Nancy stepped away from him before he could run his hand up her skirt and said, "You don't have to wave a flag when you fancy yourself. It's all over your face. Up here since just after two typing away, and a week gone by since you came back here swearing and cursing with the cold from a trip to the North Lobb. It's all right. I'm not asking any questions."

"You'd get no answers. But hear this, whatever it is, I get a bonus. Fifty quid. What about a few nights in Bristol?"

Nancy said, "I'll ask Mum. Maybe she'd like to come too."

"Oh, sure. Bring her along. We can always push her over the Suspension Bridge when we get there."

Nancy grinned. Moving to the door she paused and said, her mood changing swiftly, "If it is who I think, then I'm sorry about it. She's a nice lady. Not like some that come in the shop that I could name."

Billy said, "Niceness is nothing to do with it. Everyone is people and people, God help us, well . . . they're just unpredictable. I could tell you things that would make your hair stand on end——"

But Nancy wanted to be told nothing. She had gone. Billy took a mouthful of madeira cake and went back to his typing. The bonus would come all right, but there'd never be a weekend in Bristol so long as that tough old mother of hers was around. Right, now where was he?

He began to type again.

> On 27th inst. followed subject to car park at 4 p.m. but she did not park car and took old military road between dunes and golf course and Lobb marshes. I followed on foot and from high dune observed progress. Subject parked outside cottage on marsh owned and occupied by one, Maxie Dougall.

He paused. Lord knows what had got into them. They took no damned trouble to hide a thing. Like a couple of kids . . . just like a couple of kids who've just discovered what they've got it for. Well, he wished her joy, he really did, and she'd better make the most of it because for certain there was trouble coming to her.

\*    \*    \*    \*

Margaret lay on the big, old-fashioned bed, the patchwork cover pulled up under her armpits, covering her breasts and leaving her shoulders bare. Outside a half-gale, strengthening towards full force every minute, was roaring in from the sea. Now and again it shook the cottage, rattling the door and windows, setting the curtains pulsing gently from the draughts that came through the ill-fitting frames. The big curtain which divided the long room had been pulled partly back so that she could see the table at the far end. It was set with a white cloth which she had brought down to the cottage and with Maxie's cutlery and crockery. On the hearthstones of the fire stood an uncorked bottle of claret which she had taken from the

82

small cellar which Bernard kept at home. Neither she nor Maxie drank much, but tonight was a celebration for she was going to stay with him until the morning for the first time.

Through the open doorway she could hear him, busy in the kitchen and whistling to himself. She had come to him in late afternoon and they had made love while the gale had risen around them, made love as though their passion drew some strength from the wildness of the wind itself.

Lying now while Maxie prepared the evening meal, refusing to let her help in any way, she tried in the calm which possessed her body and mind to recognise the woman she had so quickly become. Her hunger for him matched his own for her, they were starvelings let loose at a banquet. Her delight in him was his delight in her. She had not known she could be so uncaring, or had so much wildness in her, nor so much frankness of body and speech. But it had all been there, waiting for him to draw it from her. They were like children, every wild instinct dragooned too long, who were now turned out to the rich acres of a joyful liberty arrived at last.

In her mind Bernard was rejected. She lived only for Maxie. She made some small concessions to discretion, but they were few. For days now she had looked nowhere but towards Maxie, had lived only when he was with her, had dreamed while he was away. There was neither care nor caution in her. She wanted no one but him, no time but when he was with her; wanted no satisfaction except his satisfaction and carried not even the pale ghost of a memory of Bernard or her past life when Maxie was with her, covering her with his hard brown body. Discretion had fled before the changing delights of being with him. Two days ago in the afternoon, he had taken her at high tide to watch the great flocks of waders and seabirds, forced from their feeding grounds by the rising waters, wheel in vast cohorts through the air as they came inland to the marshland to roost and work the ditch-cut land, to settle in head-to-the-wind phalanxes and wait for the turn of the tide. Knots, dunlin, redshank, curlews, sanderlings, black-headed gulls and widgeon, teal and shelduck . . . she had leaned back against his chest, watching them through his glasses as he pointed them out. Then, as she had turned to ask him some question, hunger for her had shadowed his eyes. Without a care for the world around, he had pulled her down to the dune grasses and he had taken her, quickly and fiercely.

Maxie came into the room now from the kitchen. Wearing only shirt and trousers, he padded barefoot across the room and stood beside her. Smiling down at her, he bent slowly and kissed her lips and then pulled the patchwork quilt away with a flick of his hand so that she lay naked.

"Everything's ready, girl, except the steaks. They'll take five minutes. Up with you, that's an order."

Teasing him, she said, "I don't want to eat. I just want to stay here. I want you here with me."

He bent quickly, rolled her over and smacked her bare behind.

"Up."

Without another look at her, he moved back to the kitchen. But she went with him in his mind. His woman, naked freely to his eyes, his woman to take and to order, to do with as he willed. He had known it would happen one day, had sat in this place and imagined it, and now saw it in truth.

CHAPTER FIVE

BERNARD TUCKER FINISHED changing for his weekend in Wiltshire. His small case, already packed, lay on the bed. In the street one of the official cars was waiting for him.

He took his keys from the dressing table, pocketed them, patted his suit to make sure that he had his wallet, and then strapped on his gold wristlet watch. It was a specially adapted wristwatch which contained a tape-recording device on which he could register conversations and his own personal observations. He took a last look at himself in the full-length mirror. On the scales that morning he had turned twelve stone. A couple of pounds to the bad. Gone were the days when he had been all bone and muscle, could eat like a horse without putting on weight, go nights without sleep and still face the new day bright-eyed. Life was re-shaping him. He was built for desk work now, not bridge work.

Although he was surprised, he gave no sign of it when he found Quint in the back of the car.

As the car drove off, Quint said, "Warboys told me to come. Something for you to read in the train." He handed Bernard an envelope.

Quint looked at his watch. "You're leaving it a little fine, aren't you, for that train?"

Bernard shook his head. "No. I'm not catching it. I checked your times. The whole journey can be repeated two hours later. It won't make any difference the other end."

Quint smiled to himself. Trust nothing, trust nobody. The precaution, he knew, was not directed against any lack of

85

faith in him. It was just a routine act. Live and work long enough with Warboys and Tucker and the thing was commonplace. He should have expected it. His only consolation now was that he had shown no surprise, made no question of the re-adjustment. He said, "You've got two hours to waste."

"Tell the driver to take me to the Constitutional. I'll have lunch there."

Quint leaned forward and re-directed the driver.

Not caring much, certainly not annoyed, Bernard accepted the fact that his intention of making the driver stop at Graingers in the Euston Road so that he could go in with the excuse of buying cigarettes and see if there was any mail for him from William Ankers had to be abandoned. He was more and more convinced, anyway, that he was wasting his money on the Ankers service.

The car dropped Bernard at the bottom of St James's Street. He went into the club, left his case with the hall porter, and then telephoned Margaret. He held the calling tones for some time, but there was no reply. He put the receiver down and went into the bar for a drink. Never once had he ever called Margaret from his flat. Calls could be checked and traced. Margaret knew the address of his flat, but she never wrote to him there or telephoned him. It had been eight years since she had last been in London. In the past he had made explanations and had invented excuses for the anonymity that surrounded his London life. Now, and for many years past, she docilely accepted any dictate he issued. They lived their own lives. Usually he telephoned her when he was coming home, but if he could not get her he just turned up.

He tried Margaret's number again after lunch, but there was still no reply. There was no real curiosity in him about her.

Sitting in his train he thought about her for a while before opening Warboys' letter. It was no good telling himself that she had trapped him with her stupid, immature scare of being pregnant. Without that, in the state of mind he had known then, he would have married her. He knew perfectly well now, that he had been looking for some gesture—not complete—that would betray him into a total rejection of the work into which Warboys had drawn him. There had been an early period when he had hated it, and yet had been unable to control his pride in his very real capacity for the work. Marrying Margaret, giving himself, as it then seemed, the impossible task of keeping his marriage secret had been all the defiance he could muster, a substitute for a frankness of decision which could not be drawn from his nature. He had wanted to be found out, and cast out. Had handed the choice to fate. Against all odds fate had cherished and compounded his deceit. And now . . . well, he was glad that it had been so. He wanted Warboys' place, and the places beyond it. Ambition thrived, concealed in him. The only casualty had been Margaret. She had failed him by not being the means of a wanted escape. She should have had the spirit, if not the need, long ago to have deceived him, to have found some retired army type, some widowed business man, someone of her own class for whom her money would have been a real help. Then—without rancour—they could have been quietly divorced in one of the county courts, their names lost in a long list of others, attracting no publicity.

He dismissed Margaret from his mind and opened Warboys' letter.

It read:

*There is something in the air suddenly and it has made the P.M. anxious. This may have got through to the Wiltshire end. If it has humour it and—to save me premature badgering—stay away from town and assess your findings. I don't want to see or hear from you until you bring your report to me on Tuesday at noon. I have an appointment with the P.M. at half-three. There could be another side to this, one that does not use kid gloves. I don't care a damn about the P.M.'s ditherings, but I will not have this Dept. made a target for mud-slinging.*

Bernard was unmoved. At a few rare times in the past they had touched this kind of work. Nobody liked it, least of all Warboys. He knew that the man was only marginally concerned with self-interest and his hopes of a knighthood. The department had a curious ethic, but it was a sincere and powerful one. That the Duke could be sound he was prepared to accept. It would have been impossible to find anyone on the department's staff who felt the same about the newspaper proprietor involved.

He walked down the corridor to the toilet, burnt the letter over the lavatory bowl and flushed the ashes away.

For the next three hours he resigned himself to the tedium of branch railway lines and the changing of trains. At Salisbury station there was a notice on a blackboard by the exit which read—*Commander Tucker. Car—BOU 151 M—waiting.*

He went out and found the car, and a young man standing by it. As they drove off, Bernard thanked him for waiting.

The driver laughed. "His Grace's instructions. If a party's not on the train arranged, wait two more, and then they must fend for themselves."

"Does that go for him, too?"

"Not likely. You wait until the last train, or else."

At Vigo Hall he was looked after by the butler who explained that the Duke was pheasant shooting and would be back for dinner at eight.

He was shown up to his room where a gas fire burned cherry-red, making the place tolerably warm. He told the butler that he would unpack his own things, and refused the offer of tea since, as it was well past six o'clock, he preferred the alternative of a drink. The drinks were laid out on a small stand at the side of the dressing table.

When the butler had gone he poured himself a whisky and soda and examined the room. It was large and solidly furnished with a mahogany bed, a massive wardrobe and chest of drawers and an oak dressing table that rocked a little on the uneven floor boards when touched. The bathroom, partitioned off the

88

main room, was small and narrow. The bath was deep, standing on wrought iron ball and claw legs, and one of the old-fashioned water taps had leaked gently for years, leaving a long scar of rust mark on the enamel below it.

Bernard unpacked, reaching occasionally for his drink, and then sat by the fire to finish it. Outside it was dark. He had seen little of Vigo park as they came up the driveway and of the building had only an impression of heavy grey walls.

As he got up to get himself another drink, there was a knock on the door.

"Come in."

Lady Cynthia Melincourt came in. He recognised her at once from her photographs. She was a tall woman in her late thirties with a long, thin almost masculine face and a slight stoop to her narrow shoulders. She introduced herself, and, seeing the glass in his hand, she said, "I'll join you. This place is always bloody freezing." She nodded at the gasfire. "That denotes your ranking. Benson has been told by father obviously that you must be cosseted. We live in a barracks that's falling down around our ears. If you want anything like comfort you have to pull your rank."

As he poured whisky for her he wondered whether her initial run of chatter came from nervousness or from loneliness. She sat down in the spare chair by the fire, collapsing her long length into it and pushing her feet close to the warmth. She wore a green pullover above a red shirt, and wrinkled corduroy trousers tucked into the tops of short rubber boots.

"Been working," she said, seeing his eyes run over her. "There's an old walled garden at the back of the chapel. As a penance for something I've forgotten or for the greater glory of God, I don't know, I've decided to restore it single-handed. Look—" she put down her glass and spread her hands, "—tough as leather. I can pull nettles now without feeling them. Would I be flagellating myself?"

"You could be enjoying yourself, Lady Cynthia." He liked her and was amused by her but—and no power could undermine his training—he was by no means ready to accept his first impression of her.

She shook her head. "That's too simple. Enjoyment you can buy in any market." She paused, eyeing him, then drew generously at her whisky, and went on, "So you're the man brother Bobby could never keep out of his letters. He thought the world of you. You liked him, or did he bother you?"

Bernard laughed. "No, he didn't bother me. And everyone liked him . . . so much that he never had far to look when he got into trouble. It was a bad day for all of us when he went."

"It's a good epitaph. So . . . you're the cloak-and-dagger man. Oh, don't look so surprised. I don't know anything about you but I know my father." She stood up. "When he is up to something he is always good-tempered because he is delighted at the prospect of mischief. And when he describes someone as being 'a highly placed civil servant' with almost a touch of reverence in his voice instead of saying 'some idiot of a desk wallah from the Foreign Office' then I look for all the signs of another of his little charades. A boring little one-act bit of nonsense entitled 'The Power behind the Throne'. He won't worry you, Commander, but watch him. He attracts disaster like a damp wall does moss. My brother liked you. You were good to him." She made a mock curtsy. "For that, I owe you my frankness for which you do not have to thank me."

Bernard said, "Thank you. Some time, too, you must finish telling me about your walled garden."

There were five of them at dinner, well spaced, almost uncomfortably remote around the long table. The only light came from the candelabra on the table. The Duke sat at the head. He was a small man, his black dress tie twisted askew from the jerking of his head as he turned, birdlike, from one face to another, dark eyes missing nothing, a ready aggressiveness waiting in him to question any opinion that differed from his own. He was jockey-sized and, Bernard knew, had been a well-known amateur steeplechase rider in his young days. Lady Cynthia, in a rust-red gown that left her bony shoulders free, sat at the end of the table, lost almost in the waving shadows thrown by the candle light. She said little, but Bernard could see that her attention was on the servants and the food. She knew her role from her father and, from long domination by him, was—in company at least—reduced of any importance. Felixson, the newspaper proprietor, a youthful forty, bland-faced, clothes immaculate, onyx links and buttons to his shirt, talked too much. This clearly riled the Duke, who had to make a more than seigneurial effort to seize the platform for himself at times.

Warboys had been right about Sir Harry Parks. Bernard sat opposite him. They had been introduced over drinks before dinner. He was a tall man well into his sixties, but looked even older. His face was a complex of worn angles and deep creviced wrinkles, his skin chalk white; a dead face in which only the large, luminous, fast blinking eyes signalled that there was intelligence and a certain sage humour alive in him. Years ago he had schooled his speech to acceptable form, but nothing had taken the North Country accent from it.

The talk was unexceptional apart from Felixson's sallies, and when Lady Cynthia left them to their port there was no improvement. They all knew that they played a charade, that the real business was to come. Back in the long, picture-hung library Lady Cynthia stayed with them for coffee and a liqueur and then, needing no signal from her father, withdrew.

Bernard found himself isolated at the fireplace with Felixson while the Duke at the far end of the room was showing Sir Harry Parks a collection of old medals and antique coins.

Felixson said, "This place is like a morgue. Needs half a million spent on it. The old boy's got it, too, but doesn't care a damn. Why should he? There's no son to pass it on to. You knew him, didn't you?"

"Yes. We served for some time together."

"Out shooting this afternoon, you could see it needs thousands spent about the place. Damn shame. If you own something you should keep it in good shape."

"A fair philosophy—for those who can afford it."

"There are always ways to find money. What most people don't realise is that they've all got something which they can turn into money. Something to sell . . . service, brains, aptitudes or sheer damn buccaneering expertise. Which in converse means that, with cash, if there's anything you want you can always find it and buy it." A faint smile just touching his bland face he nodded with the merest slant of his head towards the Duke and Sir Harry Parks. "He's selling. We're buying—if the stuff is right."

"And your motive?" With little effort Bernard thought he could dislike the man.

Felixson chuckled. "Patriotism? Keep the Reds out? Or maybe just the familiar itch for a good story. I'm a newspaper man. Began on the—" He stopped, grinned, touched his hair gently in almost a feminine gesture, and went on, "You tell me."

Bernard smiled. "Auckland. A throw-away sheet. Twenty years ago. You were sacked for, frankly, bloody rudeness in a pay dispute. So you borrowed—could it have been pinched? —enough money to start a rival sheet. You never looked back."

Felixson laughed, delighted. "Pinched," he said. "Not borrowed. I didn't know then that was the easier way. All right, I'm not worried about you. Warboys—though a touch of the old woman is creeping into his style the nearer he gets to that Honours List—would never have sent a boy to do a man's job. But—" all expression left his face—"we're going to have to take your word that the bomb we will buy is genuine. It's got to be no booby trap that could go up in our faces. Sir Harry Parks the man—not just his wares—is your baby. We act, or we don't, on your say so. I don't want my face blown off, and, I imagine, you don't want the chance of inheriting Warboys' seat blown out from under you." He paused, and then a smile reaming across the varnished face, he added, "Too frank?"

Bernard said, "Perhaps Warboys should have sent a bomb disposal squad." He walked to the fireside table and began to help himself to brandy.

92

Later the Duke buttonholed him. The Duke took him into a small room off the library to show him a collection of seventeenth- and eighteenth-century Dutch and Flemish seascapes and ship paintings.

"Started to collect 'em when Bobby was a boy. He used to spend hours in here. When he went . . . well, it wasn't the first time in this family, Commander. We've spilt the family blood all over the world. But I don't believe in snivelling around. Family's one thing, but your country is another. And this country today—full of snivellers, bloody state-supported snivellers. They're rust on a good crop. Reds, demonstrators, student agitators, bomb-slingers, hi-jackers . . . you name them and we've got them, and sitting right on the top are all these damned trade unions holding the country to ransom with strikes the moment someone treads on a shop steward's toe or they find out that forty-hour-a-week Joe is having trouble keeping up the payments on his colour television and all the other bloody gadgets they fill their houses with. Oh, I know, there are some good trade unionists. Honest chaps. But, by God, I find it hard to be civil enough to pass the time of day with some of their leaders I meet around Whitehall."

He stopped, shook his head like a terrier just come from a briar tangle, and suddenly smiled. "Sorry... This time of night I rant a bit. Drink touches up one's feelings. Anyway, you know what I mean. Something's got to be done for this country. We've got to have the right ammunition. . . ."

There was, thought Bernard, with the Duke and Felixson an almost childish preoccupation with warfare metaphors. Bombs, guns, ammunition, explosions. Frankly, in as much as he allowed himself any political feelings—and a reason why he disliked this job as much as Warboys—he thought that the last people to be trusted with subversive arms were types like the Duke and Felixson. In their own coverts if a guest handled a gun carelessly he was never invited again. Their skins and the skins of their friends were precious. But in political life they would happily light up their cigars while they sat on powder kegs.

93

He said, "I gather the real concern isn't so much whether Sir Harry's wares are sound or shoddy—but Sir Harry himself."

"Exactly. The goods you can examine and say yes or no. But why—and this niggles—are they brought by him? He's the one man I would never have tipped to come to market. We all want to know why. In a sense we've asked him, but we got no convincing reply. The P.M. has suddenly begun to waver about the whole thing. He thinks that the goods may be being planted—to go off in his face. Until he's sure of that we could have trouble with him. So . . ."

"So, you'd like me to find out."

"You're in the right position. Sir Harry knows it all rests on your word. You can talk to him in a way we can't. I know you and Warboys don't like this bag of tricks at all—don't blame you in some ways—but I know your reputations. Particularly yours. Fact I feel I've known you for a hell of a long time. Kept all Bobby's letters. Always full of you. Knew you were good to him when he kept putting a foot wrong. Damned grateful, even now. Sir Harry will talk to you because you're a professional and also because he knows you could queer his sale. We want a straight yes or no from you about him. What you say will be enough for me and the rest of us."

\*　　\*　　\*　　\*

When Bernard went up to his room, the bed was turned down, his pyjamas and dressing gown laid out, and his slippers by the side of the bed. In the centre of the bed was a shabby old box file, its edges dog-eared. On top of it, weighted down with a box of matches, was a sheet of note paper. In a neat, oblique renaissance script were the words—

*I thought it would help if you went through this lot first. I'm an early riser and like a stroll before breakfast. I'm told there's a lake in the park with a rather nice mock Roman temple. I hope it is not as depressing as I find the rest of this place.*

94

It was unsigned.

Bernard took a bath. He put on his pyjamas and dressing gown, turned the gas fire high and began to go through the contents of the box file. Everything was in a rough chronological order. Most of the letters had paper tabs attached to them, detailing the identity and history of the writer and the recipient. The neatness of the work impressed him. The brief, skeleton biographical notes were easily fleshed out by the imagination. He had an immediate respect for the mental qualities of the man who had made them. There were photographs, taken in England and in Europe—some of them patently at a first glance political dynamite. These too had their explanatory tabs and one or two ironical notes which coldly veiled a sharp cynicism. There were hotel bills, photostatic series of union accounts some dating back for fifteen years, and sets of committee minute meetings which had been held in secret. There were private agency reports on individual trade union members, and two or three sets of proceedings of secret tribunals set up to enquire into the handling of various funds and the conduct of liaison centres and communication systems with other trade union parties in Europe. The languages used in many of the letters and documents were Russian, Polish, Dutch, French and Italian. Frequently a translation was attached. Bernard read them in the original and checked the translations. He found that there were often discrepancies and clever distortions of true meanings. Within the first half hour he knew that he was sitting with a bomb on his lap. From the material he had examined so far it was clear that, with the right timing, backed by a properly conducted press campaign (an exposé laid out with all the appearance of dignity and a sense of shocked duty to the public) the labour and left-wing elements could be mowed down in any election like a mob of angry, club-swinging peasantry throwing themselves at the tight ranks of an army meeting them with massed fire and cold steel. He twisted his mouth wryly. Something of the martial imagery of the Duke and Felixson had rubbed off on him.

He read for two hours, making his own translations, entering observations in his note book. If any real emotion touched him in the cold analytical process of his work it was the slight stir of admiration for the subtlety and tactics of Communist groundwork, its use of men's weaknesses, greed, pride, ambition and appetites. One or two of the photographs could never be shown in the press, but they could be prudently described, and would be there to be authenticated by any State enquiry. Years and years ago, he realised, Sir Harry must have been well aware of the undercurrents, and had known that one day the house must be swept clean. There was no hope for the house to which honest, dedicated men had laid the foundation stone. It had to be burned down and a new house built. The prime fuel was here. All that was needed was the match. There would be many hands willing to strike it.

Despite his completely detached professional status, the disciplines which he had learnt in his early training, the dispassionate exercises of body skills and mental acuteness, and the cold assessment now called for from him, he wondered how much it would change the course of British political history if he now were to strike one of the matches which Sir Harry had kindly left and burn the lot.

When he had finished and was ready for sleep, he locked his bedroom door and saw that the windows were fastened. He climbed into bed and pushed the box down with his feet to the bottom. He could almost absolutely discount the need for fear in this house. Nothing, however, was secure, particularly when it most seemed to be.

He woke at half-past six, washed and shaved, dressed, and went down into the park, carrying the box file under his arm. It was a mild December morning, a thin mist knee-high over the ground and the sky, barely light, a gun-metal grey. He walked down a gravelled ride, leafless poplars towering over him, and found the lake. Grebe and coots moved out of the sere reeds and the bent, brown flags to lose themselves in the mist after a few yards.

In the scollop-shaped temple at the far end of the lake he found Sir Harry sitting on a wooden seat beneath the statue of a tall, plump, half-robed goddess. Sir Harry was filling a pipe. He wore an overcoat and cap.

Bernard sat beside him, putting the box file between them. As Sir Harry put the packed pipe to his mouth and patted his pockets for matches, Bernard handed him his box.

"You left them with me."

"Oh, thanks." The man lit his pipe, blowing the smoke in quick spurts from the corner of his mouth. The pipe drawing, he went on, "Since I was a lad I could never bear to lose the early morning. Even come the time when it was going through grey streets to the mill. Morning music, too. Not just the birds. The sound of people. Feet coming down the street, clogs in those days. People and their clogs, they made a music. I apologise for getting you out so soon—particularly as you must have been up some time reading." He beat a brief tattoo on the box file between them. "Dirty stuff. More than once I've had a mind to burn it."

"Why didn't you?"

"Aye, why? There's a good question. Well . . . in the beginning I had faith. I was out of the mill then—union official —working the way my father had always wanted. He was one of the early ones with Keir Hardie and the like. Then, when faith withered a bit, I still had purpose. Not that I didn't know the way some of them wanted to take us. It's always been there for some. Not an organisation of men who had a fair right to sell their labour at a fair price. . . . No, there was always some that saw it t'other way, dreamt of it as a political machine. A weapon of power. Not just to fight the bosses— though, by God, you had to fight them in the beginning even to get a few miserable bob extra. . . ." He stopped, suddenly smiled, and then said, "I'm not by nature a talkative man— 'ceptin' on a platform or at a council table and then it's my job, or was. But I guess you want me to talk. You've read the stuff there." His fingers brushed the box file. "Pandora's box.

97

If you're half the kind I think, you know it's not a box of fancy love letters. Over the last fifteen years I've hated the sight of it every time I came to put something new in it."

Bernard nodded. "No, I don't think we have to talk about the box. And you don't have to worry about the early morning. I've seen my share and enjoyed most of them." He'd seen the sun come up over seas as still as the lake before him, and over other seas that rolled and swung with gale-worked savageness. Now, but for Warboys, he could have been long retired to Falmouth or to somewhere in the Highlands with Margaret. Without Warboys—though he could find no true hate in himself for him—all that might have gone right, his stupid half-challenge for release long accomplished. . . .

"Aye, happen you have, Commander."

Bernard said, "They'll buy. Before I leave I'll give them my word. All I have to do then is write my report for . . . well, the few other gentlemen involved." Despite himself he could not entirely disguise the bitterness that marched with the pen-ultimate word.

Sir Harry chuckled. "It's me then? Why should I do it? Me that could swing block votes in their thousands once. They're thinking, they're sharp these trade union lads. Not hoiks any longer. Don't be taken in by a few dropped aitches and verbs not agreeing with their subject. That's to keep the working man feeling he's in touch. No, they're thinking, why should it be Sir Harry? Where's the trick? Where's the catch, the trap they want us to walk into?"

"Why shouldn't they? Many of their forefathers were playing those games centuries before you came on the scene."

Sir Harry shook his head. "Don't you believe it, Commander. We can go back, too—and not just to Wat Tyler. There were plenty before him. Wherever and whenever there was master and man. But I take your point and—" he smiled suddenly, the long chalk-white face cut deeper with creases and wrinkles, "—since I've got you up so early but you don't want to miss your breakfast I'll give it to you—hard and sharp. Take it or leave it."

"Tell me, then."

"Two reasons. The first few people can escape. I want the money. I've lived my life for a cause. I've a wife and grown-up children and grandchildren. You can have a cause and a family, Commander, but the family suffers. The work you do takes from them, and you give little back. You have to neglect them. You become a stranger to them. So—" he smiled ruefully, "when I go, and I don't think that'll be over long, I'd like to leave them something. Something a little extra. It's as simple and human as that. I feel guilty towards them all. Maybe they don't even see it that way. But I do. And when they get the money, for I shan't touch it, they'll be glad. Aye, they'll use it. It's convenient that that particular reason trots nicely in harness with the second and, for me, more important one."

"You want to burn the house down so that those of your kind who are left can build a new one?"

Sir Harry laughed. "I can see why they sent you. Aye, of course I want the house burnt down. It's rotten. Wood-worm in every beam. But it's owned now—" he tapped the box file with the back of his hand, "by a small clique of men who don't care a damn for democracy, for men's rights, workman or master. I don't call them Communists. They're not interested in equal rights, equal pay, the State control of the means of production and distribution. No—that's all claptrap. They worship power. They don't care a tinker's bugger for Labour or any other party. They want to sit on top of the pile and when they do—which could be sooner than a lot of people might imagine—there'll be master and man again—and God help the man! It's as simple as that, Commander. And don't call me naïve politically. There's your proof in that box. And here, too, another proof—" he jabbed a thumb against his shoulder "—me. I've brought you the kindling to start the fire to burn down the house, though I doubt I'll ever see the beginning of

99

the building of the new one. But built it will be. And if you want me to say more than that you'll not have it. I'll just get up and go."

"And take the box with you?"

"You're a saucy bugger, aren't you? No, Commander, I'll not take it, and you know why. There's no other market for it. Chuck it in the lake."

Bernard took the box and stood up.

"When all this is unloaded. Press, television and radio. They'll know it must come from you. They'll massacre you— one way or another."

Sir Harry shook his head. "No, they won't, Commander. They'll deny it all, of course. Call it all fraud and forgery. They're not stupid. I'm a figurehead still. They'll want all the union solidarity they can find. They know they'll have my backing. While it lasts, I'll be called back. You'll see me on television, hear me on radio, press conferences, election platforms. Honest Harry—they'll need every figure of repute they can get. But make no mistake about this—if over the last weeks they'd had any idea of the course I was going to take, of the stuff I had. . . . Well, then I could easily have had a car or street accident and that little box would have disappeared." He stood up. "Now it's in your hands. You watch yourself, lad. Desperate situations call for desperate remedies. The desperation of men who see their violent hopes about to die doesn't have any limit to it." He smiled. "But I guess you're used to that kind of situation or you wouldn't be here. Aye, and in many ways I wish you weren't here and me neither." He looked at the lake. "A nice, quiet, kindly winter morning. I wish though that I'd never lived to see it."

\*   \*   \*   \*

He kept the box by him while he had breakfast. He was by himself. The Duke and Felixson had breakfast in their rooms. Sir Harry had parted company from him at the end of the lake and had gone off for a walk in the park. Bernard guessed that the man would have no appetite for food.

He sent up a message to the Duke. They met in the Duke's study an hour later. Felixson was there, too.

Bernard put the box file on the top of the Duke's desk. Felixson sat on the window seat and the Duke stood with his back to the large stone fireplace in which a couple of logs burned on a bed of white ash.

Nodding at the box the Duke asked, "That the stuff?"

Bernard nodded. "He left it with me last night. I've been through it all."

"And?" The Duke half-turned and prodded one of the logs with his foot.

"There's no doubt in my mind that it's all authentic."

Felixson began to rise. "Let's have a look at it then."

Bernard put his finger tips on the box and shook his head. "Sorry. No. My brief is that I was to let no one else see it. I've got to work up a detailed report on it, to put it in chronological shape and to lay it all out so that it can be summarised in readable terms. Then I hand it over to the head of my department. So far as His Grace and yourself are concerned I have one instruction: to let you know whether the goods offered are authentic, will produce the result you want, and— a corollary you've both stressed personally to me, though it was also part of my brief—whether Sir Harry was selling from genuine motives. I'm sure you understand that I can't go one inch outside that brief."

"Of course," said the Duke. "So tell us."

"It's authentic. It'll do everything you want."

"And Sir Harry?" Felixson came round the desk and stood, his eyes on the box file.

"I spoke with him this morning. I'll put a précis of his personal and political reasons for his act in my report. But you can set your minds at rest. He's not planting anything on you which, to be graphic, will go off in your faces. He's using you, yes, but in order to destroy an organisation which he knows, in its present, distorted form, is a grave danger to this country."

Felixson made a move as though to say something, but the Duke shook his head.

"There's no need for any more. Thank you, Commander. And thank God it really is all that we want. Now, I suppose you'd like a room somewhere so that you can get down to this report in peace?"

Bernard shook his head.

"No thank you, your Grace. I'd like a car in an hour's time to take me to the station."

"But why can't you do it here?" asked Felixson, his eyes going from Bernard to the box file. "Nobody's going to interfere with you."

Bernard shook his head. "Sorry. I just have to follow my instructions."

"Of course," said the Duke. "Damn it, Felixson, this is nothing to fool around with. You're not going to see or be told anything until the right time comes. The Commander has his instructions. Just be content with what you've got. The stuff's good and so is Sir Harry."

Bernard had expected one of the estate staff to drive him into Salisbury. But it was Lady Cynthia, who explained that she wanted to go into the town to do some Saturday morning shopping.

On the way in she said, "You're a man who believes in very short weekend visits, Commander. I should have liked to have seen more of you."

"Ask me again some time, Lady Cynthia. I'll make amends. Perhaps when you've finished restoring your walled garden."

She left him on the platform for the London train. When she was gone Bernard took a sheet of paper from his pocket and studied a list of train connections he had worked out for himself some weeks before.

CHAPTER SIX

THAT AFTERNOON THEY had driven in her car up on to
the moor. For two or three hours they had walked together, her
binoculars slung around her neck. Although Margaret had
walked the moors and the beaches many times before, it was
only now with Maxie that she was realising how little she had
seen. He could pick out with his naked eye things which to
begin with she had trouble in pin-pointing through her
glasses, the dappled form of a deer lost against the background
of dead bracken, the faint, dark crescent of one of the coast
peregrine falcons sliding between the clouds thousands of feet
up, and the white rump flirt of a stonechat flicking from gorse
bush to boulder on a valley side. He lent her his eyes and brought
new delights to hers. Just, she thought, as he had taken her
and given himself to her and awakened and enriched her body
and spirit. He had shown her the plum and grey beauty of the
flocks of fieldfares, the military echelons of golden plover
standing head to wind on the sheepbitten grass, and the boldly
blazoned back of a jack-snipe a moment or two before it took
flight from the heather almost at their feet.

Coming back she had made a detour and shown him the
house which she owned on the banks of a small river that flowed
down from the moor, Although he seldom asked her direct
questions about herself, her past life, and never anything about
Bernard, he said then. "For God's sake, love, why do you live
where you do now when you could live here?"

"I think I might have done. But Bernard didn't like it."
She had not told him that she let it fully furnished and that
the present tenants were soon leaving.

He grinned. "There's times—not many—when a woman should override her man."

Then, without any sense of forcing him or shyness, since with the passing of their bodily restraints so too had gone any bar to their talk, she said, "Would you live here? With me?"

He said, "Aye, I would, girl. You say the word and I'll throw your tenants out and we'll move in. I've always wanted to live by a river and lie awake at night and hear it talking to itself. The sea's one thing, but it's a giantess that even when she sleeps never takes off her armour. How can you love something like that? But a river, there's a real woman for you. All right, she has her moods, floods in anger sometimes, but for the most part she goes her way biddable and serene."

She laughed and teased him, "You should write poetry. You shouldn't be content to sell those ridiculous paintings."

"They sell because they are ridiculous. And I eat from them. And if there's any poetry in me, it's not for writing, girl. It's something you bring out. You should have handled your Bernard better and made him live here."

"You don't know Bernard."

"Oh, I know him." He reached across the table where they were sitting now after supper and took her hand. "I know him and I'm grateful to him because of the way he's wasted and starved you so that I could take you and feed you with my love. He's gifted you to me and I'll always thank him for that, though I could kill him for the years of wasting he put on you."

As he spoke, he stood up, still holding her hand and she knew from the look on his face what was in his mind. She could never mistake that look now. He had taken her before they had started from the cottage on their trip, and again on the moors when the swift need in them both had dragged them down to a bed of crumbling dead bracken.

She shook her head. "Not now, Maxie, darling. I told you. I said to Bernard I'd be back by eight."

Bernard had telephoned just before she had left the house, saying that he had had to come to Bristol on business and would be home that day for a long weekend. She had said she was going out with friends but should be back by eight.

Maxie smiled and shook his head. "How often has he kept you waiting? Let him rot." His last words held an unexpected touch of contempt which surprised him. Normally the thought of her husband roused no emotion in him.

She shook her head. "You're terrible. But I really can't. Oh, Maxie. . . ."

He moved quickly, picked her up and was carrying her through the half-open curtains and the warmth of his arms took all resistance from her.

Half an hour later, he stood at the cottage gate and watched her drive away. The stars were misted by faint drifts of cloud. The wind was changing. By morning he knew that it would be raining. He watched the tail lights of her car pass out of sight on a curve of the old road. She came and went openly now. Neither of them made much attempt to avoid attention. Some people must already guess, perhaps even know, what was happening. He was unworried because it suited his book. He wanted her committed to him. One day her husband would know, must know. The thought held no fears for him. Over the days and weeks he had made her happy. There was no difficulty there. They wanted one another, and she was beginning to speak his language and to think she understood him. Maybe she did, but no more than he wished her to do.

Lying in the aftermath of love-making she had talked, needing no forcing from him. A few things had surprised him, though he had not shown it. He had half-known, half-guessed, that she had plenty of money. But now he realised that she had far more than he had ever imagined, from her father and then much more from her aunt. Telling him about the house on the river today had been a surprise. He already knew that she owned property in Scotland as well. When she talked about money or possessions he envied her. Not just for the possession of these things, but because she could talk of them as though they were of little importance. They were there. There was

105

nothing unique about them. God had ordained it. Just as God had ordained that he should walk in an orphanage crocodile and ever since have been seeking some escape to which even now he could not give a final shape. He had taken her, and would take more. She was already enmeshed in the half-illusion, half-reality of loving him, had put passionate words to it, and had taken his words, too, in exchange. But he was never going to love her or anyone else. Love was a dirtiness which had created him. No matter what all the poets and philosophers in the world said, it was no more than the twisting and turning and naked lusting that made the old patchwork quilt slide to the floor and left them both spent in a now familiar limbo.

He eased himself away from the gate on which he rested, spat, and walked slowly up the path to his cottage.

\*      \*      \*      \*

The taxi from the station dropped Bernard at his house just after six. Margaret was out, spending the afternoon with friends she had said on the telephone. He went up to his bedroom and dropped his case, with the box file inside it, on his bed.

He changed his clothes, then opened the small safe in the wall by his bed and put the box file in it. He would work on his report the next day.

Habit taking him, he went to Margaret's bedroom and looked around. There was a faint trace of perfume in the air which was new to him. On the dressing table he found a new bottle of Arpège. For years and years she had used Christian Dior. Idly he wondered what had made her change. He opened her bureau and looked through her diary. There were no fresh entries from the time he had last looked. In the drawer, too, lay a couple of paper-back novels. The same ones he had seen on his last inspection. The Churchill volume was by her bedside but with it now was another book. It was a book on Devon birds which he had never seen before, new, with the leather fringes of a bookmarker hanging from it. He opened it to the marked page, and read.

REDSHANK   *Tringa Totanus*
*Resident and winter visitor, breeds*
*During the present century this bird has made a remarkable recovery and is now well known as a passage migrant and winter resident. . . . The only breeding known to D'Urban was at Slapton in 1894. British Birds Journal recorded a pair first nesting at Lobcombe Burrows in 1908. Since then pairs have nested regularly until the severe winter of 1962–3 and none has bred since. Although there has been a progressive recovery the number of winter visitors and passage migrants is still below the 1962 level.*

A pencil mark had been made against the Lobcombe Burrows mention. Skipping through the pages, he found other passages marked. He replaced the book. Bird-watching. Well, if she had found something new to do, to give more interest to her walks, he was pleased. Birds and collecting shells and pebbles. She was a child, shaped like a woman. He was touched for a moment by an unexpected tenderness for her. With the books on the table lay a couple of seashells and a thin beach stone, shaped roughly like a heart. He picked up the stone and fingered its smoothness. He should have handled it all differently, he felt. Most of the fault was with him, but the trouble was that a true perspective only came with looking back, not forward.

He turned away, shrugging his shoulders. Well, Felixson and the Duke and the others would have their dynamite to blow the whole edifice sky high. But there would come a time of re-building. How long would Sir Harry's hopes for the future last, how long before it all began again?

When Margaret came in he greeted her and kissed her with a shade more easiness than he usually did, but he knew that it went unnoticed by her.

He said, "You're a bit late. What have you been doing?" He handed her the glass of sherry he had poured for her.

"Oh, nothing much. I went to the garden centre and ordered some plants. Then I had to go up to the Stonebridge house. The thatch has gone badly in a few places. I've kept putting it off, as you know, but it really will have to be done soon."

"It'll cost you the best part of a thousand pounds. How were they?" The house had been let to a retired colonel and his wife.

"Not too happy. They're leaving. Mild as they are, they don't like our winters. I fancy they're thinking of going abroad. I'm sorry I'm late, but they wouldn't let me go until I'd had a drink with them. And then on the way back I thought I'd take a short cut through the lanes——"

"And got hopelessly lost."

She smiled. "You know me and my sense of direction. However, here I am. I'll get you some food. You must be starving."

She left him, smiling still, to go to the kitchen. She had lied to him easily, something which in the past had filled her with a sense of shame. But now there was nothing left for him in her. Love gave the tongue a smooth turn in deceit because she had no fear of being discovered. Why should she fear something which she was going to tell him anyway before he returned to London? The only problem was choosing the right moment to speak.

Over dinner, Bernard said, "I'm afraid I've got to spend most of tomorrow on an important report my people want. It's a bore, but I'll finish it in a day. We'll have Monday free. I'm going back on the last train." Coming as near as he ever did to any real truth about his work, he went on, "Times are pretty bad for business. The miners aren't getting the results they thought they'd get with an overtime ban. We'll have a full strike before the winter's out. Then you watch—they'll all join in . . . railwaymen, power workers and the engineers. How can you run a nation like that? Or a business?"

She said, "Yes, it must be difficult." But she was miles from him. She would tell him tomorrow, when he had finished with his work. That would leave them a full day on Monday to sort things out. She had no idea how he would react. But whatever he said or did he would have no choice. It was odd that now, for the first time in years, when she knew the break was inevitable he should have been fractionally pleasanter to her. She went on, "I hope you don't mind, Bernard, but I've taken to using your old fieldglasses. I've taken up bird-watching and I'm going to join the Royal Society for the Protection of Birds. I must get out and do things. Get outside myself and find new interests. That's what the doctor said. God . . . I see now I was sticking in a dreary rut. That's why I had these stupid turns. Thank the Lord there haven't been any since I saw Harrison."

"Good. I think you're very wise. As for the glasses—you have them. Keep them."

He cut at his steak, eyes from her. He was thinking of the binoculars . . . remembering the first day of possession, the pride and pleasure in handling them, and the days thereafter when they had almost lived around his neck. He'd bought them from Warboys, cheaply, secondhand . . . too cheaply, and protesting so, but Warboys had been unshaken. He knew now that it had been one of the small acts of ensnarement which would eventually bind him. The curious thing was that he had—in different terms—far more affection and loyalty towards Warboys now than he had for this woman who sat across from him and who, except for a time of pregnancy panic, had known no really high emotion, whose dullness of character and body had within a few early years made themselves plain to him. You pay your money, he thought cynically, and then you have all the time in the world to regret your choice.

*     *     *     *

During the night the rain came. It rained all the morning as Bernard worked on his report in his study. Margaret went to church by herself, but he was hardly aware of her leaving or of her absence. Now and again he glanced at his wrist watch to see how the time was going.

First of all he rearranged the contents of the file in an order which would make reference to his report easier. Then he fashioned a rough draft, giving a broad outline of the story which the contents of the file told. After corrections, he wrote out a clean copy of the précis and burnt his draft in the fire-place. There were those, he knew, who would never read the full report, would rest content with the cold, sharp conciseness of the précis.

The full report took him much longer. He had only half completed his notes for it when Margaret returned from church and it was lunch time. Before lunch he locked all his material and the file in the study safe. Security, even when he felt most secure, was as natural as breathing to him.

Over lunch he was withdrawn, almost resenting the time he had to take with eating, and was soon back in his study, not bothering to stay and take coffee with his wife. For Margaret his behaviour was nothing unusual, and today there was not even a shadow of resentment in her at his quick withdrawal. Her time was coming.

The rain eased for a while after lunch and then returned, bringing a strong wind with it which set the trees and shrubs in the garden swaying and tossing. The brook below the house rose in spate and the field and road ditches ran dark with storm water.

At six o'clock Bernard finished. He burnt the rest of his notes and drafts, poured himself a whisky from his study tantalus and sat and read through his full report. He was pleased with it, more than pleased. He could log in his mind even now the reaction of Warboys and the P.M. Ambition stirred strongly in him, and he fed it in some distant part of his mind as he read. He had done good work before, but so had other people. But this would mark him. Warboys would go higher and he would follow him . . . and people like Felixson and the Duke would always have him in mind. Political and governmental gratitude was measured on delicate scales . . . a breath of doubt or a whisper of inadequacy could set the finely poised beam trembling to the wrong side. Never for one moment would his name be mentioned publicly but the people who mattered would know and remember. At Vigo Hall he had said *Yes* to the documents and *Yes* to the good faith of Sir Harry Parks. He had given his word without hesitation. Many men would never have frankly and quickly committed themselves to a *Yes*. They were the *Maybe* men, the *Perhaps* men. There was a limit soon set to how far they would ever go.

Satisfied with his work, he put his précis, the full report, and all the documents, letters and photographs back into the box file. He took the file up to his bedroom, locked the door, though he had little fear that Margaret would come in unexpectedly, and put them away in a hiding place which he trusted far more than any safe.

He went down to the sitting-room, poured himself a drink and sat in his armchair, letting his body and mind relax, suddenly aware of the drain on both during the day. Margaret came in. As he moved to stand up and get her a drink she shook her head at him.

"You're tired. Stay there."

She went to the sideboard and poured her drink. As she turned he saw at once that instead of her usual sherry she had poured herself a glass of whisky—poured it, he noticed, with a small shock of surprise, generously and now held it, uncut by soda or water, in her hand.

He said, "What on earth are you drinking whisky for? Unusual isn't it?"

She raised the glass to her lips and sipped at it.

She said, "Yes, it is."

He still looked up at her puzzled, and she knew that he had given her an opening which, if neglected now, she might have agonising trouble the next day in finding. By drinking whisky—which she sometimes did when she was on her own—she had signalled the unusual without intent and was now easily able to commit herself.

She went on, "It's unusual because . . . well, perhaps because things are unusual. I want to get things straight between us . . . finally."

"What on earth are you getting at?"

"Us. This life we live. Or rather—don't live. It hasn't made me happy. You must know that. And I'm sure the same must be so with you." She paused and moved to her armchair, perching herself on the side of it, carefully balancing her drink on her crossed knees. She watched him and saw without concern the shades of caution, almost wilful muteness, slide across his face. Bernard, she guessed, was on the point of making some rough, brusque move to turn away from awkwardness. But this time she would not let him. She was in control of herself and her words came easily, unflawed by nervousness. Behind her was Maxie's strength and love for her. She went on, the wraith of some inner irony moving her, "I'm afraid there are things you have to know. It's no good trying to avoid them. I'm not a child. You've got to listen to me and——"

He made a hopeless gesture with his hand, tipped his head back and breathed deeply.

"Margaret . . . just hold on a minute. I've had a hell of a two days before I came here, and I've been at it all day today. I'm flogged." He reached for his drink. "Whatever it is, let's talk about it tomorrow. It can't be anything so important that it won't wait until then." He was running away. He knew that. Whatever was on her mind its importance was clear in her manner and her words, but he was just too damned dog-tired at the moment to want anything but to sit quietly and let the turmoil and strain of professional work ease from him.

"No, Bernard. It won't do. I'm going to say what I have to say. I'm sorry I've picked a bad moment for you, but you mustn't stop me now."

"Look, Margaret, nothing can be so important that it can't wait until tomorrow."

112

She shook her head. "No. This can't wait."

She sipped at her drink and then put it on the table behind her. The movement drew her skirt slightly above her crossed knees, firmed the lines of her body and breasts as she half-turned. For the first time in years he was sharply aware of her. For a moment, though the thought was clouded with his own rising irritation, he held a picture in his mind of her naked and the abrupt knowledge, too, that it had been years since he had seen her naked. Transiently he was facing a desirable stranger. Her next words blacked out the imagery in his mind.

She said, "You have to know, Bernard, that for many weeks now I've been unfaithful to you. I love another man. I want a divorce so that we can be married."

Of all the things she might have wanted to talk about this had never even peripherally been in his mind. It was impossible to cover his surprise. His stillness and his silence signalled it as though he had been struck some numbing blow. Oddly, underlying the surprise, he felt anger rise in him against Ankers. The damned, inefficient fool. What he had known might happen, wished to happen, had come without the stupid man being aware of it. He had lost the main advantage he had always wanted to have—that he should know everything while she still thought he knew nothing. It was almost as though Quint or Warboys had shamelessly betrayed him professionally.

Margaret said, "Well, Bernard—why don't you say something?"

And that, too, from her wounded him. He, whose whole professional excellence allowed him to handle the subtleties of deceit, the deployment of special knowledge, like long practised weapons, now sat here as dumbfounded as some village shop-keeper that the whole district knew for a cuckold, sat, mouth dropped open, idiot, moon-face blank, while some cruel-kind neighbour told him the truth. Anger in him suddenly broke its banks, overflowed its courses and swept him away.

He stood up and almost shouted, "What in God's name are you talking about?" There was no sense in his words. They were just a noise, a cry of pain that came from his wounded professional pride.

Firmly, Margaret said, "About another man. I love him and I want to marry him. If it's a surprise to you, I'm sorry. But I don't see why it should be. There's been nothing between us for years. You live your life and I've lived—or perhaps gone through the motions of living—mine. Now I want a real life with a man I love. I'm sorry to have dumped it on you at a bad moment. But when would any moment have been anything else but bad?"

He moved away from her and went to the whisky decanter. He no more wanted a drink than he wanted to fly, but the movement of habit, the turning momentarily of his back on her gave him a brief sanctuary. Now, rapidly, he began to marshal his powers and gather the lines of control in his own hands, where always—but for that fool Ankers—they should have rested. The advantage was with Margaret, her knowledge of it instinctive, and marked clearly by a firmness new to him. She was rational, unflustered and determined—aspects long lost to him, just as for a moment the image of her naked body had long been foreign to him. Now some other man knew her body, appreciated it, had a continuing hunger for it—an irrational jealousy stirred him. He held it down, controlling it though it struggled fiercely.

He turned to her glass in hand, in some control now. Needing some material sign of the reassumption of his powers and authority, he said quietly, "Sit down. Properly in the chair . . . please."

She moved into the chair, sensing the beginning of a new phase, the civilised ordering of the situation. For a moment his eyes, watching her move, watching the long lines of her legs as she crossed them in the chair, stabbed him with the thought of another man's hands on her body. He pushed it from him. Physically she meant nothing to him.

He said, "Just let's sort it out calmly. How long has this been going on?"

"For well over a month."

"Where?"

"He has a cottage on North Lobb marshes. I go there."

"Never here?"

"No. . . ."

He knew at once that she was lying but it was of no importance, a concession to his *amour propre*.

"Tell me about him."

"He's called Dougall. Maxie Dougall. He's thirty-five and he's a naturalist and a painter of kinds . . . and . . ."

He watched her, listened to her struggling now for some rhythm and meaning in her words to describe the man who should take his place. He knew he wanted her to be confused, to make a mess of the picture she had to paint. But, after a few hesitancies, she surprised him. She talked firmly and coherently —qualities he had long lost sight of in her. And she talked with love and affection, demanding from him, it seemed, something of her own response and joy in this man. But there was in him only a violent antipathy. In the past, imagining other men who might attract her and want her, he had felt no doubt about their kind. He would have laid bets on the truth of his predictions; a retired army or navy man, some well-heeled estate agent or solicitor from one of the towns around, a comfortable widower, full of years still, with a large house and gardens, a stretch of fishing on one of the rivers and the occasional day's hunting. But this man was a tramp! A knowing, cunning one, bright-colour him though she did. He could read his motives as she never could because he had enchanted her with the rainbow hues of a freedom and fulfilment which— whether she would ever admit it or not—served only her physical, long-starved appetites. How typical it was, he thought, calmer now, that when she should come to make her first real claim for happiness she should have picked a worthless bastard who probably walked the world with a permanent chip on his shoulder because he had been an orphanage boy . . . she was a prize for his twisted ego, an easy sweetener for his daily bitterness. He would take all she could give and then abandon her.

He broke into her words, and said, "What does he know, really know, about you?"

She looked surprised. "What does he have to know? He knows he loves me, and that I love him."

"I'm ready to grant that. But what I mean is, what facts does he know? Does he know how wealthy you are?"

"Well, I suppose so. Yes, he must know I've got a lot of money. But what difference does that make?"

"All the difference in the world, I guess. You wouldn't want me to be less than honest about my feelings, would you? All right, it's true—our marriage has gone, has been gone for years. I'm sorry about it, but I don't think there's any point in a post-mortem. But, dead though it may be, that doesn't stop me from having a real responsibility towards you still. Years ago when we first met we made a mistake. The mistake was largely mine and, frankly, I don't think I was particularly generous or understanding about it. I made a mess of it. The last thing I want now is for you to leave me—and find yourself in a bigger mess."

"There's no fear of that."

"I think there is. Margaret, you must look at it sensibly— not like some stupid, immature girl! If it had been anyone else —someone of standing, somebody who had money and responsibility, I could have raised no objection. But, if we're going to break up, I've got to know that you're going to be happy and well-cared for."

"That's just what will happen. Oh, you've no idea how Maxie——"

"I think I've every idea. And I'm going to be quite brutal about it, because I want you to have your eyes open. You're a wealthy woman—and you needed love. But getting into bed isn't love necessarily. You can't spend the rest of your life frolicking about the sands and dunes watching birds, or taking long nature walks across the moors. For Christ's sake, Margaret,

grow up!" Despite his wish to remain calm, anger at this
unknown man and her juvenile infatuation with him rose in
him like bile. "This man's years younger than you. He's never
done a hand's turn in his life except paint a few clumsy bird
studies to sell to the visitors, to make up some small allowance
he gets from God knows where. Don't you see? You were a gift
to him. He's given you what your body wants and he's charmed
you with his sort of back to nature life. But if you go off with
him, he'll end up by bleeding you dry. He'll take your money,
as much as he can get and when he tires of being in bed with
you he'll find other women. For God's sake—you can't take
that kind of risk! I won't let you and I'll be frank about why. I
mucked up your life to begin with. I'll never have any forgiveness for that, nor deserve it—but I'm damned if I'll stand by and
let you walk off into another life, to another man who in a
couple of years will make you desperately unhappy and wishing
to God you'd had the good sense to realise what a damn fool
you were being!"

Margaret stood up. "There's no need to shout. And there's
no need for you to think I haven't considered all you've said.
I'm not a fool. But you've got it all wrong. I know Maxie
and you don't. I want a divorce and I want to marry
him!"

He said harshly, "You'll get no divorce from me. You'll
find no grounds. And I won't divorce you. If you want
to be free to marry him, then you'll have to wait five
years."

"You can't do that to me. You don't love me. You don't
want me. Maxie and I want to be married."

"Then you'll have to wait. Just go and ask your solicitor. If
this Maxie wants you legally, he'll have to wait five years. All
right live with him. Long before the years are up you'll know
exactly what he is—and you won't bloody well like it!"

Margaret shouted, "Maxie's not like that! He's not!"

It was then that her stupidity, her blindness, really stirred
him, his own guilt towards her forcing him to a sudden need

117

to draw some amend for the past he had given her. He stepped forward and took her by the shoulders and shook her violently as he cried, "Go on then! Live with this oaf! Sweat it out until you come to your senses. You stupid, silly bitch!"

He pushed her from him, throwing her roughly back into the armchair, her head thumping against the wooden frame above the velvet padded back. Without another look at her he went out of the room and into the hall.

Angrily he took down his raincoat and hat and left the house. Out of the darkness, a slash of cold rain beat into his face and above the crest of the hill at the top of the drive, he saw the black, top limbs of the trees, etched against a fleeting moon, shaking and tossing in the strong wind.

\*　　\*　　\*　　\*

A few moments after Bernard had left the house Billy Ankers walked through the sporadic showers to the top of the drive. He had left his car two hundred yards down the road in a lay-by. Buffeted by the wind, rain seeping under his collar, he cursed the boredom of a Sunday evening which had left him the victim of an impulse which came from his own frustration. He was shrewdly self-analytical enough to know—and to find little worth in—the motives which had brought him out into the night. Nancy had been due to arrive at his flat at six. It had been a long time since she had spent an evening with him. He had sat toasting his feet in front of his fire, sucking at his pipe, and enjoying the slow growth of erotic fancies which crowded his mind as the minutes towards six had passed.

At six there had been no Nancy. The letter-slit flap of his door had clanked and a moment or two after he heard the outer street door bang shut.

A note in a dark-brown envelope lay on the mat. It was from Nancy.

*Sorry, Billy. Boy from next door is bringing this. Ma's been terrible with the wind and stomeck upset since dinnertime so she cant go down the road to the Harpers for the evening an I cant leave her not the way shes carrying on. Some other time love. Yours Nance. And it's no good thinking I don't feel just as upset as you do reading this.*

Her mother was a stupid bitch, he thought angrily. Stuffing her bloody self with food at dinnertime, no doubt, as though she hadn't eaten for a week while she was still getting over a damned great breakfast if he knew her. And now here he was left half-way up a tree on a wet Sunday evening. She never gave a thought to anyone else, never thought that other people could have appetites, fancies, and what-have-you. If Nance had had any feeling for him she would have poured a hefty dose of bicarbonate down her Ma's throat and left her. But not Nance. That was a woman all over. She liked it as much as he did, but she could take it or leave it. Switch it on or off like an electric light. Didn't she know that a man couldn't do that? If you were looking forward to it, been promised it, you couldn't switch it off just like that. What the hell was he to do now? Some people had all the luck. Got just what they wanted, whenever they wanted it. A picture came into his mind of Maxie Dougall's cottage, of moving thighs, restrictedly seen through a thin break in drawn curtains. Now, there was a bastard who had the luck of the devil.

Ten minutes later, knowing quite clearly and without shame that he went as a voyeur and not an investigator, he was on his way to North Lobb marshes.

He left the car a safe distance up the old road and walked to the cottage. Before he reached it he knew that he was going to be out of luck. The place where she normally parked her car was empty. The cottage was in darkness. He walked round it, satisfied himself that no one was there and then went back to his car.

Calmer, it occurred to him that so far it had always been

Margaret Tucker who went to Maxie. It might not increase his bonus payment to be able to prove that the bastard went up to the house to her as well, but it would prove that if he did a job he did it properly. In your own house, too, Mr Bloody Bernard Tucker. That could make any man see red.

So Billy Ankers slipped inside the drive gate, moved on to the turf edging and went carefully towards the house. There was a light showing from the hall and from one of the main ground-floor windows through the curtains. He lodged himself in the wet cover of a group of rhododendrons and considered his next move. Maxie must be there. But if anyone thought that he was going now to wait until one of the bedroom lights went on they were wrong. All he wanted was one peep through a curtain chink to put truth in the place of a guess and he could imagine the rest and get back off home to some warmth and dry clothes.

He was about to move closer to the house when the front door opened. Outlined against the lights in the hall he saw the figure, unmistakable to him, of Margaret Tucker. She was wearing a raincoat and a dark-coloured beret. She closed the door and went along the side of the house, her figure silhouetted momentarily against the dim light through the main room window. Then the darkness hid her from Billy Ankers.

Billy was puzzled. If Maxie was in the house why had she come out? And if he was not in the house—and certainly not in his cottage—where on earth was she going? To meet him somewhere? To bring him back here? That seemed hardly likely. Clearly she wasn't going down to his cottage or she would have gone to the garage and got her car.

Baffled and wet, the goading of his disappointed flesh long gone, his limited integrity as an agent finding no response to the questions that filled his mind, he suddenly swore gently to himself and went back up the drive, his mind already on the pleasure of reaching his room and getting warm again.

\*     \*     \*     \*

The walk in the rain and wind had done him good, Bernard told himself. And by good he really meant good because in a very short space of time he had seen how wrong he had been. This was not the first time that he had walked out of the house to avoid a discussion or real confrontation with Margaret. Always before he had left her because he had known what was coming and known even more surely that there was nothing to be gained by anything he could say or do for her. The escape she so clearly wanted had always been within her own power. Yet the moment she had found it, why had he reacted as he did? He had faced her without charity, with a conventional response which had centred not on her happiness (to which he owed any contribution he could make, and more) but on a concern for her money chiefly, a stuffy warning for her to watch out or she would be robbed, a stiff-necked, violent disregard of any joy which rode with either the truth or the illusion which had changed her at last from a puppet into a human being. All he had been able to find for her was an angry denial of all she believed she had found, and a stupid material caution to watch her bank balance.

As he picked his way along the rain-slippery path on the edge of the steep combe which ran down from the house the thought, for the first time during his angry, disturbed walk, came to him that there were other factors and emotions which had coloured his unexpected reaction to Margaret. Jealousy and pride were there, but most potent was his surprised sense of the sudden, and real, appreciation in value of a property already half-possessed by another man. He had to acknowledge the instinct to hoard and deny to others the thing which he knew he would never want to use himself. Discount it how he might, it was a revelation to him, pain-edged, because it showed that his passions held a primitive control over his intellect. The clarity he could use in his professional life was denied him in his personal life.

Perhaps after all he did love her . . . that it had taken all these years and one simple act of courage on her part to bring him the only important discovery of his life, a discovery that might hold the prospect of a peace of mind which he had known in the days before he had met Warboys.

A cloud bank moved away from the low-lying moon. In the pale wash of its light he saw Margaret step out from the shadows of a tall growth of elderberry bushes. As he half-turned to her, a spontaneous movement of relief and welcome filling him, she put out her hands and pushed him violently. Taken utterly by surprise he stumbled and slipped on the mud-greasy path and then fell, grasping at the thin thongs of a broom bush on the combe edge for support. The broom growths broke away in his hand and he rolled backwards over the edge of the steep fall. As he went he saw Margaret's face, hard-set, as though she moved in the bondage of some dream, her skin like wet ivory, her long hair free of the beret, loose in the wind, turned to a dull silver by the brief moon whose light cast deep pits of black shadow under her eyes.

He fell outwards over the thirty-foot drop of craggy, granite outcrop towards the combe bottom, rock-strewn and noisy with the turbulent waters of the flood-swollen brook.

He died fifteen minutes later, and until the last few minutes he was conscious. But, before those last few minutes came, the instinct for order and the need for a just resolution of his problems by the simple rule of the facts known which had characterised his professional life stayed with him—raising his wristwatch to his mouth, he flicked the recording catch and began to speak.

\*     \*     \*     \*

A few minutes later Margaret returned to the house. In the hall she slipped off her coat and hat and hung them up, then she took off her half-length rubber boots and put on her house shoes which she had left below the coat stand. She went into the sitting-room, picked up her whisky glass which stood on the small table behind her chair, and then sat down.

She sat for a long time, staring straight in front of her, unthinking, seeing but not seeing, possessed by a familiar isolation which had its own strange form of caressing, all-shielding comfort which sustained her, as it had done so often before, in the immaculate cocoon of a peace which neither fear nor memory could penetrate.

She came to life some time later with the warm taste of whisky in her mouth, the glass, half-empty in her hand, and for all she knew it had only been a few minutes since Bernard had left her. She felt exhausted, the back of her head still hurt a little where it had struck the wood of the chair. She thought over all he had said, forming his moods and words slowly in her mind, and she waited for him knowing that when he returned he could well have out-walked his anger and might have decided to withdraw his opposition. But if he were the same, it would make no difference. She would leave this house, go to live with Maxie and, no matter how long the wait, prove that Bernard had been wrong.

After an hour, when Bernard had not returned, she went up to bed, leaving the light on in the hall for him. He had walked out of the house before when she had tried to talk with him about their life together. There was no set time for his moods to last. He went as he wished and he returned when he would. Tomorrow he must be calmer. They would talk again.

She bathed and then lay in the darkness, listening for his return. But sleep overrode her vigil, her hand touching Maxie's beach stone under the pillow as she drifted away.

When she came down in the morning the hall light was still burning. Bernard, she thought, must have forgotten to switch it off. She made herself toast and coffee in the kitchen and sat with the radio turned down softly. Sleep had reformed her, and there was a new courage in her that came from having brought into the open her relationship with Maxie. Whatever Bernard might say or do, she was now her own mistress. Deceit and the shams of the past between them had gone. He

123

must—and would—do what he would, but her path was quite clear.

She made coffee for him, as she always did when he was home, and took it up on a tray to his bedroom. She knocked, waited, habit still firm in her, and then knocked again and went in.

The bed had not been slept in. From below came the sound of the door bell ringing.

CHAPTER SEVEN

A FARM WORKER had found him in the early morning as
he came up the combe to look over some sheep on the higher
pastures above the brook.

He lay a few feet from the spate-heavy brook, between
two large boulders. His body was soaked with the rain which
had fallen intermittently all night. The farmhand, recognising
Bernard Tucker, and assuring himself that he was dead, left
him and went back to the farm and telephoned the village
constable. From there the morning had slowly taken its course
sweeping shock, dumb, momentary disbelief and the forced
actions of circumstance and convention before it like drift wood.

Real grief was denied Margaret. Unsuspected in her was a
core of honesty that kept her silent where others might have
paid lip service to the outward aspects of tragedy. The moment
of opening the door to a detective-constable from the town had
been the worst. From then on she wrapped herself in a stillness
of spirit and limited thought. No matter what impoverishments
had marred their relationship she knew that at some time she
would weep for Bernard, acknowledge an anguish which
would all be for the brightness and hope of their early days so
soon shadowed, and for him as a man, a life gone.

She had identified him; the corner of a rough-washed sheet
pulled briefly back from a wheeled trolley that was bier in a
small, stone-flagged room.

She sat now, in another room of the police headquarters,
high up in the Civic Centre, its windows overlooking the long
stone bridge that crossed the river, the tide out, sand and mud

banks exposed and a vortex of gulls screaming over the rubbish that drifted downstream. There was an untouched cup of coffee before her. The young detective-constable sat across from her, well aware of her standing, of her wealth and social position, and of her grief which he had to reduce to official form and order.

He asked questions, a pad of notepaper before him, and he wrote her answers down slowly and carefully, almost as though the act of writing was a strange labour for him. She would have to go through it all again, he knew, but he did not tell her this. For the moment all he wanted was the rough picture, knew that it was too soon after her grief and shock to expect more. He selected his questions with care and respect. He was young and she was a good-looking woman still, tragedy marking her with a remote nobility and waking in him an unprofessional tenderness.

She said, "He had been working all day . . . on some business report. Then he came from his study at half-past six to have a drink with me." She paused, watching his writing hand, noticing a slight fraying on the inside edge of his cuff.

"How many drinks, Mrs Tucker?"

"One or two . . . nothing unusual. We talked and then he said he was going for a walk and went out." She would have to tell them, she knew, about their quarrel, but she could not face it now. She had a solicitor, almost a friend; she felt she must see him first. And firmly, she knew this was no moment to bring Maxie's name into the light.

He finished writing and said, "He wasn't worried or upset about anything . . .? You know, his business affairs or things like that?" The last was a useful compendium phrase. It opened the way for people to give or to hold back. You could usually tell.

"No . . . but he was preoccupied. I think he was still wrapped up in the work on his report."

He stood later before his Inspector. As the man finished reading his report, they looked at each other without need to

126

speak the question which at these times always hung poised between them. He said, "It's not that some people are odd. They all are. She knew very little about him, or what he did. He works in London but she doesn't know the name of his firm. Something to do chiefly with tea-broking—she thinks. You know him?"

"Of him. They've been here for a good few years."

"He's not often here, or wasn't. My guess is they went their own way. No quarrel, she says. No upset. He just went out for a walk."

"It was a bad night for it—and a long walk. I see she went to bed before he got back."

"Not unusual apparently. She had just taken his morning coffee up to his empty bedroom when I arrived. Separate rooms. Either a cold fish or he had someone else in London."

The Inspector shook his head. "You run too far ahead. Leave it with me. I want the doctor's report as soon as it comes, and you'd better warn the Coroner's clerk." He sighed. "He went for a walk in the dark, slipped on a muddy path and fell over twenty or thirty feet to the rocks. I'd go for more height than that if I wished to do someone in."

"She never left the house. Personally I think——"

"Don't. We're too busy."

*　　*　　*　　*

Nancy bringing Billy Ankers his mid-morning coffee kept it from him until she was at the door, about to go.

She said, "Someone in the shop a little while ago was saying your Mr Bernard Tucker's dead. Went for a walk last night and fell over some rocks or something. He paid you up to date yet?"

Surprise not really with him yet, Billy said, "You sure of that?"

"That's what they said. Nasty thing to happen, isn't it? Poor devil."

His mind and attention not with her, already his real

127

concern spreading rapidly over the ready list of possibilities which his self-interest instantly conjured up, he said, "Even if a man dies the law protects his creditors. I'm not worrying about that. Sad, though. Oh, yes, very sad." And then— because Nancy was rigidly conventional about the proper responses to the news of death, near one, relative, friend, local worthy or national figure—he added portentously, "God rest his soul."

Nancy eyed him for a moment and then said affectionately, "You bastard."

When she was gone Billy eased himself back from his table, stretched his feet to the electric fire and, while he waited for his coffee to cool, began to think about Mr Bernard Tucker and allied matters.

And as he sat there, Margaret sat at the long table in Maxie's cottage to which she had come direct from the police in the Civic building.

Maxie had been painting when she arrived. Propped before him was a half-finished picture of pin-tailed duck, a part-formed clumsiness which was transformed in his mind's eye to the real thing as he listened. The moment of her unexpected entry was over, the incoherence which had broken from her and then been smoothed away in their embrace, was gone. She was calm now and sat apart from him, not reaching for his hand across the table, needing, he knew, only his presence there to give her the steadiness which at first her words and action had lacked.

He listened to her, the black and white absurdities of the half-painted duck transformed, memory's vision exact and clear. He had the growing sense of a friendly, watchful genius signalling to him, clearly and promisingly, that this day was marked for him. He realised, as she told him of the quarrel with Bernard, that she had gone further in stating their relationship and intentions than had ever been established between them. They had talked romantically and wishfully of being together, living together, of going away and finding some

128

new setting in which their love could flower untouched by any blight from this familiar environment. Marriage, yes . . . but only as a wish, part of the chorus of her bliss. But for himself he had made no commitment beyond feeding her fancies as she lay talking on the bed with him after love-making, or as they walked the sands or some moorland river bank. He had expected opposition from Bernard, but had known that she would come to him. Now—without any move from him, like manna from heaven, unexpected—all his hopes were fed.

He smiled to himself as she said, "I told him everything, Maxie darling. That we wanted to be married and all he could find to say after all these years of neglect was that he had to protect me against you. And not knowing a thing about you. Stupid talk about your being after my money, would take it and then tire of me. . . . Oh, Maxie, I hate myself even to repeat it."

"Don't bother about it, love. There's plenty of men who grudge what they can't or won't use themselves. But you should have told the police about it."

"I couldn't. Not then. I wanted to see you first."

"Yes, I know. But you should know—and you do—that there's nothing lost by honesty. It can lead you up some rough paths, but in the end it takes you where you want to be. We've nothing to hide, least of all our love for one another." He got up and walked round to her, stood at her back and put his warm palm on her cheek, cupping it gently. "When you see your solicitor, tell him everything. There's no shame in anything we've done or been." He slid his hand down the line of her neck and under the top of her blouse, his fingers stroking the first fall of the valley of her breasts and the odd wonder took him that once, long ago, this dead Bernard must have touched and caressed her so and then, still living, had passed away from her. That was really when he had died for her. Her grief now was only the last gesture to rites almost lost in her memory. He said, his accent strengthening without deliberate imposition by him, for once the warm, country earthiness entirely natural, "God took him. 'Tis no good trying to blind our eyes to the freedom that gives to us. Neither of us would have wanted the gift at that price. But there it is, girl. There's birth and there's loving and mating and there's death. And there's a due season for them all, except dying. . . . Aye, that's a happening for which no man can see his time."

She stood up and came into his arms, her head against his shoulder and he held her warmly to him and there was a tenderness in him for her which flushed rapidly to a blood stir for her in his body. But he held it down, surprising himself by the ready schooling of his body's rude hunger. Although he didn't know the man, had rarely seen him, he knew that the tribute of self-denial was this day the only prayer he could form for him.

When she was gone he went back to his painting. He touched in the bronze-green wing patch and, with a fine-pointed brush, in black, the scientific name—*Anas acuta*—because he had discovered that the visitors for no reason he could see liked to have it. There were always a few of the birds from October until March out on the estuary waters. After that they were away to their nesting in Iceland or the Continent. . . . By March, too, he could be away, married to Margaret—that would have to come now and there was no turn in him against it. He would paint no more birds. . . . He would be a married man, his wife a woman of property. . . . She would eventually make a will in his favour, and his favour would be her favour for as long as her body held him. No matter how strong the salt of its present season in his blood, he knew that it would run its due course and then die. And when that happened . . . then she, too, must die, liberating him to his freedom and her fortune. The thought of that time to come wreathed in his mind like a snake, elusive and never still. . . .

\* \* \* \*

Her solicitor, Andrew Browning, after the formalities of condolence, and the practised paternalism towards a wealthy client, not friend, but long known, respected, privately assessed and judged as worthy, and the marital conditions no surprise to him because they paralleled a hundred others and more that came across the table to him, was entirely reassuring, which, he knew, was all that she wanted at the moment.

He said, "The police will have to know about the argument between you and your husband, of course. And about your friendship with this Mr Dougall." He had seen him once or twice when he was playing golf at North Lobb. Sometime, years ago, he seemed to remember that the fellow had occasionally been among the caddies at the clubhouse. Not her type. But so far as that was concerned, he was beyond surprise. Legally, if she stayed with his firm, he would do all he could to protect her. But give a starved woman a new lease of life and her generosity could smash all the flood gates of prudence. "I think, perhaps, later on, I should have a talk with him. However for now, don't worry about the police. It is entirely right and proper that you should have held your counsel until you could see me." He knew the Chief Inspector, played golf and bridge with him, and sat with him often at Rotary lunches. "I'll have a word with them. Of course—since there must be an inquest—you'll have to make a complete statement."

"An inquest?"

"Naturally, Mrs Tucker. It wasn't a natural death. The Coroner must handle it. But there's nothing to upset you in that. Leave it to me." He smiled thinly. "You're all right, of course, financially, as I know. You may or may not know that your husband's will is lodged with us. Probate, of course, takes some time, but it's not a complicated will and, of course, everything goes to you."

"Yes, he told me that long ago."

"And that he was a man of considerable substance . . . ?" It was less question than a floating bubble on the surface of the conversation.

"Yes . . . I always assumed so."

"He had a flat in London, I think?"

"Yes, a furnished one. There will be some things up there."

"Would you like us to handle that? With your authority we could send someone up. No doubt the keys will be . . . available among your husband's effects down here."

She said, "Maybe . . . I'm not sure. Could I let you know about that later?"

"Of course. Do you know the name of the firm he worked for? They must be told. There will be various matters to clear with them, and they with us."

Bluntly, the memory of the long-standing offence firming her words, she said, "I've no idea. He was always evasive—secretive—about it. I could never think why. Once he did say he worked on a private, sort of free-lance, basis for various firms. I never pressed him. Bernard wasn't that kind of man."

"I see." He was surprised but would have thought poorly of his professional poise to show it, had become with the years almost incapable of showing it. His own emotions were best kept out of his clients' affairs. "Well, it won't be a difficult matter. There will be something in his flat or at home among his papers which will give us that. The main thing at the moment, Mrs Tucker, is to look after yourself. Leave everything to us. If anything bothers you or you need help just give me a ring either here or at my home."

He went to the door with her, holding it, mouthing the smooth farewells and stood for a moment watching her cross the hallway. She was a good-looking woman, well-built and well looked after, full of years in which she would be attractive to men. Pity she had picked on a man like this Dougall. Not that he knew anything against him, but it was enough that he wasn't her type or class. Odd fish, her husband. He'd only met him briefly a few times. Something tightly contained there, words well chosen, controlled. Secretive, she'd said. Maybe, but it was more than that. Some kind of professional remoteness . . . banker, property speculator, negotiator . . . oil or chemical industries? Marked all over him. Well, sooner or later, when they went through his papers they would know.

Thirty feet drop—he knew the place . . . public walk—to the only few rocks in the whole top end of the combe. Luck was against him. Nine times out of ten it would only have meant a broken arm or leg or a few cracked ribs at the worst.

*     *     *     *

It was no good pretending that the house was empty without him or that she missed him. The house was as it always was. She went into his study where he had worked all the Sunday. The desk was neat and tidy, no loose papers around. The remains of the coal fire were dead in the grate. She pulled open the drawers of the desk. They were either empty or held stationery and impersonal stuff . . . nurserymen's catalogues, a local house directory, and a *Whitaker's Almanack*—two years old. It was remarkable how he could have inhabited a room, though sporadically, over so long a time and leave nothing of himself in it; no pipe, no favourite worn-covered book, no broken cigarette lighter nor the odd feather picked up on a walk and stuck in a vase . . . nothing of Bernard, either of his coming or going.

She went up to his bedroom. The safe was locked—as was the one in the study. The papers he had worked on over the weekend would be in one or the other. She had a momentary curiosity about them because they were tokens of the man she had never known. Well, when she got his keys from the police, she would see them. The cover on his bed was partly turned down waiting for him. He had done it himself because he didn't like her to come into the room to do anything for him when he was at home. Everything had the neatness of an ex-naval man, used to small spaces and the wisdom of neatness; a place for everything and everything in its place so that the hand in the darkness could find what it wanted without delay. The dressing table held its toilet things in exactly the same places as she had always known them to be. The drawers of his chest were full of meticulously marshalled shirts, pants, socks,

133

handkerchiefs. His suits, coats, and ties hung in his wardrobe each precisely aligned, all ordered, not one sign of haste, carelessness or indifference in their ranging.

On the mantelshelf over the disused fire were the only real signs of the man himself and his life and affections. There was a silver-framed photograph of her taken on their honeymoon. He kept it there for her sake, she knew. Next to it in a battered leather frame was a picture of himself and another naval officer on the bridge of a destroyer, duffle-coated, binoculars about their necks, his companion's peaked cap set a little rakishly, and Bernard wearing a balaclava knitted helmet with his naval cap stuck on top of it, grinning at some joke that had passed between them, gone now, dead for ever. Two other photographs—group ones—of different ships' companies, Bernard somewhere in them all. And in pride of place, taking up the centre of the mantelpiece, was the symbol of a love which had been stronger and more lasting in him than any other—his first command, a frigate, long before she had known him, modelled in teak and metal, resting on a wooden cradle from which it could be lifted. This creation of metal and wood on its painted wooden sea was the altar at which he had worshipped the love outstripping all others, cherished beyond all others. . . . Seeing then, not the mature man in uniform who had come up the loch shore to greet her, but the young man, the young officer who had been piped aboard his first command, the Bernard she had never seen in life, and already committed to his first and only love, she began to weep. She sat back on the edge of his cabin-neat bed and let the tears come freely for him.

\*  \*  \*  \*

On Tuesday afternoon at six o'clock Warboys' buzzer went for Quint. He put down the *Evening Standard* he had been reading—the last, he knew, that he was likely to see for some time since the printers were going on strike in all the major cities, obeying the call of their union, the National Society of

Operative Printers, Graphical and Media Personnel. A nice mouthful, he felt. And anyway, no papers would be a relief from reading about bad news, trade recessions, balance of trade deficits and all the rest. Though the televison would do its best, no doubt, to fill the gap.

Warboys was leaning forward over his desk, his arms cradled on it, hands clasped as though he confined some small creature in his span and watched it, unamused at its attempts to escape. At his nod Quint sat down.

Briefly cocking an eye at him, Warboys went back to the contemplation of the phantom captive on his desk.

He said, "You gave Tucker my letter before he went?"

"Yes, sir."

"Did you go to the station with him?"

"No, sir. We dropped him at his club in St James's. He was having lunch there. Although he was going to follow the train schedule I worked out for him, he'd decided to take a later train but use the same routings."

Warboys raised a hand to his chin, breaking the barriers about his captive, and stared into space above Quint's head.

"How was he?"

The question confirmed to Quint that something was wrong. It was a strictly professional question, hard with interest but carrying no human concern with the simple state of a man's health.

"Just the same as ever, sir."

"How big was the case he carried?"

"Weekend. One I've seen him use often." There was no hunger in Quint to know why the questions were being asked. To have put a question himself until the invitation was handed to him would have been a breach of all his training.

"There's been no communication from him while I've been out?"

"No, sir."

"You can get into his flat?"

"Yes, sir."

135

"Go over now and have a look round." Warboys sat back slowly in his chair and shrugged the collar of his black jacket up round his neck. "I shall be here until late. Come back and report." He clipped his nose between thumb and forefinger as though to suppress a sneeze and added, "He had an appointment with me today. He hasn't shown up. There may be something, small if there is, in his flat. That's all."

Quint took a taxi a hundred yards away from the building, and he dismissed it some streets away from the apartment block where Tucker lived. During the ride he kept his speculations well within bounds. He did this out of cold knowledge. For all he knew—and they had played some twisted tricks for exercises on him before—it could all be part of the now sophisticated training schedule which they still had for him. It could be that he would walk in and find Tucker there, grinning at him and no explanation ever given, and himself going back, containing his private confusion, to report to Warboys and be dismissed still without satisfaction. Could be—but he was wiser now in their ways and fancied he could scent, like some maturing hound dog, the true trail from the artificial.

He walked the stairs to Tucker's first-floor flat and opened the door with the duplicate key which every staff member had to provide of his or her dwelling place. Ultimately there were no ivory towers, no private lives in the service.

He went through the flat methodically and expertly and without hope. If Tucker had had anything which could only be hidden in the flat he doubted whether he would find it without tearing the place apart. At the back of his mind, however, he half-knew, half-guessed that Warboys was reaching not for something, some sign, deliberately and fastidiously secreted, but for some trivial mark or object left exposed because at the time of leaving not even Tucker could have known that future events would load it with some slim significance. He found one only, and this only of minimal interest.

He was about to leave when the door bell rang; three short rings, a pause, and then a long ring. Quint made no move to the hall door. Bernard Tucker would never ring his own door bell. Quint had no intention of opening it. He went quietly into the bedroom and stood behind the half-drawn curtains and watched the broad flight of steps at the front of the apartments, lit brightly by the overhead door light and three small flood-lights in the narrow garden. It was almost seven o'clock. After a moment or two a man and woman, arm in arm, turned in from the street and entered the building. Had they been going out he would have marked every detail of their dress and appearance and never forgotten it. He would have assessed their age, type, and class with a smooth expertise that had taken him years to achieve and which others above him could still easily overmatch.

Quint waited, puzzled a little that any caller should only ring the once. Then, through bedroom and lounge doors which he had not shut, he heard the firm slam of the hall door. He went quickly back into the lounge, standing shielded by its half-open door.

A woman came into the room and closed its door with a little nudge of her left shoulder which swung her round so that she was facing Quint.

He gave her marks for only the briefest upswing of an eyebrow, the shadow of the parting of lips in a quickly killed expression of surprise. She was bare-headed, glossy black hair, a touch of the evening's sporadic drizzle laying highpoints on it under the light. She had a pretty, petite, heart-shaped, slightly too thin face and skin with a dying tan. A fur coat made her body shapeless though he knew from her legs that it would be shapely enough, and he knew who she would be; Bernard's woman, the Slav talker, the bachelor's solace. A special bell ring, and then wait four or five minutes before letting herself in with her own key . . . Warboys must know about it and tolerate it as a privilege of rank. His, Quint's, own amours were scat-tered, brief and scarred no emotions.

137

He knew he would have no trouble with her. She would not be standing where she was, with a red nylon string bag of groceries hanging from her right hand, unless Bernard had trained her to contentment with a limited alliance. Her long acceptance of those conditions fashioned the cool—accent touched—words that came from her.

"Good evening. Were you waiting for Bernard?"

"Yes, I was. He said he would be here at half-past six, but that he might be a little late. That's why he gave me this." He opened his right palm and showed the front door Yale key.

She smiled. "He can be erratic about time." She moved, put her string bag down on a chair and slipped off her fur coat. The dress underneath was simple, but was no copy pirated from a famous house. It belonged to her and was her almost as naturally as her dark hair and, revealed now, the small-boned grace of her slim, wide-hipped body. She moved towards the sideboard and without looking at him said, "Would you care for a drink while you're waiting?"

"No, thank you. I'm afraid I must be going. I've another appointment. Perhaps you'll tell Bernard?"

She turned, dark eyes on him, and smiled, nodding.

"Of course."

He moved towards the door, saying, "I'm sorry if I gave you a surprise."

"Not at all." She paused, the smile given more and deliberate liberty and added, "I'm used to it."

For a moment he wondered if she was fooling him and he was supposed to know it. That this was why he had been sent—another hundred metre post on the long training track. An ordinary person would have asked his name, given a name, too. She could be one with him and Tucker and Warboys. A deep flick of anger stung him, and then pricked him again as he realised that when he reported to Warboys he still might not be enlightened. Then the resentment was gone. They trained you hard, and went on being hard. It was too late to cry out for

138

some easing up. You had to stay fit, always strung to competition point, neither below nor over, always finely on the precise pitch of absolute performance.

When he was gone she walked into the bedroom and watched him go down the entrance steps and as he reached the pavement turn and look up at the window. He couldn't see her, she knew. But he would know she was watching him. He and Bernard—they played games whose names and most of the rules she had guessed long ago. It was this esoteric, shadow play which had kept her moderately faithful to Bernard for so long and gave her, no matter the wide spaces of ignorance and mystery he retreated into at times, a deep and compassionate pity for all his kind which was a form of loving. All men were boys and never recovered from their juvenile blood-and-thunder reading which fed some primitive hunger in them and even in later years forced them to join some society, secret or overt, where they could go on acting out mankind's torrid ancient dreams.

She took her shopping bag into the kitchen, slipped on an apron and began to make preparations for cooking a dinner in which Bernard had said he had every hope of joining her. Hope was a commodity of spurious worth with him. She had cooked many a dinner for which he had never appeared. Whoever the man was, she had not liked the look of him; young, in his late twenties, tallish with a long, prominently boned face, the skin like hard-honed leather, firm, unwrinkled, and brown, rarely blinking eyes with little humour in them.

\*      \*      \*      \*

Warboys was sitting as he had left him, arms half-mooned together on the desk, head lowered, only a glimpse of his eyes coming up now and then as he talked. It would have been easy to imagine that he had remained in a state of trance, unmoving, since he had left him were it not for the position of his desk telephone. It stood now four inches closer to his hand. He wondered what conversations had gone on while he had been away.

He said, "I went through the flat. Everything was in order. But there were two things which . . . well, might have some relevance." He regretted the lame phrase as soon as he had used it.

Warboys said, "There's no question of relevance so far as you are concerned." His eyes came up slowly, and then, surprisingly, he smiled and added, "No relevance, yet, maybe. Not at all, I hope. Go on."

"In his bedroom on the dressing table he had left the watch he usually wears." He did not have to describe it because Warboys knew it as well as he did, the thin gold watch on a slim gold chain which he wore across his waistcoat or in a small fob pocket below the band of his trousers, the chain anchored to a clip on his braces. "He must have worn some other watch."

"So he wore some other watch. Have you checked the supply department?"

"Yes, sir. He drew a recorder four days ago."

"And the other thing?"

"While I was there, after ringing the bell and waiting for five minutes, a girl came in. The ringing of the bell was specific, a simple code to give her identity. In the interval before her entry—"

"—You watched from the bedroom window."

"Yes, sir."

Warboys smiled again, but although it carried no approving nod, Quint sensed that somewhere approval had been given, that there was an importance to all this which was forcing some decision on Warboys, that even someone else might have been sent on this same mission an hour before him, and he and the unknown were now being weighed, judged, on their reports.

"Girl, is that correct?"

"No, sir. A woman. Thirty odd, dark hair, attractive, heart-shaped face, slight possible Slav accent, expensively dressed, mink coat, entirely at home, carried shopping bag full of groceries. No handbag. Clearly expected Commander Tucker either to be there or to arrive this evening." He paused, and then—without any transgression of personal loyalties because they did not exist in their work—he went on, "I would say his mistress."

Warboys sat back and gave a little sigh. Then he stood up, jerked his jacket into place and said, "Stay on duty here tonight. If there's a call or any message from Commander Tucker ring me at my home. If nothing comes in by midnight come over to my flat. While you're on duty have X1351 sent up to you. Read it. You're growing up. You'll find quite a lot about the lady you met in it, but nothing to make you nervous about her . . . though quite a lot to respect. Good."

The last word dismissed him.

He went back to his office and rang through for the file and while he waited he felt relaxation sliding through his muscles and the certitude of some triumph moving to meet him. He might never see Commander Tucker's private file, but to be ordered to read that of his mistress, Tania Maslick, was enough to denote trouble, trouble that—with luck—he would have to make his own. And not, he told himself, before bloody time. The apprenticeship had been long . . . long and just and necessary.

CHAPTER EIGHT

THE INQUEST HAD been at four o'clock. Her solicitor had
used his standing with the police and the Coroner's people to
arrange everything as smoothly as possible for her. She had
given her evidence and answered the questions which were put
to her without any trouble or embarrassment. She had described
the quarrel between herself and Bernard quite frankly, saying
that their marriage had been in name only for many years and
that she had asked him for a divorce, for the opportunity to go
off and make a new life for herself. When the Coroner had
asked if there was some other man specifically concerned with
her decision she had said there was, and had been allowed to
write down his name and pass it to the Coroner. Maxie's name
had already been made known to the police in her second
interview which had taken place the day before—the Tuesday.
The police surgeon had given his evidence, describing the cause
of the death. Several of Bernard's ribs had been broken and
one of these had lacerated his right lung and the lower part of
his windpipe. Death had been due to asphyxia caused by the
inhalation of blood.

The Coroner had recorded a verdict of accidental death.
Browning, her solicitor, who had picked her up at her house,
had driven her home. In a small case were all the personal
possessions found on Bernard at the time of his death.
Margaret had asked that his clothes be cleaned and given
away.

Browning stood now, fingering a glass of sherry. Bernard's

143

personal possessions were on the sitting-room table. They were few; a ring of keys with small ivory dice on a chain as a tag, a silver cigarette case, a lighter, an ebony-backed pocket knife, a leather wallet with thirty pounds in notes, a handful of small change and a slim gold wristwatch on a black leather strap.

He said, "Would you like me to go through his stuff, Mrs Tucker? There will be things I shall have to have . . . insurance policies, tax papers and so on."

Margaret shook her head. "Not at the moment, if you don't mind. I'll collect it all for you and let you have it." She sipped at her drink, and went on, "I suppose there will be a report of the inquest in the local paper?"

Browning, knowing quite well what was in her mind, said, "You're thinking of Mr Dougall? No, there won't be any mention of him. In fact, I doubt whether there will be any report at all because there won't be any weekly paper. They're talking of striking in sympathy with the London newspaper workers."

He watched her face, wondering what went on in her mind. His experience told him that the probability of anything out of the ordinary was unlikely. Bernard Tucker had slipped on a wet path, his mind no doubt preoccupied with their recent quarrel, and he had had an unlucky fall. The police felt that, and they were content with it. With people like the Tuckers in this town you did not go beyond the obvious facts in the hope of discovering others—that way, if you made a nuisance of yourself and ended up empty-handed, lay the road to deferred or lost promotion. The smaller the town, the longer were people's memories. Though he could guess that when the police had been given Dougall's name there must have been a moment or two of heady professional speculation.

He finished his drink and said, "I'm sorry I must leave you now, Mrs Tucker, but I've a pile of stuff still waiting at the office. . . ."

"You've been very kind and helpful. You really have."

144

"Well, thank you. And, a little advice, Mrs Tucker. Try not to be on your own too much. I think it would be a good idea if you went away for a few weeks." He knew that if she did then Dougall would go with her but that was none of his business.

When Browning had gone Margaret took the keys and other odds and ends and went up to Bernard's bedroom. There was a dull lack of feeling in her which gave her the sensation of being merely an observer, watching herself, standing outside all the events of the last few days. Only once in all that time had Bernard been real for her, and then she had wept. Now, she was halted in some limbo, waiting for life to start again. That it would was certain, but for the time being she could raise little response for the prospect ahead. Her body was a stronger element than her mind and just now it was imposing its own imperatives on her. Maybe, she thought, the solicitor was right. She should go away, free herself of this atmosphere, and then there would be an end of all that she had known with Bernard. She picked up the wristwatch from the pile of his possessions which she had put on the top of his dresser. She had never seen it before. It looked very nice and expensive. It would be comforting to think that Maxie would be coming this evening to sit and talk to her. But there would be no Maxie. He had decided quite firmly that he would not see her until after the funeral which was tomorrow. He had said, "There's a right way, and a wrong way, and around these parts if you take the right way, then folk soon forget—but do the wrong thing and they'll remember for ever. The one thing they stick to about death is decorum. There's no man easier wronged than a dead one."

A stir of pride moved in her for Maxie. He was well educated though, she knew now, preferred not to show it. But there was, too, a simple, homely, country decency in him which was as strong as his physical strength. In these days, though the need for it was there at times, she knew she could attend the comfort of his presence; real solace lay in knowing that he was

145

there in his cottage on the marsh with her in his thoughts always.

*    *    *    *

There had been no call from Tucker by midnight. An hour later, at Warboys' flat, Quint had been briefed fully about the whole affair.

Warboys, in an old red dressing gown, running a hand through his lanky white hair, said, "That's it, Quint. You know everything. It's your baby. I want Tucker—and I don't want you to discount any possibility simply because he was what he was in this department. The department's fallen flat on its precious arse. The P.M. wants those papers because his future is tied to them. There's no need for hyperbole. You've got your own imagination. Tucker and the papers—your job. You can have access to anything or anybody you want, except— you won't go near Sir Harry Parks. All right?"

Quint nodded. He contained satisfaction and pride easily. But it was good to feel them there. Nothing like this had ever come his way before. It marked him now in another class. Sort this one out and he was on his way. As Warboys had talked a list of conjectures had ranged themselves in his mind, possible explanations, alternatives already in the back part of his brain being weighed, judged, discarded, kept floating. Tucker was now no longer his superior, semi-friend, leagued with him in common professional interest, but Tucker to be searched for or hunted, to be trapped, rescued . . . but, no matter which, of less value than the papers and report he had taken with him.

Warboys, standing up, preparing to see him out, said, "There is no certainty about any human being. That, sadly, is the one certainty that the years have brought me. Always somewhere there is a flaw in the purest marble."

A faint turn of loyalty moved Quint and he said, "The Commander could be being held."

Warboys gave a thin smile. "It's good of you to say so."

"Or have been run over by a bus."

"Just bring me the right answer, and quickly."

Quint went back to the office and rang for Bernard Tucker's file.

He spent the next hour reading and re-reading it. He slept on the office camp bed for three hours. The next morning he made three appointments for the day and left for the first one at ten o'clock.

He let himself into Tucker's flat, and spent half an hour going over the various rooms again. There was nothing which moved any spark of curiosity or hope in him.

At half-past ten, without any ring of the bell, the door was unlocked and Tania Maslick came in. She took off her white raincoat, gave him a little nod and said, "Would you like me to make some coffee?"

Quint closed the room door behind her.

"No, thank you, Miss Maslick."

She sat down in an armchair, put her handbag by her side on the floor and said, "All I know about you is from one brief meeting and a telephone call. I think rather more is required."

He handed her his routine identity card. It listed him as an information officer of the Legal Adviser's branch of the Home Office. It was not strictly true, but the Home Office would never repudiate it if any enquiry were made about him.

He said, "Commander Tucker is my senior officer. If you wish to check it I can give you a telephone number to ring."

She shook her head, handed him back the card, and said, "No. I accept it. I have a good imagination. My mother came here as a Polish refugee, long before I was born and my father was—" She broke off suddenly and smiled.

"I know all about you, yes, Miss Maslick. But we have no official interest in you. I just want to talk to you about Commander Tucker—unless you have any objections."

"They would mean little if I did, I imagine. No I have no objections, Mr Quint."

147

"How long have you known him?"

"Just over five years."

"How did you meet him?"

"I own this block of flats. The lettings are through my agent, but I have always insisted on a personal interview first of all with prospective tenants. That's how I met Bernard. It developed from there."

"Did he tell you what he did for a living?"

"He said he was the director of a chemical company with a large export trade. I always ask for two references—a bank and a personal one. He produced a note from the manager of his West End bank, and a letter from a well-known member of Parliament."

"How long was it before you realised that he was probably not the director of a chemical company?"

"After about a year."

"Did you ever ask him about it?"

"No. Bernard and I had a very fine sense of questions which neither of us wanted the other to ask. It suited me." She smiled. "A little mystery keeps a relationship piquant."

Quint nodded, and said, "You must know I wouldn't be talking to you unless there was at this moment some concern about Commander Tucker. I would have expected you to have asked me right away, perhaps, about that. But you didn't."

"No. I am concerned, of course, about anything to do with Bernard. But knowing him for years has taught me to sit and wait."

"Did he tell you anything of what his movements were going to be this last weekend . . . from Friday last?"

"No. I saw him on the Thursday for a drink in the evening here. Then I left. We arranged that I should come and prepare dinner on the Tuesday evening. He said nothing about the weekend." She reached over, lifted her bag and found her cigarettes. "To avoid you a little embarrassment I should explain that I had no regular nights for sleeping here. If Bernard wanted me and I was free I stayed. I could always tell within a few minutes of walking in here whether he was going to want me to stay. Then, if I could, I did." She lit her cigarette.

Quint said, "Commander Tucker was due to keep an appointment at his office yesterday at three o'clock. He did not turn up. More than that I cannot tell you—except, of course, that we want to find out where he is."

"Thank you for that."

"You love him?"

"No. Nor he me. We and our individual circumstances happened to suit one another. So, since I have no reason not to want to help you, let me tell you all I know about him. It's not much. He said he was a bachelor——"

"Said?"

"Why not? Quite a few men who have wanted to sleep with me have begun by saying they were bachelors and, having got what they wanted—though the deed of gift was always in my control—have persisted with the fiction. Bernard said he was a bachelor. I never had reason to doubt him. I knew he had been in the Royal Navy, naturally. We seldom—as a couple— met other people. I know nothing of his friends or relatives, except that he maintained a transparent fiction that he had an old mother living either in Dorset or Wiltshire. He used— deliberately—to get the counties mixed at times."

"His mother lived in Jersey and died twenty years ago."

"I am not surprised."

Quint felt that she was not going to be surprised at anything. It was clear to him that she had accepted Bernard on exactly the terms she wanted, and whatever she had guessed she had kept to herself. Knowing Bernard, he felt certain that the man would have soon learnt everything there was to know about her, and approved. Otherwise she would not have lasted five days with him.

He said, "You must have been in this flat many times on your own. Were you ever curious enough to . . . well, take a good look around?"

She laughed. "Of course. I know it all, every inch, drawers, cupboards. Even his desk there which was not always locked. So?"

"What impression did your curiosity give you?"

"That the whole flat was the way Bernard wanted it. Impersonal. There was nothing private here. No papers, no letters . . . a few bills sometimes . . . nothing. He could have walked out of here at any time without luggage and left only the barest signs of his presence or personality."

"Did you give yourself a reason for that?"

"But, of course. Because of his work. Because of your kind of work, Mr Quint. Bernard kept no bundles of old love letters, no personal documents . . . nothing. Always he carried on him whatever there was to give some lead to his place in life . . . like maybe your little identity card and so on. I was sorry for him—though he would not have thanked me for it because he valued his self-dedication. Yes, I was sorry for him, and I am sorry for you. My mother used to talk about your kind of people. She is now long dead." She blew a thin trail of cigarette smoke, and added, "But, of course, you know all about her."

"Possibly."

She laughed. "See—you cannot commit yourself to a Yes or No." She stood up. "I can't help you, Mr Quint, not the kind of help you want. I can tell you what Bernard liked to drink and eat, what wine, what food. I can tell you how he was as a lover, but not really as a man. One thing I do know is that for many, many years I am sure there had never been any true happiness in his life—somewhere, honour and true pride in himself had been taken from him without his knowing it until it was too late. He is missing. I would not be surprised to hear sometime that he had committed suicide."

Quint picked up her raincoat and held it for her. She was, he realised now, the safest kind of person for Bernard to have picked for a mistress, but she had been of very little help to him. Too high a premium was put on 'true happiness' in life. It was a will-o'-the-wisp which he had no inclination to chase.

150

He said, going to the door with her, "Thank you for your help, Miss Maslick. You must say nothing of our talk to anyone. I'll be in touch with you if the necessity arises."

She said coldly, "Bernard's lease of this flat expires in two months' time. The rent has been paid until then. The furniture and furnishings are all mine. I shall look in occasionally to see that things are all right."

He went back, sat down, and lit himself a rare cigarette. Women, he thought, always made too much of everything.

What the devil had happened to Bernard? The man, professionally, he would swear was as solid as a rock. And Warboys, for all his outward calm, had to be teeming inside with anxiety. A special assignment from Downing Street and he had fallen flat on his face. . . .

His second appointment was with the Duke of Woodford at his London house in Kensington. The appointment had been made for him by Warboys. He was conscious at once from the Duke's manner that he felt that Warboys should have come to see him. To discount this, he said as soon as he had the opportunity, "Mr Warboys has had a high-level directive that to begin with all enquiries should be kept low-keyed, your Grace. Otherwise he would have come himself."

"Yes, yes, I see that."

"After all it's quite conceivable that Commander Tucker has had some accident. He could be lying unconscious in hospital somewhere unidentified."

"Surely he'd have some identification on him?"

"I'm afraid not. It's a Department rule not to carry any identity—unless it's a false one—on certain assignments. We're making a check as far as we can of all accidents, but that's a long job, your Grace, when it has to be done discreetly. The main thing I wanted to ask you was how you felt about Commander Tucker while he was with you."

"Don't follow you, man."

"I know you didn't know him, but one gets a sense sometimes of, well, uneasiness in a man. Something on his mind.

151

Or, maybe, just an intuition difficult to base on anything but an instinct. That—or anything which struck you as odd or unusual might help. At the moment we're in the dark and we can't rule out any possibilities."

"I see. Well, frankly, I thought he was a damned good chap. Knew something of him through my boy, of course. They were both in the Navy together. No, given the circumstances of his visit and its importance, he behaved exactly as I would have expected anyone with his responsibility to have done."

"Your daughter took him to the station on Saturday morning. Did she wait with him until he got his train?"

"No. Asked her that myself. She just left him at the station, waiting for the London train. Which of course he may not have taken."

"That could be. He had an important report to prepare. He would have arranged somewhere quiet to work on it. Also he had specific instructions not to return to London until the Tuesday morning. He gave you a clearance on the material Sir Harry Parks had brought, and also on Sir Harry. You accepted this, and so did Mr Felixson. I'd like to know, sir, whether there was in any slightest way any element of unease about Commander Tucker in your mind—no matter how small or transient?"

"None at all. I thought Commander Tucker was a first-class man, right on top of his job. You can tell these things at once. Same goes for Sir Harry Parks. I don't approve of the man in some ways, but his motives were, I am sure, genuinely sound. If you want my opinion in case Warboys hasn't passed it on to you, I don't think there's any question in all of this of treachery by Sir Harry or double-crossing by Commander Tucker. I think the reason he hasn't turned up is that something as natural as death or an accident has prevented him from doing so. If I'm wrong then there's going to be a lot of trouble for some people. There's nothing else I can tell you."

Quint got much the same response from Felixson when he went to see him at his London flat. At the end of their meeting

Felixson said, "Well, I hope you find him soon, and the stuff with him. The P.M.'s said that we have to honour our contract with Sir Harry. It'll be a new experience for me paying money for something I'm not going to get. So try and make me happy, will you?"

"I'll do my best."

That, he thought, as he went back to the office that afternoon, was an understatement. His best and much more than his best were called for. He was going to find Bernard. Warboys had dropped this into his lap like a gift from the gods. There were a dozen other people who could have been given the assignment, but Warboys had picked him. That choice carried a promise which only failure could kill. An embargo had been placed on any approach to Sir Harry Parks. The man did not know that Bernard had disappeared. He would never know anything, except that he had been paid. If the documents and report were never found he might wonder why they had never been used as designed by him. He might ask, but he would be given no satisfactory answer. He had never been given any specific promise that the stuff would ever be used. Nobody in the political world or in his, Quint's, would so rashly overcommit themselves as that.

Back in the office Quint found a sealed memorandum from Warboys to him. It read—

*You'll need a partially briefed assistant on all this for the spade work. I've assigned Lassiter. He knows Tucker is missing and that he was on an important mission at Vigo Hall, and that he had with him documents, etc., of high importance. At your own discretion you may, if circumstances warrant it, enlighten him further. But on no account must he become privy to the ultimate political implications.*

Half an hour later Lassiter reported to Quint. They knew one another but not well, and had never worked together before. Quint knew that Lassiter, twenty years older than he was, was the thinly fleshed epitome of failure. His abilities were

153

unquestioned, but they had always stopped short of the point which could have made him a Tucker or a Warboys. Lassiter had been given his chance at some time and had failed—that mandate once issued was never revoked—and now he lingered on, comfortable, competent, but confined for the rest of his working days in a fixed grade. He accepted it with a cheerfulness which could be irritating at times to Quint because he wondered whether, if he should reach the same dead end, he would be able to match the man's comfortable equanimity . . . ambition long kissed goodbye, and the acceptance of this covered by a good-natured irreverence. Lassiter, thought Quint, a spectre to haunt the young and the ambitious.

He was a small man with a thin, richly veined face that came from hard, home drinking. Jockey-sized, long armed, impeccably neat in his dress which in the office was always a navy blue suit and a dark tie with highly polished brown shoes, his first words were, "So, the good Commander has either defected to the other side, taken his money and popped off with some floosey or been run over by a Green Line bus in the country and now lies——"

"Shut up." Quint said it quietly and without malice.

"Sorry. But it's the kind of thing dear old Bernard could have said himself. Great sense of humour—with the right people."

"When did you see Warboys?"

"Before lunch. And what have I done since—apart from a beer and a sandwich? No police checks, missing persons. That's out from on top. But I've given the sign to passport controls, airports, harbours and so on—discreetly. I've got a girl ringing through a list of hospitals for casualty admissions. That'll take days." He dropped a sheet of paper on Quint's desk. "There's a list of all connections, local and mainline, from Salisbury station around the time Tucker was dropped there until four o'clock in the afternoon. He could have gone anywhere, but he couldn't have gone on travelling on the Sunday by train because of the ASLEF Sunday ban. I haven't checked Somerset House for deaths yet but I will do in a few days. Regional notifications take some time to come through. Also I've been thinking about him. He was told not to come back until Tuesday. He could just have taken the stuff home to work on."

"Home? But he lives in London."

Lassiter smiled. "He keeps a woman in London. He could have another in the country. He's not *our* Commander Tucker now. He's *our* problem and so gets no special concessions. Tania Maslick is not the first mistress he's had. He likes women. For all we know he could be keeping a wife somewhere."

Quint smiled despite himself, but underneath he was annoyed with himself. Lassiter had given him a sharp lesson in the powers of imagination. Tania Maslick had said that Bernard had created a transparent fiction about having an old mother still living whom he visited on some weekends. There was no reason why, in fact, he could not have a wife somewhere.

He said, "You've known Bernard far longer than I have. You think that could be possible?"

"No, I don't, but we can't ignore it. Nevertheless, I'll run a check." Lassiter lit a cigarette and slid his lighter back into its little suede cover. "I'll get someone on to marriage registrations at the Registrar General's Office here and in Scotland. I'll fix the rest of the routine things, too. Try and pick up his movements from the station. Some porters have long memories and passengers are the only things they have to look at. What about the opposition? I gather there is one."

"I doubt whether they could have been off the mark so quickly. I'll look into that. There's something else, too. I want to see every one of our regular drivers with their duty schedules over the last month—but only the ones who drove the Commander."

"Will do. So there it is . . . a pretty vivid bunch of probabilities. He's done a deal with, or been grabbed against his will by, the other side. Or—he's lying dead, or unconscious, and unknown in some hospital. Or—he's all the time had a secret life somewhere with a wife or mistress and he went back to it to do his report—and something has happened there."

"Loss of memory?"

"Why not? There's plenty on his mind and on ours that we would like to forget."

*　　*　　*　　*

The funeral was on the Thursday at four o'clock. Billy Ankers parked his car a little way back from the entrance to the crematorium and watched. Somewhere in all this business he knew that there must be money to be made. Somewhere if he played his cards right there had to be good pickings—and no trouble for himself. His magpie instincts were alert, and so was his own sense of self-safety. Until he had worked out a sure line of approach he was content to remain an observer. Although the local paper had not appeared, the verdict had become known in the town. Accidental death . . . well, well.

He saw Margaret Tucker drive into the crematorium in her own car, wearing a black coat and hat. A little later her solicitor arrived, and then came another car with the secretary of the local golf club and two other men. Last of all came the hearse.

Billy Ankers sat sucking his pipe for a moment or two and then drove off. Although he couldn't see his way to it at the moment there had to be something in all this for him. Mr Bloody Tucker owed him money, but that was small beer and could wait. He could bring that up after a decent interval and in private with her solicitor. No Maxie Dougall at the funeral. That would have set too many tongues wagging.

Impelled by curiosity and distant self-interest, he found himself driving out to the house at Lopcommon. Margaret Tucker wouldn't be back for some time. Wonder how she was feeling now? Glad to have him gone, the field opened up wide for her and Maxie. He'd had a chat in a pub on the evening of the inquest with the local reporter—an occasional contact of his—who had given him a fair account of the proceedings. No mention from Margaret Tucker that she had left the house after her husband had gone out. So far as she was concerned she had stayed in the house and waited for him and eventually gone to bed. Domestic quarrel over a marital problem. The reporter had been a bit guarded about that. But he, Billy Ankers, was miles ahead in that game. Gone off to bed had she? Tired of waiting. Well, he knew better than that. He was going to have to handle this properly. No rushing. And no question of trying to get at her through Maxie. Maxie was uncertain and he could be violent. No, he'd have to go to her when the moment was ripe. Meanwhile, since an empty house was an empty house, there wouldn't be any harm in having a quick look round. Everything at sixes and sevens . . . there might be a few quick pickings which would never be noticed.

He parked his car in the layby at the top of the hill and went down to the house, approaching it along the footpath at the top of the combe. As he passed the spot where Tucker had fallen to his death, untouched by any emotion, he told himself that if she had pushed him over she had picked the best spot. Stand in the bushes to one side of the path and—over you were before you knew what had touched you. Not much of a fall though. But there you are. Life always turns up the unexpected. And—Good Lord!

He stopped suddenly. Maybe that's how she'd done it. Just like with all that pinching business. He could see the look on her face now as she moved down some crowded store, a miles-away look in her eyes, and nicking stuff as cool as a cucumber. That's what could have happened here. Quarrelling over Maxie had touched her off. And then—not even knowing it— she had gone after him. . . . Well now, that was something that could be worked on.

He put his pipe in his pocket and went on to the house. He got in through sliding the catch on a back window with his knife. He spent ten minutes in the house, held there largely by his consuming curiosity. He could have loaded himself with stuff, but there was no need now to take more than a token to satisfy his magpie complex and ease the itch from his fingers. There were bigger, easier and safer pickings waiting for him. . . . Oh, yes, big pickings. Still, even with that in view, a man shouldn't leave a job empty-handed. Ten to one she'd never miss it. All wrought up with death and funerals and the thought of bright days ahead with that Maxie Dougall. . . . A nice watch it was. Obviously the old boy's, just kicking around on his dresser top with the other stuff, keys and wallet. Nice touch that to leave the wallet with its money. . . . Yes, ten to one she'd never know it was gone. Her mind wouldn't be on his things. She'd have nothing but darling Maxie in her thoughts. . . .

CHAPTER NINE

THAT THURSDAY HE had a job helping to load a gravel barge out on the westerly point of the dunes where the two rivers met. The barge had been floated ashore on the high tide and as it ran out had been left on the crest of the long, sloping sand bank. He hadn't wanted the money and had only marginally been interested in obliging the barge-owner, a friend of his. The day being what it was, he felt the need to strip down and exhaust his body with the heavy labour of shovelling gravel and sand aboard. More than any other, more than the day when he had spoken his first few words to Margaret, and the day when she had finally come to him, this was the day when the pattern of his life began surely to fall into place, piece fitting piece, colour blending with colour, like a jigsaw surrendering itself. He had been to a crematorium once to the funeral of a boy—grown man, dead in a road accident—who had been at the orphanage with him. The clinical ceremony had had no meaning for him. It was no more than a graceless tidying away of life. Better, he thought, to burn a man on a pyre on the beach, see the flames taken by the wind, the charred wood flakes fly up to heaven, choired by the screaming of the wheeling seabirds. One should go out with colour and song, grief overlaid with the pride of a primitive return to the ancient dust. No man could avoid his undignified entry to life. But his going, at least, should be a fitting pageantry that would mark itself in the memory of the people who loved him. Someone, even Margaret for a time, had loved Bernard Tucker. Not he. But he could not avoid feeling some pity for the way of his going, dropping like refuse into a disposal unit.

Working, sweating, feeling the grit of sand between his hands and the heft of the spade, he wondered why he should find time for Tucker in his mind. Tucker was gone. The way was opened for him. He had never seen it this way, never dreamt of it this way. His musings had been darker, himself forced to action and strategies which had coiled and stirred amorphously in his mind, lacking positive shape, resting and waiting on time to help him. He had that help now. It was all too easy, as though some deity, distrusting his abilities, had taken the matter in hand. He resented that.

When the sun was gone, the tide turning to drive the shore birds from their feeding grounds, he walked back through the fast gathering dusk to his cottage. Above him, unseen, he heard the whistling of wings as a flight of duck went over, and distantly the cry of curlews. There was a light showing through the curtained window of the cottage. The dark bulk of her small car merged with the shadow of the garden wall.

He went in, hooked his cap on the back of the door and shucked his pilot coat, dropping it to a chair as he turned to her. For a moment or two they looked at one another without speaking. She was suddenly a stranger to him, and he had a feeling that he was caught up in some drama shaped to his purpose but no longer controlled by him . . . his original creation taken from him and reconstructed for his better benefit.

Her coat was off, resting across the end of the table, a little black hat neatly placed on top of it. She sat at the table wearing a plain black dress, her hands in front of her, just touching the black gloves she had too discarded. Her fair hair was salon-schooled, her face moved slowly to a smile that did not banish the lingering solemnity of the day's rites, and her body had the stiffness of one who still played a given part. The embarrassment of the artifice he sensed in her passed to him. He knew then, again, that this was not the way he had seen or wanted things to run. He was diminished because he sensed that he no longer completely commanded the destiny he had outlined for himself.

160

Then she stood up swiftly and, with a little cry, came to him. He put his arms around her and the warmth of her body against his broke the bonds he had fancied held him and gave him back the illusion of direction he coveted. He kissed her, and then ran his hands through her hair, spoiling its imposed form. Then, holding her again, he felt the need in her body for him, and, because he would be master again in his own time and style, he reined back the instinct to lift her and carry her through the drawn curtains to his bed.

He eased her away from him and said, "Girl, I'm all mussed up with work. Get yourself a drink while I clean up."

He went to the fire and threw kindling on the white ash, kneeled and blew with a soft whistling breath until the embers glowed and the kindling took, and then piled split logs on the flames.

Behind him she said, "Do you want me to talk about it?"

"No. 'Tis done and it was none of our doing. But it sets us free to be ourselves. That's enough."

He stood up and seeing she had not moved from her chair he found the bottle and a glass and poured her sherry. He sipped it himself first and then handed it to her, and was suddenly happy and restored to himself for he was in control, pleased with the artifice of his reply.

He went into the kitchen, stripped his shirt from him and washed in the tin bowl in the sink, speaking to her as he towelled himself.

"Since noon I've been out on the bank, shovelling sand. You could slice it like a cake and then see it slowly crumble as you tossed it aboard. There's something about earth or sand that works like that. Snant they call it in these parts. . . ."

He came back and into the bedroom end of the room and changed into a clean shirt and trousers and went back to her. He sat at the table, slewed sideways to get the heat from the growing fire and poured himself a beer.

She said, "Maxie . . . will you do something for me?"

"What?"

161

"Just something." The edge of a teasing smile which he had come to know marked her lips. "There's something I want to do for us. Something I've been thinking about in these last few days. But I don't want you to say no to it. You've given me so much, I want to give you something. Will you do it and not ask any questions . . . not now, anyway?"

He nodded. "If it's something you want . . . something you specially want."

"It's for Saturday. I want you to be ready in the afternoon. Just pack some clothes and be ready to come with me. Don't ask where or why or for how long. Just be ready."

"Why not? I enjoy a surprise as much as anyone."

"Oh, thank you, Maxie." She came round to him, sat on his knee and put her arms about his neck, her lips touching the side of his forehead. He held her and was happy because things were coming back to his own ordering again. He could read her mind and indulge her. He knew the strain which had been with her, knew that it sought some ease which he alone could give by the promise he had made. What she had in mind would be no surprise to him. He knew that for a while there was nothing for them either here in his cottage or in her place up at Lopcommon.

They sat for a while talking, and they both knew that they needed no more of one another now than that . . . knew that the future would begin for them when she called for him on Saturday. They could both wait because there was now nothing to keep them apart.

As he watched her car drive away he sensed that the withholding of themselves one from another was a poor rite to mark her husband's passing, but a due one. Death was no atonement. Only a going that wiped the slate clean and put all living debts into limbo.

*　　*　　*　　*

It all came to a head on the Saturday. In the morning Quint interviewed the last of the motor pool drivers who had

162

just returned from a week's driving duties in the North of England. The man had been with them for years.

Quint took him through the driving duties he had had with Bernard over the last month and the driver—an elderly, heavy-faced man called Harris—answered Quint's questions briefly and accurately, remembering dates, places of put down and pick up and giving no sign that he was well aware—even though he had only been back a few hours—that something was in the air about Commander Tucker. Though he ranked low in the order of the department's personnel, he shared the common law of answering a question but never asking one until invited . . . and that invitation sometimes signalled in the faintest tremor of an eyebrow, a pause where one should only half be, or a stillness which waited to be disturbed.

Finishing going through the schedule, Quint said, "That's it then, Harris. All routine stuff?"

"Yes, sir. That's it for the last month."

"Did Commander Tucker talk to you much when you were driving him?"

"Sometimes, sir. He'd sit up front and have a chat. Just about general things. Nothing . . . well, ever personal or work-wise. He was always very correct."

Quint caught something in the tone of the man's voice as he spoke the last sentence—or he could have imagined he did. Anyway, he kept back the framing of some words of dismissal and held Harris's eyes, watching the slight nervous motion of two thick lips moving over one another, the tip of a tongue barely breaking through them. There could be more Harris wanted to say, but he knew it would not come uninvited. Harris was an old naval man. He had a loyalty to Tucker and a loyalty to the department. He could guess how finely they were weighed against each other. Dropping any thought of finesse, he said bluntly, "All right, Harris, you can go." He waited as the man stirred to turn away and then added, "Unless you have anything to say which might help us."

Harris's body poised to move, relaxed. He rubbed a big

hand over his chin, and then said, "There is, sir."

"Let's hear it then."

"I may get into trouble over this. Not that I really did anything wrong. I'm very fond of Commander Tucker. He's a fine man. I suppose you could say. . . . Well, maybe it comes from working in a place like this, you see things differently, begin to think, well, in the way you, sir, and Commander Tucker have to think. After all we are trained to keep our eyes and ears open."

Quint, having let him run long enough to clear his embarrassment and firm himself for whatever he wanted to say, cut in, "All right, Harris. Just tell me about it."

It came then briefly and plainly. Harris had frequently driven Tucker home, to the corner of the road in which he had his flat. But on one or two occasions Tucker had asked to be dropped in Euston Road. On one of these occasions Harris had been held up at the traffic lights and had seen Commander Tucker go into a tobacconist's shop a little way up from the lights. On another occasion he had dropped Tucker and had gone on up the road, found a turning place, and coming back had seen the Commander getting into a taxi. He hadn't thought much of all this until the third time when he dropped the Commander and was held again by the lights. There had been a long delay because the police were hand-controlling the lights to regulate the evening rush hour traffic. Harris had seen the Commander come out of the shop and get into a taxi on the far side of the lights just as they had changed. He had driven on, following the taxi at a safe distance.

"I don't know why I did it, sir. Except, well . . . I was stuck in the traffic stream anyway and then. . . . Well, working here, there's times when you get a bit fanciful in your thinking. Anyway, I followed the taxi and it dropped Commander Tucker at the end of his road. It happened once more, about a week later—only this time there weren't no hold-up at the lights. I just went ahead and parked well up the other end of the Commander's road and saw him come up in a taxi like

164

before. I don't suppose I'd ever think much of it—him hopping out to get some cigarettes, maybe, and sending me off because there weren't any parking spots. But there are. Shop's on a corner of a side street. I could have pulled in and waited and then gone up through the back streets to his road. I know it's nothing much, sir. But it struck me as kind of funny. Why waste good money on a taxi, when I could have parked and waited for him to take him home? If he'd gone off anywhere else, sir, I could have understood because maybe he didn't want me to know."

"Well, we'll leave that, Harris." Once they had got something off their chest they liked to embroider things. Quint had no time for that. He asked, "What was the name of this shop?"

"Graingers, sir. Lefthand side, just below the underground station."

He would have sent Lassiter, but Lassiter was out. So he went himself. Bernard smoked his own special brand of cigarettes and pipe tobacco made up by Dunhill's. In the flat, when he had searched it, there was a cabinet stocked with a good month's supply—Bernard was not the man to let his stores run out. He would be unlikely to need to buy cigarettes casually on the way home. But tobacconists had other uses.

It was a small, rundown shop, hardly bigger than a kiosk. The man behind the counter could reach practically all his stock without moving.

Quint said, "Have you any letters for Tucker? Mr B. Tucker?"

The man said, "Who are you?"

"I've been sent by him to collect."

"Oh, yes. Well I know Mr Tucker. Never forget a face. And 'is instructions is—personal collection only. So shove off."

Quint put his identity card on the counter, and said coldly, "Don't play around with me." He tapped the card. "You can read. Hand over his mail and I'll give you an official receipt.

Make a fuss and I'll have a police car here in two minutes."
He laid his hand on the dusty, finger-marked telephone at the
side of the counter.

For a moment or two the man looked at him, and then
with a sigh reached under the counter and brought out a long
cardboard box, split into sections by alphabetical tags. It was
half-filled with letters, some of them stuck in on their short
sides because they were too long to fit the width of the box.
Quint pulled the box to him against a half protest from the
man and began to thumb through the Ts. There was one letter
for Tucker. He took it and pushed the box back to the man.

"What about the receipt?"

"It will be sent to you officially."

He went back to the office. There was satisfaction in him,
but no elation. He knew better than to indulge that. Experience
had taught him that an easy break was often the beginning of
real trouble. Nothing was ever neatly dished up, ready for
consumption. But even with his limited knowledge he could
not suppress his wonder that a man like Bernard could have
tolerated in his private affairs a sloppiness which would have
been unthinkable professionally. He had to know that all the
drivers and low grade employees saw themselves as extensions
of those they worked for. You could not train them to keep
their eyes and ears open for the unusual, to train even limitedly
their senses to recognise the small flaws in set patterns without
creating in them some ambitious dream of usefulness, uniquely
manipulated and ending in a triumph which would mark them,
raise them higher. The place was riddled with tuppenny
numbers who felt that they deserved to do something more
important. Harris would get his credit eventually and it would
probably ruin him as a driver for ever.

He slit the envelope open and read the letter from William
Ankers.

An hour later Lassiter came back. He hung up his hat and
coat and then sat down at Tucker's desk and said, "Funny
thing, isn't it, when a man wants you to find something, puts

166

it right under your nose and you go blindly by it? He got himself married and said nothing—at a time when there was a strict rule against it. Stay single or get out was the order. Christ—he must have really wanted out at the time and nobody obliged him. In one way or another, I suppose, it's a phase we all go through. Well, perhaps not all." He pulled a sheet of note paper from his pocket.

Quint knew what was coming, knew that 'it' was not ever any phase he was going to go through, and knew too that he would never allow any shadow of his own satisfaction in having beaten Lassiter to the post to show. That was a pleasure which was heightened by not being revealed.

Lassiter came over and dropped the paper in front of Quint. "There it is. A copy of the certificate is being flown down from Edinburgh. He was married in Scotland when he was on a special course donkey's years ago. Still in the Navy then, but officially attached to us, and had been for a long time, for special duties. Margaret Fiona Donaldson. A bonnie Highland lass, no doubt. And for my money she's still alive."

Quint touched the paper, his eyes taking in the pencilled information and he said, "You've done a good job. She lives in North Devon. Mrs Margaret Tucker, Lopcommon Barton, near Braunton." He nodded to a pile of Kelly's local directories which were piled on his desk. To ease a disappointment which Lassiter must have but would never show, he added, "It all came from a line I picked up from one of the drivers. I'll tell you about it later."

Lassiter's eyes widened a little and he faintly blew out his cheeks, holding his breath, a deliberately comic face.

"So," he said, "what do we do? Find the phone number and ring up and ask if the Commander's there?"

Quint smiled. Lassiter had taken it well. He said, "I've got the phone number already but it won't be used unless Warboys says so."

"Which he won't. I wasn't being serious."

"I know." Then as a sop to the man, charity which he

could easily dispense now, Quint passed the letter to him. "You can read this."

Lassiter took it and sat down at the other desk. The paper was headed with the name of William Ankers, his professional style and his address. It read—

*Dear Mr. Tucker,*

*Further to my last, and hoping to recieve some communication from you or the pleasure of a visit when you are next here for the benefit of new instructions consequential to the facts as set out under.*

*Since last report have had the subject under observation more closer owing to her change of habits, chiefly concerning the Lobb burrows and dune visits. Recently subject has taken to being away for customery walks much longer. One day in particular (20th) leaving at four she did not return until after dark (7.30 p.m.). The same again two days later, and the following day after that. Each time I went out after a proper interval and tried to locate subject without success.*

*On 27th inst followed subject to car park at 4 p.m. but she did not park car and took old military road between dunes and golf course and Lobb marshes. I followed on foot and from high dune observed progress. Subject parked outside cottage on marsh owned and occupied by one, Maxie Dougall. Subject was inside for half an hour and then left. Said Dougall is man well in his thirties. He earns a living casual labouring, but not often, selling things, gifts and such like to holiday people. I know nothing against him personally but he has a reputation for various things. Enough said, but if you should wish for more I will tender with pleasure a separate report.*

*Two days later I followed subject No. 1 to Lobb Burrows where she repeated visit to cottage but did not emerge as I kept observation. When it came dark this is on the evening of the 29th inst at seven o'clock I approached the cottage and through a chink in the curtains of a lighted window managed to look into the ground floor bedroom. Both subjects were on the bed. Both subjects were unclothed and they were in the act. More than that I need not say. I withdrew at once, but I felt it my duty to you to confirm the same goings on on a further occasion and can swear to times and dates. I now await your further instructions or the favour of personal visit from your good self.*

*In addition I have to report that during all this time since last report I have seen no sign of Subject No. 1 having any of her shoplifting fits. Also I will think you will agree that the agreed bonus for results are fairly earned.*

Yours at your service<br>
William Ankers.

Lassiter dropped the letter on the desk and rubbed the back of his hand across his lips. For Quint he felt nothing. Nobody need do. He knew where he was going and would get there. But Tucker . . . an early marriage in Scotland, the only move he could think to make, probably made on an impulse, to get him out—plenty of people here had known that desire. Not bloody Quint. He was hand forged, anvil-beaten and tempered for this job. From that moment of marriage in Scotland he knew, as certainly as though Tucker were here telling him, that something had gone soft in him which he wanted uncovered. And nobody would do it because nobody could imagine its existence. It was difficult, too, to imagine the Tucker of later years as a young man without the guts merely to hand in his notice openly. Maybe he had been going to do that and then, suddenly, had changed his mind—and luck had stayed with him. Funny, someone you had always thought to be so solid should all the time have been all messed up within. Sad, too. But there was plenty of sadness around, well covered up. But Jesus, what kind of contained despair was in him to send him to any William Ankers—though, God knows, the man had done his job? And Margaret Fiona Donaldson with her Maxie Dougall? Any charity for Tucker most probably would have to be shared with her. Quint's voice came through to him.

Quint said, "I asked you what you thought of that?"

Lassiter knowing, though he doubted if Quint did, that Tucker had been Warboys' creation, guessing long ago at the love behind that act of creation, answered, "I'm glad you've got to drop it in front of Warboys, not me."

Quint said, "I'm seeing him at four o'clock. He'll be pleased I've broken it so soon."

Lassiter nodded, half closing his eyes. The '*I've*' meant nothing to him because he had long ago ceased to look for, or want, any mead of credit. He was thinking of Warboys. He'd take it, of course, without a sign, but the scar would come and be there always though hidden.

\*     \*     \*     \*

She had been busy all day Friday, the arrangements she had to make filling her day and, in a curiously soothing way, making the last days remote. Bernard was gone, but the finality of that knowledge now lost all trace of real meaning because he had always been gone. She had no sense of loss because she had lost nothing. At first that thought had made her feel guilty, but it was not a guilt she knew now that she could honestly accept. For his death, the going of a man who had once meant something in her life, she had paid all the respect demanded of her and had found a moment of true grief. Beyond that there could be nothing, no claim which still lingered to impose itself on her from their life together.

She had unlocked the two safes, collected all the papers and documents she could find and had taken them to her solicitor to deal with. All his personal stuff she had left in the house. She could collect it later or dispose of it. She had made a collection of such things as she wanted from her own possessions and clothes and removed them. She was leaving, never to come back to Lopcommon to live. The arrangements for ridding herself of the place would come later. Her life had been given a new beginning and a new direction. There was little of the past she wished to carry away with her.

In the early afternoon on the Saturday she drove down to Maxie's cottage. When she arrived he was standing by the pool at the side of the house, a loaf of bread ·under one arm, another loaf in his hand and he was breaking the bread and throwing it to the ducks and geese. He wore a black, polo-necked sweater, clean corduroy green trousers and there was a soft suede jacket lying across the wall behind him. She smiled to herself, loving him, relishing this moment of arrival.

The wind was southerly down the estuary and mild in her face as she got out of the car. He raised a hand to her and went on feeding the ducks and geese, finished the loaves, and then came across to her. He put his hands on her shoulders and kissed her. There was nothing now to hide. What the world might have guessed, the world could now know. This kiss, this greeting, belonged as much to the world as to them.

He said, " 'Tis no use letting the bread go stale while we're away. Wait there. I'll get my case."

She said, "I've arranged it all. You don't mind that, do you, darling? Just this once?"

He rubbed the back of his right hand gently across the tip of her nose. "If you want to be a masterful woman—that suits me. Just this once." And, going to the house for his case, he thought without concern that it was easy to give in order to receive, easy to obey rather than command if the moments were right. And this moment was right. She had gone through more than he could ever have imagined would have happened to her. She had to find something now to mark the ending of a captivity and the beginning of freedom. There was no sense in not humouring her, nor hardship either. She had been a caged bird, now unexpectedly free, wings strong, pinions eager for flight. Away up, girl. Fly high, and I'll be with you. The hollowness and artifice of his conceit made him grin and the grin was still there when he came back, suede jacket over one shoulder, his old suitcase in his hand.

When she made a move to get into the driving seat, he said, "No. I'll drive. You know where we're going. You can tell the way. You've got a man now to do the dirty hard work for you."

She sat beside him as they bumped slowly up the old military road and she kept her head lowered for a while so that he would not see the wetness of unbroken tears in her eyes. And then, because she knew he would know they were there, she half turned and smiled, a tear breaking down one side of her face.

The sight of her tears moved him strangely into a moment of confused emotion. He said, "The year's too mild. There's frogs' spawn in the ditches two months ahead of time. And I picked up three starlings' eggs on the field out back where they come to grub. I've never done that before the beginning part of February before. You want me to turn left or right on the main road?"

"Left."

As they crossed the car park to take the rise to the main road, the orphanage crocodile was coming down to the beach, the wings of the nuns' bonnets flapping white in the southerly wind, the hem of their robes flicking the dust. Seeing the children, she thought of him years ago in a similar file. She said, "What was she like, the Irish nun who named you?"

He said, "She had a terrible temper if you crossed her. She came from a poor family in County Clare and she was the seventh child of a seventh child which meant that she was full of magic. She was and it was all white not black. You know what they say around here about a fisherman who's like that? Seventh of the seventh. All he's got to do is sit in his boat out there when the fish are running and whistle. The salmon line up to jump aboard. She had hard-worked hands. But they never seemed hard to me. And she had a knack of tucking you in at night so that the blankets kept their place against any bad dream or nightmare. And I loved her almost as much as I love you. . . ."

"Oh, Maxie, that's beautiful."

And he knew it was because he had meant it to be. When the time was ripe, words made stronger bonds than iron chains. But just for a moment he wondered whether at times there wasn't a magic in words, too. You freed them from your mind to serve you, but the moment they were out, like new fledged birds from the nest, they were away to a liberty of their own which you could never control.

They slept that night in a small hotel in a Welsh valley with the sound of a river fall drumming at their window. The hotel register marked them as man and wife under a name which they had chosen as they drove. She slept in his arms, her slow breath touching his face, and he lay listening to the call of a pair of tawny owls in the woods across the river, shrived now of all thought that fate had worked too easily for him.

\*     \*     \*     \*

Quint watched as Warboys read first the brief summary of his findings, and then turned to the Ankers letter which was attached to it. The middle finger of Warboys' right hand tapped in a long-intervalled movement against the tooled-leather top of his desk. A browning bloom of a pot of white cyclamens on the desk dropped off. Absently Warboys reached for it, teased it into an untidy ball with his fingers and then dropped it on the desk. His finger tapped again. Finally Warboys pushed the papers from him and looked across at Quint.

He said quietly, "You've done well, Quint. And you've done it quickly."

"Thank you, sir."

"Have you taken any action on it?"

Warboys heard himself speaking, the Warboys who was entitled to sit in this chair, the Warboys who not for a moment was going to share the agony of that other Warboys who had taken another's comradeship, friendship and admiration and had corrupted them. He would have to be entertained later.

"No, sir. You said to keep this low-key. I could have phoned

173

Lopcommon Barton . . . Commander Tucker or his wife might have answered."

"Quite right." Bernard, though, would never have answered. Warboys was sure of that. Had he been ill at home he would have called long ago. He had either to be dead, unconscious or absconded. He made no choice in his mind about the possibilities.

"If I may say so, sir, I would suggest that a confidential call to the Devon Chief Constable at Exeter might be the way."

He watched Warboys run his fingers over his thin white hair. He was taking it well. But at that moment he was far less interested in how Warboys was taking it than in waiting for his reaction to his suggestion because it was the first time he had gone beyond the bounds of his brief. No suggestions, no questions until they were clearly called for. He waited for Warboys to say, 'Just leave the suggestions to me'.

Warboys said, "Yes, I think so. Who is the Chief Constable?"

The answer liberated Quint from a grade long held. The one freedom licensed others. He said, "He's an old friend of yours." He put a piece of paper on the desk in front of Warboys.

Warboys glanced at it, nodded, and said, "All right. I'll have a word with him. I'll let you know. Is Lassiter in?"

"Yes, sir."

"Tell him to stand by. You'll have to go down. It's Sunday tomorrow—no trains. He can drive you."

When Quint was gone he put in a personal call to Devon for the Chief Constable. "Wherever he is. If you have any trouble come back to me." He got up and went across the room to a wall cupboard and poured himself a drink.

He sat at his desk with it, waiting for the call to come through. At the moment he could dispense with all concern with the present fate of Bernard. That would be known soon and dealt with. In his mind was thought only for the man all those years ago who had broken a hard rule, whose breach

174

even now would have marked him enough to have denied him the future rewards and position which he had come to covet. One act of revolt, long dead, but hung about his neck forever . . . like that bloody albatross. The word brought back a host of sea images; the bird itself hanging low over the water off their port bow in the southern seas. He had loved Bernard, and had wanted him. And Bernard had known it, known the response in himself, hard-schooled it, and given it no licence. Lacking that, but not hope, he had taken him with him . . . forced him, subtly but ruthlessly. And all the time Bernard had wanted to escape, but had no power to match the persuasions which he could deploy. Could do nothing but make this stupid, immature, half-quixotic gesture. Praying that it would be noticed; praying that discovery would give him freedom. And Fate had thrown dust in the eyes of all around him. The hundred to one chance had succeeded.

The telephone rang and he spoke to the Chief Constable. The conversation finished, he sat and waited. Memory served him well. He had made two visits to the Scottish training centre. The night before he had left, after his second visit, there had been a dinner for some local people, part social, part politic because there had been some feeling against their presence. A young woman called Margaret had sat on Bernard's right. Back through the years he could recreate her, summoning her up from the fringes of limbo; a tall, fair-haired young woman, an unbroken, gawky grace in her body, near nervousness or shyness keeping her mostly silent forcing a mechanical deliberateness into her actions as she ate and drank and mostly listened. Some sign there must have been then for him to catch, but he had seen none, regretted it now, but was far too gone in age and all the succeeding years to blame himself or to find any anger for or condemnation of Bernard.

An hour later, the telephone rang again and the conversation was brief. When it was over he put his empty glass back in the cupboard and then signalled for Quint; Quint who would

175

never make another Bernard Tucker, either in failure or success, but Quint who had been born destined to find some cold goddess to serve and had been rewarded by an early revelation and had made his vows eagerly.

To Quint, sitting across from him, Warboys said, "I've spoken to the Chief Constable. The police there are expecting you. They will book two rooms at the Empress Hotel. They've no brief—except what you give them. They know, naturally, that it concerns Commander Tucker, but his status has not been defined nor should be. They'll assign you a man and give you all the assistance you ask. I want Sir Harry Parks' papers and, if it exists, Commander Tucker's report. Nobody down there knows the nature of these. Nobody must know. All right?"

"Yes, sir."

Quint sat unmoving. The question was in him to be asked, but he knew that there could be no surer way of marking himself than by asking it. He knew, too, that the pause while he sat, watching Warboys' face, was limited in precise professional fractions of time. He could not take a few seconds' unlicensed grace before he moved, and he knew, too, that Warboys was deliberately running him up to the limit. To hell with him. He put his hands to the desk edge, shaping to rise from his chair.

Warboys said, "Commander Tucker's dead. Accidental. You'll get the details. The inquest was on Wednesday, and the burial—cremation—was on Thursday. That's all."

"Yes, sir."

Quint left the room. A lesser man, he thought, might have begun to express some conventional sorrow, surprise, or appropriate condolences. A lesser man would have made a big mistake. Warboys' face, immobile from a swift inner freezing of the spirit, had asked for nothing. Quint put his coldness down to an icy professional concern for a highly important mission so unexpectedly disrupted, not knowing that the man was imprisoned in a glacier of grief.

\*　　\*　　\*　　\*

They left the hotel the next morning, and drove along the Sunday quiet of small mountain and country roads deep into the high heartland of Wales. They ate lunch at a small inn and then left the car and walked, dressed securely against the squally weather, up the course of a mountain stream until they came to a hill tarn, cradled between the shoulders of high peaks. The wind bowed the shore reeds of the lake and worked thin furrows of foam-edged waves across its surface. As though some conventional, romantic sentiment in Nature indulged them, a wild squall of rain sluicing across the waters swept over them briefly and then the sun broke brightly from a break in the clouds behind them and created across the far end of the tarn the perfect arc of a rainbow.

For Margaret, standing at the water's fringe, Maxie's arm around her, steadying her against the wind that spun spume drift off the waves into the air, it was a moment she knew she would always remember. To be held and coupled to a man by the strength of his arm, to stand with a man who loved and asked nothing of her but her love in return, was a joy not rare, but unique, which only the perfect splendour of the rainbow could commemorate. It was hers for as long as she lived, to become imperishable in her memory.

As the rainbow died slowly like a wraith against the far peaks, Maxie said, "Look. That's the first time I've ever seen one. For a moment I thought it was an old buzzard. But look at its tail."

Away to their left, wheeling slowly, low over the shore was a kite, fork-tailed, head dropped low as the bird scanned the ground, the long, slender wings motionless except for an occasional flick of the sharply angled wing tips.

Maxie took the field glasses from his pocket, watched the bird for a while and then handed them to Margaret. She focused them and the bird came up clearly in the lens. She could see the yellow-rimmed eyes and the matching yellow cere on its beak, the faintly streaked, greyish-white head and the rich, ruddy plumage of its wings and body.

Beside her Maxie said, "There used to be hundreds of 'em. All over the country. Scavengers in the filthy gutters of old-time towns. Now, they're just here in Wales. A handful. But they're coming back. When they do, then folk will have to look to the washing on their lines."

Margaret gave him the glasses, and said, "What do you mean?"

Maxie grinned. "They build a big, old untidy nest and they line it with mud and paper and rags, girl. If you were an educated type like me, you'd know that from your Shakespeare. Somewhere in one of his plays that I had to do at school he says, 'When the kite builds, look to lesser linen'." He looked across at the wheeling bird and went on, the burr strengthening in his voice, "Aye, girl, there's something marks ever the good days in a body's life with a special sign. 'Tis a pity most folk don't use their eyes to find it."

"And that's our sign for today?"

"Aye, it is that."

She smiled, loving him so much when his voice took on its accent, knowing now that he did it deliberately at times for her pleasure, and knowing, too, that the kite was his sign for this day, but not hers. This day, for her, had already been marked by the rainbow.

She turned herself against him, putting her rain-wet lips against his. Across the lake, unseen by them as they embraced, the kite dropped earthwards and on the fringe of the lake took a water vole among the sedge grasses, its scythe-tipped talons killing it instantly.

CHAPTER TEN

THE YOUNG DETECTIVE constable was the one who had originally interviewed Margaret. His name was Kerslake and he was waiting for them when they arrived at the Empress Hotel. He sat now by the wide window that looked out to the broad, tidal reach of the river above the old stone-built town bridge. His official brief was limited. Unless these two men decided differently they wanted to avoid police headquarters. He knew nothing about them, except the identity cards which they had produced after first seeing his. He was not here to ask questions, but to answer them and to render all the assistance he could. Curiosity he had, but he kept it to himself. He knew that in some way their presence was connected with Mr Bernard Tucker—Commander, it seemed. Apart from that he indulged his own imagination and speculations privately, but was determined not to let them interfere with his role. Others could have been assigned to them, but he had been given the job. Promotion rested on such small preferences.

Quint, the tall, dark-haired, younger man of the two, was reading the reports of the Coroner's inquest and of the two police interviews with Margaret Tucker. He had a lean, hard face with dark, still eyes, a face that was cut in sharp, flat planes as though some sculpture had overworked it almost to near caricature. Fancy thought, Kerslake told himself; but the presence of these two men from a world which was a distant spin off from his own stimulated his imagination. The other one, Lassiter, sitting on the edge of the bed was older, the florid touches in his complexion instantly recognised and,

179

maybe, giving the clue to his subordinate position. A long-armed, short-legged monkey of a man, neat as a pin, reading the reports that were handed back to him by Quint much quicker than Quint had. Lassiter, Kerslake guessed, he would get on with easily. He would get on with Quint, too, but it would be deliberate, nicely calculated work.

Quint finished reading and while Lassiter caught up with him, lit a cigarette, offering one to Kerslake who shook his head gently. Finally Lassiter handed the slim bundle of reports back to Quint who slipped them into his brief case.

Quint said, "How long have you lived in this town, Kerslake?"

"All my life, sir. But I worked for eighteen months in Exeter when I first started in the force."

"What's been done so far?"

"Nothing, sir. Those were the instructions."

Quint said, "When we're in private you can cut out the 'sir'."

"Thank you." It was a cold concession but Kerslake appreciated it. It put him on their side. From little acorns great oaks grow . . . maybe.

"Was it generally known that Mr Tucker was a retired naval man?"

"No, it wasn't."

"Tell me what you know about Commander Tucker and his wife—other than the stuff in the report."

"Very little. Never any trouble with us. Well off. Big house at Lopcommon. No children. He came home infrequently. Worked in London. Company director or some such. Nothing specific. He was a member of the golf club for a little while. Few social contacts. Much the same for his wife. Little social life. There must be dozens more like them around here. Mostly retired or semi-retired people who've come here within the last ten or so years."

Quint gave a little look in Lassiter's direction. The man on the bed swung his short legs and kept his eyes on his neat, finely polished shoes as he said, "You any thoughts about the Coroner's findings?"

Kerslake knew at once what they were after. This was no official, protocol dominated interview. Neither of these men ultimately would care a damn how or where they got whatever it was they were after. But once they were gone he would have to live in the town. His job and its prospects had to be protected. He said, "Only what's in the official findings."

Lassiter looked up and grinned. "A very proper answer."

Quint gave a bleak smile and said, "But not much good to us. Between the three of us, Kerslake, you can go off the record —as a policeman and as a local resident. Nothing will come back to you——"

"So," interrupted Lassiter, "if it should become necessary to let us know your Chief beats his wife and has three mistresses you can say so without fear. Is that clear?"

"Yes, sir."

Quint stood up and switched on the lights against the growing dark in the room. Kerslake rose and pulled the window curtains. As he turned back Quint said, "What do you think— did Commander Tucker slip or was he pushed?"

"I think he slipped. Nobody in their right senses would push him over so small a drop. Apart from that I don't see Mrs Tucker in the role of . . . well, a pusher."

"How do you see her?"

"A neglected, unsatisfied woman, turned in on herself, who finally got hooked by this Maxie Dougall. It wouldn't have to be from pity on his part. She's still a very attractive woman. I'm only surprised it hadn't happened sooner."

Lassiter asked, "Why was his name kept out of the inquest?"

Kerslake gave a minute shrug of his shoulders.

"Her solicitor is a friend of the Coroner and of my Chief. This is a small town comparatively. We don't like offending our people or embarrassing them unless it is essential."

Quint nodded agreement. He was happy to let Lassiter come in with his questions because the switch in attention by

181

Kerslake from one to the other might unsettle him—in which case he would be relegated to no more than a driver and errand boy. He said, "Maximilian Dougall?"

"Single, mid or late thirties, lives alone in a cottage out on the dune marshes. Naturalist, bird-watcher, that sort of thing but only in an amateurish way. No known parents. Brought up in a local orphanage. Rumour says he has a small private income from somewhere. Local story that he's the discarded bastard of some wealthy or aristocratic family. Doubt it myself. Clever. Grammar school scholarship. Makes a living selling paintings and odds and ends to tourists, casual labours in the off season. Used to poach. No convictions. Attractive to women, but so far as known has always stuck to the willing visiting types. No local scandal until now." He paused and then added, "Likeable—but a dark horse."

Lassiter said, "Any other interests? Local politics? Sports or social activities?"

"No. He's the hermit type in a sense."

"Sure?" The question came from Quint.

"Yes, sir." Kerslake had no idea what they were after. For a moment—despite all his professional gratification at this contact with them—he was seized with the outrageous fantasy that if at this moment it suited their book they could wipe him off the face of the map with never a question being asked. Ridiculous, but coldness centred like a freezing hand between his shoulder blades. And, as the illogical sensation stayed still with him, they added a confusion to it. Only a moment of iron control stayed the show of his surprise.

Quint said gently. "Now tell us about William Ankers."

Lassiter gave Kerslake silent credit. He handled himself well. Not far buried in Kerslake was material that Warboys could have shaped and which Quint could not fail to recognise. Kerslake, he thought, would do well to make a mess of things at some point. He would stay happier that way than any quiet recommendation from Quint to Warboys could ever make him.

Kerslake, deliberately suppressing the reiteration of the

man's name, said, "He has an office-cum-flat in Allpart Street. Calls himself an enquiry agent. But he's chiefly a debt collector and tally man for a credit firm. He's dishonest when it suits him. He has a mistress, woman called Nancy Barcott, who works in the baker's shop under his rooms." He touched his upper lip with the tip of his tongue, not in any slightest token of salacity but to give himself a pause to flatten his voice as he went on, "He's no outside interests, sporting, social or political. He's thirty-nine and has lived here all his life. No living parents or family, except a brother who's a river bailiff in South Devon."

Quint nodded, noting the performance, filing it against the barest possibility of recall, and said, "Andrew Browning?"

Kerslake answered, "Sixty, senior partner in. Browning, Rolls and Weare, solicitors. Established here for donkey's years. Married, wife living. House on Old Quay. Two sons, long grown up and married. One's army and the other farms in Essex, I think. Solid character, Rotarian, well-liked, knows everybody. Acts for the Tuckers. Plays golf, sails, local councillor. Well-liked, a kind man, but professionally a shade lazy. Second or third class brain."

Lassiter chuckled, but Quint's face remained unmoved. He said, "What car does Mrs Tucker drive?"

"A blue Mini. AMW 993 L."

"Is that a local number?"

"No."

"When you get back to your office put out a confidential notice on it, country wide. No action to be taken. Just report location."

"But why, sir? Isn't she at Lopcommon—" Kerslake checked himself.

Quint allowed himself the edge of a smile. It took time, and training, and a special armouring to curb the brain's spontaneity. Kerslake was good but little more at the moment. He said, "No, she isn't. We called at the Lopcommon house before we came here. The garage is empty and there's a note pinned to the back door saying no milk is wanted until further notice."

Lassiter said, "It's urgent that we talk to Mrs Tucker as soon as possible."

Kerslake, recovered, said, "She's probably gone off for a few days. Either to friends or relations, or maybe just by herself. It would be natural, after what she's been through this past week. Just wants to get away from it all. However . . . I'll check Dougall's cottage.'

"I want to look around Mrs Tucker's house. Can we go by Dougall's place on the way out to Lopcommon?"

"Yes, sir." Kerslake watched as Quint turned and un-hooked his hat and coat from the back of the room door. Lassiter caught his eye and winked, smiling. He said, "Don't look worried, lad. Just a simple case of breaking and entering. There won't be any come-back."

Quint said, "On second thoughts, you'd better phone your office from here and tell them to put out that call. Just locate and report. No approach to anyone connected with it. Once it's found I want it tagged and all movement reported." He picked up the telephone receiver and handed it to Kerslake.

Twenty minutes later they were driving down the old military road to Maxie Dougall's cottage. They walked the last hundred yards. The cottage was in darkness. As they approached it a goose honked from somewhere near the pond. At the door Kerslake hesitated. Because the place was in darkness did not mean that it would be empty.

Lassiter said softly, "Just knock. If anyone is there we'll deal with it."

Kerslake knocked, but there was no reply.

Quint looked at Lassiter and Lassiter shook his head. "He's away with her."

They went back to the car, drove along the coast road, up over the headland to Lopcommon, and then openly down the drive to the front of the house.

Lassiter went round to the back. Quint, standing in the porchway with Kerslake, said in impersonal tones, "You come in with us. If we decide to take anything, you'll see what it is.

184

Everything will be listed and we'll sign for it. For the time being you're working under direct Home Office instructions."

"Yes, sir."

Quint was thinking, concern for Kerslake's feelings almost non-existent, that in all the years he had known Bernard Tucker this house had been here and the woman in it. Never once had it occurred to him that there was anything wrong with Tucker, that he had any dangerous secret to hide or private fear or agony to contain. Let it, he told himself, be a sharp lesson. With almost everyone, no matter how absurd the thought might be, there could always be something major or minor to be hidden. At that moment he was free. At the moment he was an exception—and he meant to stay that way.

The front door opened and Lassiter let them in. They went through the house quickly, establishing its layout. Then they began to go through it room by room. It was clear at once to Kerslake that they were not doing a thorough turning over job. They concentrated on the study downstairs and the Commander's bedroom. The safe in the study was locked and the flat-topped desk had many of its drawers empty. The contents of the others either Quint or Lassiter flicked through with an almost casual interest. Whatever they wanted was something which they would recognise instantly, something large enough not to be easily hidden.

There was another safe behind a picture on the wall in Commander Tucker's bedroom. This, too, was locked.

Lassiter standing near the fireplace said, "He'd have carried the keys with him. Always have them on him. Mrs Tucker could have an enquiring mind."

Quint turned to Kerslake. "Where are the Commander's clothes and stuff? At the station?"

"No, sir. Mrs Tucker didn't want his clothes back. They've either gone or are going to Oxfam. All his personal stuff was returned to Mrs Tucker. Among it there was quite a considerable bunch of keys."

"Tidy woman. Try his dresser," said Lassiter. As Quint

185

went to it, he picked up a leather-framed photograph from the mantelshelf. Warboys and Tucker on the bridge of some ship. The faded past, he thought; the bonds of friendship cemented by the trials of war, comrades in arms, and later the other bonds and the other comradeship for a war which brought little honour to anyone.

In the top lefthand drawer of the dresser was a bunch of keys, lying with a wallet, a silver cigarette case, half-filled with hand-made Dunhill cigarettes, a small lighter with the nickel plating heavily worn, and a slim, ebony-handled penknife.

Quint exhibited the keys briefly and went to the safe. He opened it. It held nothing except an empty dog-eared box file. He turned to Lassiter and said quietly, "This was it."

Lassiter, glancing at the box, nodded. He only knew they were looking for a set of documents and a report. What they were about he officially knew nothing. Privately, since he knew the personalities concerned, he had made some broad assumptions.

He said, "Bernard would be the last man to trust a safe. Particularly an old-fashioned job like that or the one downstairs."

Quint went out of the room and they followed him down to the study. The safe was empty.

Lassiter said, "When clients die their solicitors get busy because the dead live on for quite a while legally." There was a whisky decanter and glasses on the study side table, and it was a long time past his usual hour. For a moment he hesitated and then went to the decanter and lifted it. "Anyone else?"

Both men shook their heads and Quint gave half a frown. The expression left Lassiter untouched. He poured himself a drink and said, "She'd have collected all the stuff in the two safes and handed it over." There was little doubt in his mind that Mrs Tucker was gone for some time. The sitting-room and study fireplaces were cleared of ash he had noticed . . . tidy woman . . . people burnt things in fireplaces.

Quint said to Kerslake, "Ring Browning. Ask him if Mrs Tucker delivered to him all her husband's personal and private papers. If she did, wherever they are, at his home or his office, I want to see them. I'll be with him in an hour's time. Tell him it's urgent. A Home Office enquiry of immediate importance and strictest secrecy."

Lassiter sipped his raw whisky, smiled, and added, "That'll bring him." He watched Kerslake's face, gave him high marks for control, and a few more for the almost natural way he went to the study telephone and picked it up. He was a fast learner and, with their backing, quick to assess and use new authority. Andrew Browning would not enjoy being given a directive by a detective constable in the middle of a Sunday evening . . . carpet slippers, a glass of brandy and a good book in either hand and a sudden squall of westerly rain hammering at the window. He listened to it now on the study windows.

Quint said, "Let's take a look at her bedroom while Kerslake phones."

For that intentional or unintentional kindness Kerslake was grateful. Jesus . . . old Browning, at this time of night on a Sunday. Then, suddenly, he smiled as he dialled. Why not? As he listened to the dialling tones he found himself wondering how men like these two started . . . how did you get into that kind of racket? If they stayed long enough he might find out . . . might even ask; but not Quint, the other would be a safer approach.

The dialling tones stopped. Kerslake swallowed hard and prepared to give his instructions to Andrew Browning.

Upstairs Lassiter said, "For a woman who's taken off for, say, a week, even a couple of weeks, she seems to have taken a lot of stuff. Only two pairs of shoes left in the wardrobe, a dozen empty hangers, and the bed stripped down. No towels in the bathroom. She could have gone on a cruise round the world."

Quint said, "We'll see what the police call turns up. If the stuff we want isn't with that solicitor we'll have to take the place apart. Why the devil did Tucker have to go and slip over a cliff?"

The last sentence, anger-touched, warmed Lassiter with its human frustration.

He said, "Maybe he didn't slip. Maybe he jumped—just bored with the whole thing."

"That's enough of that bloody kind of talk. And don't pull that whisky trick again with me when there are people like Kerslake around. It doesn't look good."

Unrepentant, Lassiter said, "No, sir." And then because he had been saving it for a proper moment—whether it was important or not—and it was fair enough to take a small victory over types like Quint either out of envy or malice—he said stiff-faced and in a casual tone, "I didn't feel it wise to mention this in front of young Kerslake, but there's something missing from Tucker's personal effects. I understood from you that he was wearing one of our gold recording wristwatches. It wasn't in the drawer with the other stuff. Maybe—" he paused; "—she's given it as a present to her boy friend."

*     *     *     *

A sign on the farm gate had said—ACCOMMODATION. The farmhouse itself lay under the brow of a hill, low and shallow-roofed, walls pink-washed, with a belt of wind-twisted trees flanking the sloping ground which ran down through bracken and gorse-covered waste land to grey slaty sea cliffs above a sharp crescent of sand which rimmed a small bay.

It was not the time of year at which the farmer and his wife expected visitors, but after a certain amount of doubt and consultation they had finally agreed to take them. The car was put in the barn at the far side of the house and they were given a large, low-ceilinged bedroom looking down to the sea. Though neither of them had said so yet, they both felt that this was a place more for them than any hotel. Hotels meant other people, and other people wanted to talk and become friends, and hotels had public dining-rooms while here the farmer's wife had offered them their own sitting-room in which they could eat in private.

They sat now, each in an armchair in front of the log fire. By reaching out her hand Margaret could have touched him. She wanted to do this, but resisted the contact because she drew a strange pleasure from denying herself the small joy, knowing that it was always there to be had. He was reading a book which he had found on the shelves at the back of the room. She watched him, his face still except now and then for a slow pursing of his lips as though savouring the words that flowed from the page to his mind. She remembered—and that life was now so infinitely remote to her, her memory of it was already purged of all emotion—the times she had sat with Bernard like this at home, a silent barrier between them. Two men and so different. Bernard had seldom talked and even less seldom about himself. Maxie, when the mood took him, and she was beginning to understand how to promote that mood, would put his head back and talk freely . . . about himself as a boy, about his school days and, sometimes, with a frankness that disarmed her and brought no jealousy, about the women he had known.

In the books she had once read there had been women who had adored their men. She knew now what that truly meant. She worshipped him. Herself and all she could call on were his for the taking. Everything she had ever read about true love she knew now *was* true. She would have done anything for him. With Bernard there had been nothing she could do for him. With Maxie, apart from their love, her life had acquired a purpose if only so simple as anticipating his wishes and surprising him by making them come true. To do and be all this would give her life valid meaning at last.

As she stared into the fire she suddenly knew he was looking at her. She turned as he dropped his book into his lap and his hand came out to take hers. He grinned and with the bluntness which she accepted now without surprise, he said, "If that little old door had a decent lock on it, love—I'd strip you right down and have you by firelight. And I'd bet it's not the first time it would have happened in this room. No matter what they say about the Welsh, they're a people of great passion."

She said, "Is that all you love me for? Just that?"

"Aye. Why not? The body holds everything, brain, heart and soul. Where else then should a man bring his worship?"

"One day you'll run out of the right answers."

"Maybe. Then you'll have to stop the questions and we can sit in silence which will be no hardship because there'll still be thinking and loving and a great stack of memories to thresh through."

When he awoke in the morning, the bed at his side was empty of her. The wind and rain of the night had gone. Sounds of farm work and animals came from outside. He heard a starling whistle on the roof and the call of the herring gulls down at the cliffs. He sat up in bed, stretched, and ran his hands through his dark hair. The log fire in the bedroom grate was now a pile of frost-coloured ash. He smiled to himself. He had wanted to take her by firelight downstairs, and she had said nothing to him of having already asked the farmwife to put a fire in their bedroom. She had, he realised, a knack for anticipation, for quietly divining his moods and wants and arranging for their gratification. It was natural that it should come out now so strongly. In her own house with her husband she had been no more than part and parcel of the furniture and fittings. Mistress of nothing but an unwanted loneliness.

As he stirred to get out of bed he saw a long, manilla envelope lying on her rumpled pillow. He picked it up. A message was written in pencil on the outside.

*Good morning, my darling. I have gone for a walk. Won't be long. Inside is a present for you with all, absolutely all, my love. M.*

Inside was a twice folded document on thick legal stationery. He sat up in bed and read it. It was a copy of her will, dated the previous Friday. It had been witnessed by her solicitor,

Andrew Browning, and one of his clerks and left the whole of her estate, real and personal, to him. For a moment or two there was an angry urge to tear it up. It had come too quickly and without any effort on his part. It was what he would have wanted eventually, would have had to have. He swore softly to himself, fighting off the belittling impression he had known before of being forestalled by some outside Fate whose intrusion was an insult to him; a Fate which mistrusted his own powers to arrange his life.

He flung the will to the bottom of the bed. But by the time he had washed and dressed his anger was gone, dispelled partly politically and partly naturally since there was a robust self-esteem in him which could not reject the tribute of first the gift of Margaret herself, a fine, good-looking woman, ardent and desirable and since their coming together looking years younger than her real age, and now—why after all waste time on his own injured pride?—so soon presenting him with all that she owned, putting herself and all that was hers into his hands. But Fate, he thought, the humour pleasing him, should really step back for a while and let him do a little work for himself. Gifts from the gods should be treated with caution. True gain was no more than a man could earn for himself by his own sweat and craft.

\*     \*     \*     \*

Quint lay awake in bed that morning, waiting for his early tea to come and thinking about Bernard Tucker. The box file, he knew, had held all Sir Harry Parks' papers. Once he had it Bernard would never have let it out of his sight or touch until he was convinced it was secure. He'd been dropped at Salisbury station for the London train. He saw him cross over, small case in hand, and catch a train to Bristol. A change there and then down to Exeter and the branch line to this place. Either his wife had met him or he had taken a taxi home. There was no importance in that. According to the inquest proceedings he and his wife had spent a quiet Saturday evening and then gone to bed. (Separate bedrooms and bathrooms. That must have been Bernard's choice. For how many years? No matter to him. He had had Tania Maslick in London. And, late in the day, Margaret Tucker had found someone too.) He had worked all day on the Sunday in his study. Business papers and reports for his firm in London. (How could a woman have accepted all that without curiosity? No . . . not really difficult to imagine where no love existed; and Bernard had a way of choking you off with a look, a firm slam of the shutter in your face if you persisted. He had early learned never to take him to that point. So had she.) He had finished his work late in the afternoon and gone up to his bedroom. Would have taken the box file and his personal report with him and burned all his scrap notes and synopsis aids. What then? His own house. No more security risk than the minimal protection of his safe could cover. That would have been enough. But not enough for Bernard. The moment of confidence was the most dangerous one. He would have done something about that. He would have put the empty box file in the safe because even though empty it needed some shield against an alien eye. Naïvely Sir Harry had—how many years ago?—inked his initials H.P. on the cover. (This he had kept from young Kerslake's eyes, but not from Lassiter's. But Lassiter was no threat. He was old and wily enough to know now far more than he had been told. A cunning sod, too. Keeping the gold wristwatch bit for the right moment.) There was no doubt that he had hidden the papers somewhere. They weren't with the stuff which Mrs Tucker had handed over to the solicitor, Browning. (God, that had been tricky to start with but the old boy had calmed down in the end —how often had he seen it—and eventually had been beguiled by the affair's obvious importance. The old boy, too, he guessed, could have had the passing thought that help rendered in affairs of State might bring some discreet, low-grade award in some future Honours List. No stopping him after that, right up to the point of professional indiscretion.)

Since Bernard had hidden the stuff, but left the empty box file in the safe, it must mean that he had chosen a place which would not take the box file but, by rolling or folding of the papers, would take them. He'd left the house only once on that Sunday, in the evening when he had gone for his fatal walk. He would never have taken them with him. The walk was unpremeditated. Brought on by Margaret Tucker and her personal affairs. It was an almost certain assumption that the papers were still hidden in the house somewhere. And that meant they had to turn the place over today. Just he and Lassiter with Kerslake sitting on the outer doorstep with a valid warrant to search in case Mrs Margaret Tucker turned up. Warboys had confirmed that procedure at two o'clock this morning and had promised to put the wheels in motion from his end. Warboys, as tart as a damson, on the phone. Was he already scenting failure, or hung-over now more openly with shock from Bernard's treachery, so distant, but freshly wounding? But he, himself, had no time for thought of failure. Not on this one. Because this was the one from which he had to launch himself upwards and onwards.

All right. So they turned the place over and found nothing. What then? Plenty. The inquest report was concerned only with Bernard's death and the preceding family quarrel. Margaret Tucker had been questioned—but only along one line. No one had hammered her to find out if Bernard had left the house at all—except after the quarrel. All the concentration had been on the quarrel and Bernard's leaving the house for a walk. What time had he finished his work in the afternoon? What exactly had he done before going up to change for dinner? Nobody had cared about that. (But he did. If the house produced a blank, he would soon be screwing every single detail of every minute of that day from her.) There was a postbox at the top of the hill above Lopcommon. Bernard— such simple guile was so often effective—could have walked up and back in five minutes and posted the stuff off. To where? The office? Or even—God forbid—to that lout Grainger

(Though it would have been in the letter box when he searched it. Unless—and for his own sake, God forbid—being bulky, the bloody man had had it separately under the counter and had kept quiet about it.) Jesus—if it were as simple as that Warboys would crucify him. . . .

He reached for the bedside telephone and put in a call to London. He waited in mild agony until he got the duty officer at the office. He gave his instructions and told the man to let him know the outcome. He put the receiver back. Relief spreading its slow euphoria through the mind.

His morning tea came and he sat, cradling the warm cup in his hands, the winter sunlight streaming through his window. Lassiter would have seen it. Maybe had already and was deliberately holding it back a while to drop it in front of him at some chosen moment, just as he had with the watch. Lassiter the detail man. It would be a nice moment. He looked forward to it. But for all that Lassiter was the one man he, himself, would have chosen to be with him. His malice was unprompted by ambition. Yes, Lassiter was the man for him. If they found nothing in the house, he was the right type to have with him when he talked to the woman. If he had to frighten her, drive her to remember, Lassiter would be a gentle presence to hold and sustain her, catching the point of tears and confusion and offering the easy balm. Though, God knows, she might really be well able to look after herself. Off somewhere now—but soon to be located—with some damn ne'er-do-well to whom already she had willed everything she owned. Old Browning had offered that privately, diffidently breaching a professional code because . . . '. . . *since this matter is so important it might have some . . . well, I just felt that in the circumstances. . . .*' Talking in suspended phrases, inchoate almost, because at the back of his own mind he was not sure what there was to offer or whether he really had anything to offer at all. He was just the sort of bloody fool who really might have something but never think of producing it.

There was a knock on the door and Lassiter came in,

194

wearing dressing gown and pyjamas, a cigarette in his mouth, and his eyes a little fogged with the whisky which he had drunk in his room before going to bed.

He said, "A small fear that surfaced amongst my waking dreams."

"Such as?"

"Bernard could have slipped out some time on Sunday and posted all the stuff off. Not to the office, we know. But the documents being bulky, old Grainger could have been holding them under the counter."

Quint nodded, still-faced, and said, "Yes, I know. It occurred to me late last night." He nodded at the telephone. "They're going to turn the place over first thing this morning. If the stuff's there we can go home. If not—we've got to take the house apart."

"Save us from that." Crossing to the window, staring out at the mud banks of the river, Lassiter said, "They should do his flat, too. Seeing the way posts are now a letter can take bloody days. Though—even if we can't ignore it—I don't think Bernard would have done it that way. He was due to hand over on Tuesday to Warboys."

"Don't worry. I mentioned the flat as well. But I agree with you, I don't think Bernard would have used the post."

CHAPTER ELEVEN

AT HALF-PAST NINE the news came through from London that there had been nothing in Grainger's shop, and nothing at Commander Tucker's flat. Kerslake arrived with a warrant to enter and search Lopcommon Barton.

They went out to the house, but on the way made a detour to Dougall's cottage. It was still empty.

"They're off," said Lassiter, "on a bicycle made for two."

Kerslake smiled to himself. He could see that Quint was not amused.

When they reached the house Kerslake was told to stay outside in the car. They wanted no interruption from trades-men, or any other visitors. He would make his own excuses for his presence there according to the nature of the caller. It was a cold morning with a thin hoar rime lying in the shadowed pockets of the combe side. He warmed himself every so often by taking a walk up the drive and back through the garden and wishing he could be inside to see the way they went about their work. There would be no wrecking, no upturned drawer contents on the floors . . . none of the desecrating mess which so many house-breakers left and which he had seen so often. When they left a room he knew that it would look exactly as it had been when they had entered. He had seen people weep at the sight of their homes after a thief had worked it, weep not for what they had lost but from shock at the violation, the rude contamination of strange, irreverent hands. There would be nothing of that from these two.

Inside the house Lassiter and Quint took separate rooms.

Two in a room meant that something might be missed between them. Quint took Bernard's bedroom and bathroom suite, and Lassiter took Mrs Tucker's. He went unhurried through the routines of search, thoroughly, efficiently, following the precise procedures acquired in the hard training of his first days with the department and sharpened by years of practical experience. But now, for once, the searching had a paradoxical element because he searched where Bernard Tucker could have hidden, and Bernard knew all the tricks. It was almost like one of the original set exercises in searching. If the stuff were in this room and he missed it, then from somewhere Bernard would be giving him a black mark.

There was one drawer in Mrs Tucker's bureau which was locked. He got Bernard's bunch of keys from Quint. There was no surprise in him when one of them opened the drawer. Nothing in this house would be closed to Bernard. There was a leather-bound diary and two cheap paperback books in the drawer. He flipped through the two books to see if there was anything loose between the pages. There was nothing. On the cover of one was a girl, immodestly dressed, he thought, snuggling up to a Highland warrior on top of a mountain. He sat down and began to read through the diary. If there were to be a clue to Bernard's hiding place it would only come from some source which Bernard would never have considered. Wives, more so when love was gone, had sharp eyes and scored little triumphs for themselves to ease their bitterness or frustration; and why not, the neglected little darlings?

He read the diary right through to the last entry which was some weeks old. There was no mention of Maxie Dougall. He took the diary through to Quint and tossed it on Bernard's bed.

"When you want a break, I think you ought to read through this. There's a point in it which may be worth considering. Is it all right if Kerslake comes into the house for coffee? It's freezing out there."

Quint nodded and picked up the diary.

Down in the kitchen Lassiter said to Kerslake, "See if you

can rustle up some coffee. If there's no tinned milk—pop down to the village for some. You should buy yourself a book to read, too. This is going to be a long job." He fished in his wallet and took out some notes. "And a bottle of whisky. There's no reason why the lady of the house should have to treat us as guests."

"Yes, sir."

"Don't go formal. We're human—even Mr Quint."

Kerslake grinned.

Lassiter went back to the bedroom and heard Kerslake's car drive off. He smiled to himself. There was tinned milk in the house—he'd seen it the day before—but Kerslake knew his priorities. Kerslake was anxious to please, to learn, and Kerslake—it happened to so many—would be dreaming and hoping and wondering how you got your toe in the door of the department. He could read him like a book because it was what had happened to himself years and years ago when he had been with the Royal Corps of Military Police, not even Army Intelligence. Kerslake should kill his dreams. The work was interesting but dirty. He wondered how long it would be before Kerslake could no longer contain some question about William Ankers. They had questioned him about the man and then left him high and dry. That was hard on a type like Kerslake.

Half an hour later they had coffee in the kitchen. Quint drank his quickly and went into Bernard's study to work there. Lassiter laced his coffee with a splash of whisky. Five minutes later Kerslake was back in the car with the radio turned down softly and Lassiter had taken the step-ladder from the scullery and gone into the roof loft through the hatch on the top landing. He had light from a couple of strip tubes on the roof beams, operated by a switch on the landing. The place was empty except for two water tanks. The floor had been covered with a four-inch layer of insulating material, loose grey granulated stuff like dirty snow. He examined it for signs of disturbance and saw none. He lifted the covers of the water tanks and checked that there was nothing hidden inside. Then he groaned, went down on his hands and knees and began to sift and scrape through the loose floor covering.

They took three-quarters of an hour off for a bar counter lunch at the pub in Lopcommon and then went back to work. They finished the house and then the garden and its sheds and the garage. Kerslake froze in the car and became mind-sogged with the mush and music from the radio. He was twice called in to make tea. The second time he saw that the level of whisky had dropped considerably in Lassiter's bottle. He had a feeling, though he did not know why unless it came intuitively from something in the man's manner, that Lassiter was searching without any real hope of finding whatever it was that they were looking for.

He was right. Lassiter and Quint had changed their search pattern. Each now was taking the rooms and areas that the other had previously worked. Each knew that the other would find nothing, but the training method had to be followed. Lassiter knew that if Bernard had hidden his stuff in this house its discovery had to come with help from Bernard. Hide and seek. You're cold. You're hot. By themselves in this house— Bernard watching them sardonically from above—they would never get anywhere. Slowly an eagerness built up in him to meet Mrs Margaret Tucker. What they wanted was her picture of Bernard—the stranger to them. It would be from this woman that they would get their answer if only in the obliquest terms.

\*     \*     \*     \*

They had walked up over the hill at the back of the farm and across a long stretch of moor to the headwaters of a small stream which they had followed downwards into a narrow valley clothed with ash growths and stunted oaks, the stream growing to a boulder-broken torrent. There was a small hamlet where the stream met the sea. Here they had lunch of bread and cheese at an inn, and then turned northwards to walk the coast back to the beach below their farm. The wind was cold and raw against their faces.

The path was narrow and Maxie walked ahead of her. She was glad of this for, although they could not talk to one another so freely, she liked to see him there, moving easily over the rough ground. The sight of him was company enough. Years ago . . . years and years ago she and Bernard had walked together while they were still in Scotland. But even then it had never been like this.

She would never again, she thought, live at Lopcommon. Maxie would never go there and she hated the place. It was amazing how you could read one man and not another. That surely came—the sureness of understanding without words, a look or a touch enough—from love, from that part of love which hung above, beyond the body, an essence which needed only passion to create it and then rose free to live its own life. This morning she had come back from her early walk, wondering what he would say about the will, a little fearful that she had rushed things out of a love which impelled her to pledge not only herself but everything she had. She had known the moment she walked into the room that he was with her and understanding her.

He had held her, running the flat of his hand under her hair on the nape of her neck, pressing her face against him and had said, "Don't be worried. I know how you feel. A man's pride touched wrong can make him curl up like a hedgehog, all spikes to the world. But not with me, girl. You gave me everything I'll ever want when you first came to me in the cottage. Aye, you could tear that piece of paper up now, walk out on me, and you'd still leave me with all the riches a man could ask for in this world." And then he had held her away from him and with that grin, the grin of a small boy in the orphanage crocodile, had gone on, "But you disappointed me and for that you must be punished. What man wants to wake in the morning wanting his woman and find her gone? For that you have to make proper amends. . . ."

They had been late down for breakfast; and now as she walked behind him the tears in her eyes from the wind were joined by fresh tears from herself. Such joy as she now had, nothing could take it from her. Maxie had said it; whatever happened they both had all the richness which they could ever ask for.

They dropped down to the crescent-shaped beach and arms linked, bowed their heads into the wind and began to walk across it to the path that led up to the farmhouse.

That evening after eating they sat by the fire, she on a cushion at his feet, and decided that there was no desire in them to move from this place they had found. They would go when their mood changed.

*　　*　　*　　*

In Quint's hotel bedroom, the two of them were having a drink before going down to dinner. A little earlier Kerslake had left them after bringing them back from Lopcommon Barton. Three times during the day Kerslake had telephoned the police headquarters to see whether there had been any report on Mrs Tucker's car. There had been none. He had left promising to let them know the moment any positive report came in.

Lassiter, fingering his glass, was now nursing the feeling that they were going to get nowhere without Margaret Tucker. Whether Quint felt the same he did not ask. In an hour Quint was due to telephone a report through for Warboys. Quint did not like making nil returns. Even the small crumb of a result to pass on would have lifted the withdrawn mood which Lassiter knew claimed him. To have found her car, to be able to tell Warboys where she was would have helped—would, Lassiter guessed, be his hope right up to the time of telephoning Warboys.

Lassiter got up and helped himself to another drink. An enquiring look towards Quint brought only a shake of the head.

Lassiter said into the blue, "Ankers talks of her shoplifting.

It's in her diary. You read it. An almost clinical description and her own diagnosis. Frustration, change of life perhaps, boredom, no real purpose in anything she was doing. An unused woman, whose mind and body take control and force a new character and role on her when she least expects it. This bore you?"

Quint looked at and beyond him.

"It could," he said.

"It shouldn't."

"Why not?"

"Because—don't ask me for any logic behind it—she's the key to all this. Just a feeling I have which you probably don't share. But I was taught not to ignore any hunch that persists. A few moments ago I was not going to mention it to you. But you're such a picture of gloom I thought you needed cheering up."

Despite himself Quint smiled. When you worked together protocol lapsed. Lassiter had no real time for him, he knew. But Lassiter wanted results just as he did. On an impulse he held out his empty glass and Lassiter came over and took it to recharge.

Quint said, "Let's have it—and make it stick."

Lassiter gave him back his glass and sat on the bed. He toasted him and then said, "Right. There's nothing about security that Bernard didn't know—and when necessary practise. He comes back home with a bunch of important papers. So far as we know—and I'll bet against it—there's no outside opposition. Nobody else after them. Right?"

"We'd have picked up some sign if there were."

"But Bernard would have taken just the same precautions as if there had been. He never let up. He works on his report on the Sunday, finishes it and tidies it all away. Mailing it off to some address we've disposed of. Even when we covered it we knew that it was something he would never have done. Not the Commander. He was going to stick with the stuff until he landed it on Warboys' desk. He hid the stuff in that house."

"We've gone through that, and we shall go through it again tomorrow. But you know as well as I do that to be absolutely certain we should have to take it all apart, brick by brick and beam by beam. We can't do that."

"Neither could Bernard. It's somewhere handy enough to be hidden, or taken out in a few moments."

"Where the hell does Mrs Tucker come into this?"

Lassiter smiled. "We're going to accept that he put the stuff in the house or surroundings somewhere?"

"Yes."

"Then Mrs Tucker comes into it because the man she knew was a different man from the one we knew. Vastly. For Christ's sake we didn't even know he was married, wanted to be rid of her, and had this place down here. Warboys is mourning him right now—but he'll never forgive him for it, for making a fool of him and his beloved department."

"Stick to the different man Mrs Tucker knew."

"Gladly. Tucker hid the stuff that Sunday. The fact that he died a few hours later is unimportant. He would still have put it where he did because the idea of his own death would never have entered his mind. Now, where did Mrs Tucker's husband hide the stuff?"

"We're back at the same point."

"No. It's my bet that there's something she knows about Tucker—and we don't—which will lead us to the stuff. It could be something very simple, meaning nothing to her, but everything to us. How does that seem to you?"

"Reasonable."

"Thanks."

"But we can't bloody well talk to the woman until we find her."

"Don't worry. She'll surface."

"But when? Warboys is being pressed from above."

"Then keep your fingers crossed that the police locate her soon or she turns up of her own accord. They could put out a call on the radio or television for her, but I don't imagine that would be popular. The name Tucker might ring like an alarm bell, not only to Sir Harry Parks, but to some of his old friends."

"How the hell did you know about Sir Harry Parks?"

Lassiter smiled. "Bernard didn't tidy his office desk because he thought he was going back to it. I've used it these last days. There's a recently issued, derestricted biography file of Sir Harry still in it. And to make my first point again—that's just the kind of break we ought to pray for from Mrs Tucker. Something that not even Bernard could have anticipated would break his security."

\*    \*    \*    \*

Billy Ankers sat in his room, toasting his feet in front of the gas fire in the grate. On the far side of the room a small electric fire stood close to his bed. The warmth in the small room was tropical. He felt relaxed and pleased with himself. Nancy would be with him in an hour. At least, he hoped she would be. It had been a long time. If any small boy came clumping up the stairs with excuse notes from her he really felt that he would have to make the effort of finding himself a more reliable companion. It was an idle thought. He knew it would never happen. Nancy knew and understood him. To break someone else in would be too much like hard work. Good old Nance, she knew when to shut her eyes or her mouth. And so she should, seeing the kind of father she'd had. He hadn't been above or below making a quick turn in his time and he'd done his little bit of porridge now and then at Exeter and Taunton jails. Nice old codger—he'd picked up quite a few tricks from him. But not this one, not this touch of mischief which was more than half-formed in his mind. Against that the few quid which Mr Tucker had died owing him was nothing. If this came off he wouldn't even bother to claim that through the solicitors. Not bloody likely. That would be asking for it.

He relit his pipe and stared at the mantelshelf, his lips working like a bored goldfish blowing bubbles. But he was far from bored. Got to handle it dead right, he told himself. Different paper, different typewriter. Don't post it in the town. Where? Bristol would do. And really make it clear that it was a once and for all touch. No coming back again for more. Not with this kind of thing. Greediness could be dangerous—particularly with a woman like Mrs Tucker. She would frighten easily, but if you frightened her too much you might touch off something you couldn't handle. Let's face it, for all he knew she could well have pushed the old boy over. And, if she'd done it once, she might do it again with someone else . . . to yours truly, particularly if she happened to be in one of her shoplifting moods.

Wonder where she was now with that Maxie? Cuddling up in some little love-nest. The whole town knew that they had gone off together . . . nice, juicy scandal. But they would be back. When they were he'd give her a few days to settle down and then do his stuff. In the meantime he had the letter to make up. Have to pitch that just right. And the amount to decide. Five hundred? Hardly enough if he wasn't going to come back for more, and he wasn't. A thousand? About right, and she'd never miss it.

He pushed his chair back a fraction to ease the heat on his soles and forgot about the letter he would have to write as he contemplated what he could do with a thousand pounds.

Walking home down Allpart Street, Kerslake saw the light shining through the fanlight at the top of the door next to the baker's shop. He could hear Quint saying, 'Now tell us about William Ankers'. And he had told him. And then Quint had dropped it and gone on to Andrew Browning. Since then, not another word about Billy Ankers. Not that that puzzled him. He'd lay any money that Commander Tucker had employed Billy to keep an eye on his wife's doings. That was clear enough. Billy had probably sent a report on Maxie Dougall. He could guess how that would have been pitched—strong enough to fortify Tucker's angry opposition to the man. But why had Tucker wanted to have his wife watched? That was more intriguing than why he had picked a scruff like Billy Ankers to do it. Billy, he guessed, had been picked because he was the only man on the spot. If Billy had ever tried any nonsense—and that was something that the fool could never resist eventually—then Commander Tucker, seeing now who and what he was, could have frightened the living daylights out of him, and more. He smiled at the thought. And then the smile went. For God's sake, what were they up to? 'Now tell us about William Ankers', and then no more. Why hadn't they been to see him? Well . . . it was none of his business to ask them questions. Show yourself too eager, too bright (when all the bloody time you could be being stupid) and they wrote you off. And that he did not want because, who knew, he was young and there was all his future ahead of him.

He turned into the garden of his lodging house. As he opened the front door the smell of cooking drifted down the hall from the back kitchen. A bed-sitting room and meals in common with the other lodgers. What he wanted was the key of a London flat, no girl in particular, and to be able to face someone with that hard, level stare of Quint's.

\*     \*     \*     \*

They spent another two days going over Lopcommon Barton without result. The search for Mrs Tucker's car or her whereabouts had produced nothing.

Quint sat in Warboys' office now, listening to what he knew was the cold preamble to an ultimatum. For a moment or two he had a quick picture in his mind of Lassiter, propping up the bar in the Empress Hotel, and envied him. To Lassiter success or failure meant only minor elation or superficial wounds. For himself he knew that he would be marked for the rest of his professional life by the result he could produce on this case. If he gave Warboys what he wanted, and what those beyond wanted then the road ahead was clear. Should he fail through no fault of his own, he would have no defence because failure itself was an absolute that precluded all generosity and all excuses. You won or you lost here. There were no second or third places. He realised that he—who had always wanted Bernard's place—was fighting Bernard himself for it now. No outside forces, no opposition, just Bernard and the unseen, unmeasurable motions of chance and circumstances. For all he knew—and his own iron-controlled anxiety produced the fancy oddly in his mind—he could be on the point of seeing his professional ambitions harried and crippled because at some time in the past the wind had blown the last dead leaf from a tree or the mind of some man had given unexpected occupancy to a moment of nostalgia which had changed briefly his purpose and direction. That Warboys, with his own higher degree of power and cold dream of honours, would suffer with him was no consolation.

Warboys said evenly, "The position is absolutely clear. It is as near a certainty as makes no difference that there will be an election early in the New Year. And this time—and not before time—the lines of battle will be drawn up so that there will only be one choice before the electorate. Is a democratic government going to control this country or is the future of the country going to be in the hands of the trades unions and their ability to impose their will by industrial power? Forget all the nonsense of who controls the trades unions. It is the power of the State against the power of organised labour. Either government by law, or the rule of force by workers' organisations led by militants whose real purpose is plain anarchy—no matter what fancy political name they choose to give to it." Warboys paused fractionally. He had been tempted to say—as he often had done with Bernard, 'How am I sounding?' and he remembered, too, Bernard's reply the last time. 'Like a T.V. political pundit. But you're warming up, Percy.' Conscious of the sharp bite of memory, he went on, "But let's waste no more time on that. Politics stink. Sadly—this time—we are over involved and can't withdraw. Those papers are wanted. Whether or not they would ever be used is not our concern. Any of a dozen twists of expediency or electoral opinion poll ratings could keep them locked away, unused. Safe in the ammunition locker, maybe for another time. But the point is the ammunition locker is empty . . . until we get the papers. If we don't get them ever, or in time for them to be used if that decision is made—then you know the score, Quint. There will be a certain brightness withdrawn from your future for ever—and from mine." He let the words sink in, and then smiled sympathetically. "We've produced miracles in the past. Nothing less is expected of us now. Damp squibs are not wanted. So what do you say to that?"

Quint said, "When we find Mrs Tucker I shall find what they want."

"What does Lassiter think?"

"The same, sir."

"What do you think has happened to her?"

"She's holed up somewhere—not deliberately—in some place with this man Dougall. They're freshly in love. They're not flashy types who'd go for a big or plushy hotel. They're somewhere on their own. Not in a town, I doubt. Some cottage or farmhouse with the car seldom used. The numbers of wanted cars the police have to look out for are in hundreds, and there are plenty of men in the force who say 'Oh, to hell with it'—unless the car parks right under their nose. She's not abroad. Her passport's still in the house. And he has never been issued with one. Put out a call on T.V. or radio and they'd be turned up tomorrow."

Warboys shook his head. "That's out. You know why."

"Out for good, sir?"

"Yes. Within five minutes the press would be crawling all over the place. There are good men in the press. They soon read the score. Five minutes with her or this Dougall! Can you imagine? Five minutes in that town and the name Commander Tucker a gift for them. No, it's out for good. That's been categorically stated. But I'm not worried. She'll come back in her own time, or be spotted. When she does . . . well, it's up to you." He was silent for a moment or two, poised to dismiss Quint, a man he had begun to create—just as he had created Bernard but had overlooked, because of an affection never allowed to transgress its proper bounds, the basic unsuitability of his material. Bernard had cheated him, but the original sin he knew had rested in him. Sublimating a love yet keeping the object of that love near you by guile was, he could now confess to himself, a dishonour greater than reaching openly for that love and risking utter rejection . . . and that he knew was what he would have had. He went on, "The autopsy was positive that Bernard lived for some time after the fall?"

"Yes, sir. Ten or fifteen minutes." And knowing what was coming, Quint added. "I've spoken to the surgeon. He had little doubt that Commander Tucker would have been fully conscious for quite a while. Which means that the Commander would almost certainly have used his watch and recorded where he had put the papers unless—" He broke off sharply. The last word had slipped from him before he could halt it.

"Yes? Unless what?"

Without hesitating Quint, saving himself as far as he could, said, "Unless he had a good reason for not doing so."

Warboys, acknowledging to himself that Quint was growing up fast, that he would be a good man soon and, maybe, a far better one than Bernard had proved to be, said casually, "I shouldn't rely too much on the watch."

Quint said, "Mrs Tucker will know where the watch is. She could have given it to Dougall, or have it with her planning to do so."

"Her dead husband's watch to her lover?"

"I gather she is a strange woman in some ways. This shop-lifting business and a certain quiet disregard of conventions."

Warboys nodded, dismissing Quint. When he was gone— already under instructions to rejoin Lassiter at the Empress Hotel—Warboys went to his cupboard and poured himself a drink. For a moment or two he had been tempted there and then to give orders that when the watch was found he wanted it brought to him before the tape was played. God knows what Bernard might have said. The prospect of death could concentrate a man's mind in a strange direction. He had no wish for anyone else to hear any last moment message to him from Bernard, some cruel, even though true, valediction. Then he dismissed the thought, ashamed of himself. Bernard was not the kind of man to take advantage of his dying moments to wound other people.

CHAPTER TWELVE

As THEY CAME down off the moor to the wooded river valley Margaret, who was driving, turned off the main road into a side lane.

Maxie asked, "Where are you going? This isn't the way back."

Margaret smiled. "It is the way. Another way home. You'll see."

She drove carefully down the narrow country road to the valley bottom and stopped the car on the old stone bridge that crossed the river. Sunlight struck through a border of pines across the low, white-faced, thatched house, and over the grey slates of the stone-built barn at its side. The lawn sloped down to the river which was dropping fast in height now after the recent rains. A few early snowdrops flaked the river bank.

She said, "You like this house, don't you?"

"Of course I do, love."

"You'd like to live here with me? We could be happy here, couldn't we?"

He grinned. "We could be happy anywhere."

"No, not at Lopcommon. There could be no question of that. But this is the house for us. For me, and for you. Oh, Maxie . . . sometimes in the last days I felt I couldn't wait for this moment. I just felt if I didn't tell you I'd burst. Darling, it's all ours. No, all yours. . . ."

She held out her hand to him with a key resting in its palm.

For a moment he felt that he wanted to take the key and throw it through the window into the river. He was angry with himself more than with her. He should have known from the

213

time she had turned off the main road, known as they drew up on the bridge. Maybe any other man in love with her would have known; though poor himself, could have read the lines of naïve generosity which embroidered her love. To hide even the smallest open show of his feeling, he put his hand over the key on hers and pulled her to him, burying her face against his shoulder.

He said, truth and his passion for her and the anger from her generosity mixed and slow-moving in him, "Oh, girl . . . what can a man say to someone like you? Do you think there's any part of me that wants anything else than your love?" Hands on her shoulders he held her away from him, looking hard into her eyes. "If I said No to you, that we were going back to my cottage and that must be the place for our love, would you take that?"

She was silent for a moment and then she held up the key, her face smooth with happiness, her eyes shining, and she said, "Tell me to throw this in the river and I'll do it. Tell me, Maxie. . . ."

Suddenly he laughed, shaking his head, and said, "My God, you're a wild one, and a sudden one, and love has given you a bagful of tricks. Where's the woman who walked the sands lonely and empty? Where's Mrs Tucker who couldn't tell one day from another because all the days were the same? I thought I had a bird to free from a cage out of love, a bird that would be feared of flying, that would pull back from liberty. . . . And what have I got? A fine falcon that bids fair to out-fly her tiercel. A real goer that even in a cage treasured all the powers of freedom and, tossed up, takes the wind under her wings and heads for the high blue. . . . Oh, girl, one thing I ask you is not to stop surprising me with your real gifts. Not this—" he nodded towards the house, "—though it's a fine and over-generous one, but the gifts that come from yourself. . . ."

And talking, his anger smoothed away by the power of his own words—thrown out without fair thought or care for any exaggeration, just words that were more a balm for himself than

214

for her—he saw the moistening in her eyes and felt the hard movement of a doubt about himself. It was not she who was being led and mastered and made another's creature, but himself marked for that. And it seemed to him that for his own manhood's sake and the old score he longed to settle against all the deprivations of his own life's form, there must come a time when some gift must be rejected. Some act of rebellion was necessary for him against the smooth lines which Fate was laying down for him with her. He was being left no work to do, no subtleties to deploy, no crafts to display. Things which came too easily had no value . . . or was it to be, despite all the ease now with which first she, and then her gifts, had come to his hands, that in the final act of dispossession—a cloud with constant changing form in his mind—he would be left entirely alone and find himself wanting?

He opened the door with the key, picked her up and carried her over the threshold. They went round the place together. The previous tenants had left the house on the weekend of her husband's death. Already she had brought over some of the things she wanted from Lopcommon. All the furnishings in the house were hers, most of them from her old home in Scotland. She did not say so but he knew that there would be little here to remind her of Lopcommon. She took him up to the granary floor of the barn and was full of ideas for converting it to make a study or a studio for him. . . .

"We can put in a large window. You'll be able to sit and work and watch the river. We're twenty miles from the town, and the village is a mile away. There won't be any embarrassments. I shall sell Lopcommon Barton. . . . Oh, Maxie, Maxie, my love! We shall be so happy here."

She was like a girl, a young girl with a first love colouring all her days, and his heart warmed for her. As she talked away, opening doors and cupboards and picking up ornaments to show him, he felt a sudden fondness for her, a deep unexpected affection. The snows of her loneliness had melted and were running down the high brooks full of chatter and brightness

215

under a too long absent sun. He reached for her suddenly and spun her round, holding her close to him.

She knew the look in his eyes and she said, "Oh, no Maxie, not now. There's so much to do. . . ."

He grinned, picked her up and said, "Aye, that's true, and things must be given their proper priorities. This is our house. Love comes first in it."

He began to carry her up to one of the bedrooms.

\* \* \* \*

Kerslake, wondering how Quint was going to take the news, picked his words very carefully.

He said, "Yes, sir, she's back. But not at Lopcommon. I had a call from her solicitor a short while ago. She phoned him to make an appointment to see him tomorrow. Apparently she's been back three days, living at a house she owns over near Stonebridge. That's about twenty miles away."

"Three days?" Quint made no attempt to hide his anger. "How could she be living three bloody days within twenty miles of this place and her car not reported? For God's sake! We've been sitting around here for days and when she comes back it's three days before anyone lets us know. What kind of force have you got here?"

Lassiter at the bedroom window, the light fast going from the sky, turned and said, "Did the solicitor know she owned this house?"

"Yes, sir. Apparently she lets it furnished. The last tenants left just before she went away with the Dougall man."

"And it never occurred to the fool to let us know that?"

"Well, sir, I suppose he didn't think it was relevant. As for not picking up the car . . . well, it was reported. Ten minutes after Browning spoke to me."

Lassiter smiled to himself. Kerslake had done no wrong, but he was loyal to his kind. He said, "She's back. That's the main point. The man Dougall's living with her, I presume?"

216

Kerslake nodded.

Quint said nothing. Days of frustration, days on which at every evening report to Warboys he had sensed his frustration and growing anger, and these an indication of the concern of the men behind him, harrying him, no doubt, with less subtlety than Warboys would ever use to one of his own agents. And three of those days wasted because of the damned stupidity of a country solicitor and some stupid village policeman.

Lassiter said, "Do you know the house?"

Kerslake said, "Yes, I do. Would you like me to phone and make an appointment for——"

"There's no need for an appointment," Quint said. "You go down to the car. You can drive us out. We'll be with you in a minute."

"Yes, sir." Kerslake left the room.

Quint said to Lassiter, "When you go to get your coat in your room phone London and tell them we've found her. That's something Warboys can pass on at least."

"There's something more important than that."

"What?"

"How you tackle her. It's no good glaring at me. You've got to settle it before you get in the car with our young friend. Waiting around has put us both on edge, but that's nothing to do with her. If you pitch in right away—and you've no reason to do that—you could get her in a fine state. She'll be damn-all use to us like that. And don't get edgy with me. I'm thinking of you and the job."

"For Christ's sake what do you think I am? She's done nothing criminal. We just want her help."

Lassiter smiled. "I think you're so relieved that you'd enjoy being hard with her—and regret it within ten minutes. So I suggest you leave it to me, for the first few minutes. There's no need—unless we're forced to it—to go into the business of Bernard marrying and keeping it secret. She's going to have enough to cope with. We want her on our side. Don't forget——

217

she's Mrs Bernard Tucker. She's got a lot of surprises coming to her."

For a moment or two Quint said nothing, then he smiled and nodded. There were plenty of other men he could have had with him who wouldn't have risked offering the advice or would have deliberately withheld it to enjoy the difficulties he could make for himself. But not Lassiter—and Lassiter, he knew, was not doing it entirely for him. Lassiter had done it for the sake of the job more than anything else.

He said, "You're right. Though I should have calmed down in the car. We'll just play her gently—and not too long. Let her get the picture and then have a night to sleep on it."

Lassiter went to his room for his coat, poured himself a drink, and sipped at it while he waited for his London call. Mrs Tucker, Bernard's wife, the wife of a man who had been one with them, and more than them. She deserved a little special treatment and, for all he had said, he knew that Quint could have been a long time coming to that. The curiosity about the woman which had been slowly building in him over the past days was suddenly stronger now that he knew he would see her soon. He had seen photographs of her, turned her house over three times, read her diary, poked around the cottage of her lover and—after a personal call from Warboys to the man— he and Quint had talked to her doctor about her absent-minded stealing fits. Quint—beating his heels, frustrated, his mind turning to any bizarre possibility—had wondered whether she might have known Bernard's hiding place. In one of her states she could have taken the papers and either destroyed or hidden them—a wildness of thought which Lassiter did not share. Now, in a little while, he was going to see her and talk to her. As that happened he knew that a great deal of the dead Bernard would be alive for him.

When they got to the house she answered the door to them. Kerslake had been left to sit in the car. Lassiter handed her his card, introduced Quint, and said that they were old friends of

Bernard's and also business associates. They would be glad if she could spare them some of her time. There were various professional matters which Bernard had left unfinished and they hoped that she could help to clear them up. He expressed sympathy for her in her loss and regret that they had to disturb her so soon after her husband's death.

The oaklined hall was decorated with holly and Christmas hangings for the festival which was little more than a week away. Margaret looked at the card and said, "The Home Office? That's the Civil Service, isn't it?"

"Yes, it is, Mrs Tucker. We'll explain about that."

She led them into the sitting-room. A log fire burned in the open grate. She offered them drinks which they both refused. There was no sign of the man Dougall.

Margaret, confused, said, "Why did Bernard never tell me he was in the Home Office? I understood from him that he worked for a business firm . . . something to do with tea-broking."

"Yes, I know," said Lassiter. She was taller than he had imagined from her photographs, and looked younger; a well-set-up, fine-bodied woman. Not beautiful, but with a good face. It was not difficult to imagine her as she must have been when Bernard had first met her. A distant loyalty to Bernard and a genuine concern for her peace of mind moved in him. He went on, "Bernard had no personal desire to mislead you. It just so happened that his position in the Home Office was a highly confidential one. He worked in the most delicate areas of the affairs of State. Whether he liked it or not he was obliged to practise certain . . . well, polite fictions. Shortly before he died he was given clearance to let you know the real truth. Sadly . . . well, he died before the opportunity came. Later we'd like to come and talk to you again and then we'll be happy to answer any questions about Bernard's life that we can, and help you with any problems you have . . . I mean concerning his flat in London, his personal effects, and financial matters connected with his employment. But for the moment, Mrs

Tucker, we must limit ourselves to a single matter of importance in which we need your help. It concerns some very important State papers which were in your husband's possession and which we must recover."

Margaret said, "You mean he did secret work . . . well, like the things you read about?"

Lassiter smiled. "In a way. Though it was all perfectly straightforward and correct. Commander Tucker was a man highly regarded in his profession. Had he lived he would undoubtedly have been knighted for his services. I should tell you that we've read the report of the inquest on his death. We don't want to embarrass you, but I hope you will be kind enough to answer a few questions for us—questions that have nothing to do with his accidental death. A loss, I may say, which we all in the service greatly mourn."

Lassiter paused. He did not care much for his last sentence, but then you never knew with women. It could be something which she expected, even though she had meant to leave Bernard. There were conventional expressions which the living—no matter their true emotions—expected about the dead.

Margaret said, "I'll help you as much as I can. But I really knew nothing about Bernard's work. And I understand now why." She understood the plain, brief facts, but not, she felt, the necessity for a man to shut off the major part of his life from his wife. For a moment or two she was seized with compassion for the Bernard who had been obliged to close so much of his life to her. The man Lassiter, kindly and considerate, went on talking, explaining to her about the papers which Bernard had brought home to work on, explaining how carefully he would have guarded them, how they were now missing, and that a duly warranted search of Lopcommon while she had been away had failed to bring them to light. He was frank, but unemphatic, and this to some extent cut away the beginnings of resentment she could have felt for the intrusion. Instinct prompted her to the knowledge that behind

220

these men rested a great source of power and influence. Dimly now, she realised that the same kind of aura had hung about Bernard.

Lassiter finished, "Well, that's the position, Mrs Tucker. So far as your personal life is concerned—while naturally we have become aware of the circumstances—that is not something which concerns us. All we are concerned with is these papers. My colleague, Mr Quint, worked directly under the orders of your late husband. So, I think it's best if I leave it to him to do the rest of the talking."

Margaret nodded. She liked Lassiter, but for the other she had no feeling. He had sat silently watching her, a lean-faced, dark-haired man with a quality of stillness about him as though he were tightly wound, tensed against the thrust of strong inner energies seeking exercise. As she turned slightly to him, he gave her a faint bow of the head and smiled.

He said quietly, "You weren't at home when Commander Tucker arrived on the Saturday. Had he telephoned to say he was coming for that weekend?"

"No. But then he seldom did. He just turned up, mostly without warning."

"On the Sunday he worked most of the day on these papers?"

"Yes. At least I imagine they were these papers. He said it was a big business report he had to prepare."

"Did you see them at all?"

"No."

"Where would he have kept them on Saturday night?"

"I imagine in his safe. Either the one in the study or the one in the bedroom."

"During that Sunday did he go out at all? I mean leave the house—until he went for his walk in the evening?"

"I don't think so."

"You're not absolutely sure?"

"No. But usually he would come and tell me if he was going anywhere."

"He finished his work not long before you usually have drinks in the evening. Did you see him go up to his bedroom?"

"No, but I heard him. I was in the sitting-room and the door was open. I imagine he went up with his papers, put them away, changed and then came down for his drink. It was then that——"

"Yes, we know. The point is, Mrs Tucker, that it is a fair assumption that Commander Tucker went up to his bedroom with these important papers. He put them in his safe—or left them in the safe in his study. But the papers were not to be found in either safe, and not to be found in the course of very thorough searches which we have carried out at Lopcommon. That suggests, in fact, that either he didn't put the papers in one safe or the other, or that he did and they were subsequently taken out by someone."

"I can't imagine by whom."

"Neither can I. I don't think they were taken out because I don't think they were ever put in any safe. Commander Tucker hid them—almost certainly in the house somewhere. Have you any idea whether he had any secret hiding place around the house? Particularly upstairs?"

"Not that I know of. I opened both his safes myself. The one in the study had private papers which went to my solicitor. The bedroom one just had an empty box file. I left it there."

"Yes, we saw it. The papers were in it originally. I gather you don't intend to live at Lopcommon again?"

"That's right. I shall sell it or let it furnished—as I used to let this house." She was easier with him now, but she knew she would never like him. When he spoke to her his eyes never left her face. Lassiter, she noticed, seemed at times to be paying little attention. He stared at the ceiling or his eyes went slowly round the room. Seldom did he look at her. She had the odd feeling that he was bored and could not care less about these papers.

"When you came here—just before you went away—you brought a certain amount of stuff from Lopcommon?"

"Yes. Chiefly my own personal stuff."

"Did you bring anything of Commander Tucker's?"

"Well, not really. He kept very little at Lopcommon except his clothes."

"You brought nothing from his bedroom or study?"

"Yes—from the bedroom. There were one or two photographs of him in his naval days, and a little model of his first frigate, and a photograph of the both of us taken just after the wedding. Oh, yes, and a big family bible that he kept by his bedside."

"How big?"

"Oh, about that size. . . ." Margaret gestured with both hands to indicate the size of the bible.

"May we see it?"

Margaret got up and left the room.

Quint said, "She's cool."

"Why shouldn't she be? Bernard didn't die a fortnight ago for her. It happened years earlier." Lassiter eyed a silver tray on the window table which held decanters and glasses. Bernard had set her a problem and also them. She was well on the way to solving hers. Maxie Dougall was a lucky man; a fine woman, a fine house and a fine fortune, right into his lap . . . he wished her all the happiness she deserved. He went on, "Keep the rest of it down to ten minutes. She's going to lie awake for a long time thinking tonight. Tomorrow is another day."

Margaret came back with the big family bible, its covers held together with a wide brass clasp. Quint opened it, and ruffled through the foxed pages, and then handed the book back. He said, "It was just a thought. For your information the papers, folded in two, would fit into something of that shape and size. Rolled up . . . well they would go into something the size of a tall vase or a round table leg. You brought no furniture here?"

"None."

"You'll forgive this question I'm sure, Mrs Tucker—but Commander Tucker's personal stuff, the clothes he was wearing and the things like his wallet and so on which were with him at the time of his death. What about them?"

"The police arranged for the disposal of his clothes to some charity I imagine. I've left what he carried on him at Lopcommon. I really haven't got round to thinking about them."

"You wouldn't have given or be thinking of giving anything, say his wallet, cigarette case or a watch, to any of his friends down here as a memento?"

Margaret shook her head. "Bernard had no friends down here. If there's anything you or Mr Lassiter would like or someone at his office . . . well, I'd be glad for you to take what you want. I just couldn't think of anyone here who would want anything like that, absolutely no one."

Lassiter stood up. For the first time her voice had hardened, for the first time something of the quiet despair and waste of her past years had deliberately been displayed. He said, "You've been very co-operative, Mrs Tucker. We won't bother you any more this evening. But could we ask you to think where Commander Tucker might have hidden the papers? Perhaps, too, we might be allowed to come and see you tomorrow." He smiled. "We shall eventually find the papers, of course. I think when we do it will be because something has occurred to you . . . some small thing whose importance won't be apparent to you but will be to us. The only thing I would ask you—because of the importance of this matter—is not to discuss this business with anyone else except Mr Dougall. I can understand that that would be reasonable. But please ask him to use the same discretion as yourself."

For a moment a little smile, a moment of clear gratitude, showed on Margaret's face. He was sounding like some benign family lawyer, he knew. He hoped, but not with much optimism, that their relationship could always be kept that way.

Margaret said, "Thank you, Mr Lassiter, and you Mr Quint."

Kerslake drove them to their hotel. They sat in the back and there was no talk between them. There was a lot Kerslake would have liked to have known. He sensed that if he ever came to work with people like them there would often be similar situations. For a man with a strong sense of curiosity that would be hard to take, but with practice one could learn to keep to any rules. If not from Quint, then minimally from Lassiter, he had got the impression that they liked him and had no real complaints. The stupidity of Browning and the Stonebridge police constable was nothing to do with him. He drove, permitting himself the wild dream of doing something, taking some initiative which would mark him forcibly as their kind of material. God, they looked nothing, but they were men with real power behind them. He was young, there was nothing in this town for him. . . .

Over their whisky in Quint's room before dinner, Lassiter said, "So, she doesn't know that the gold wristwatch has gone."

"She could have been hoping that Dougall didn't walk in wearing it."

"That how you read her?"

"She's a woman. Oh, she was helpful, but then she wasn't being pushed. The documents are the important number. We'll come to the watch later. I know you're thinking that Bernard may have recorded where he hid the papers."

"You want to bet on it?"

"Which way?" asked Quint.

"I'll take you an even fiver. He'll have said nothing."

"Why on earth not?"

"Because I think I knew him better than you. And we're learning a lot more about him. Those papers are dirt. Warboys normally wouldn't have touched this business with gloves on. But he had to. Bernard would have felt the same. He will have said nothing about them. For his money death would have been a little more acceptable to him that way. Bernard won't help from beyond the grave. Fundamentally he hated the whole service. He wouldn't waste his last breath on it. . . ."

*　　*　　*　　*

225

Maxie Dougall lay in bed alongside the sleeping Margaret. Outside, in the tall firs by the bridge, a pair of owls called to one another now and then, and from the woods rising beyond the river he heard the short, fierce scream of a vixen and the answering bark of a dog fox. Although there had been intermittent wind and heavy rain for weeks, the weather had been unusually mild. These spells were not uncommon in the West and Nature responded to them. Birds began to pitch an occasional courtship call; deep in a hedgerow the small white face of a wild strawberry plant would bloom palely. Today he had watched a couple of crows carrying dead sticks to an old nest and, when they had reached it, drop them to the ground as though their original intent had faded from their memory. Plant and beast had a long way to go yet. There would be hard frost and snow to come in the New Year. The ground would be iron-hard and drift-covered and there would be no question of courtship or blooming.

He lay listening to the sound of Margaret's quiet breathing. To have a woman who slept by him breathing gently, lying securely at his side, was a new experience for him and one which so far time had not made commonplace. There were pleasures in having a woman, he was beginning to realise, that had their own even joys which lay far away from the flesh and the strong emotions of mastery and possession. It was a rare knowledge and a fine experience, and, he guessed, a combination which could carry its own seduction. This, he imagined, was how happily married people were ... passion not spent but shaped to a different proportion; new, smaller joys surfaced on the long stream of daily life. He could understand it, applaud it even, but knew that it was not for him. To be accountable, no matter in how small a way, for the rest of his life to another was not for him.

She had been upset by the visit of the two men. He wished that he had been with her when they had come. She needed him, not only against them but against the truths they had given her about Bernard. Thinking about all she had told him,

226

he could only have a sad curiosity about the man. How could any man have shaped or let his life be shaped in the way his had been—to take a wife and hide so much of himself from her? He had never spoken to the man in his life and only seen him infrequently. He stirred now with a quiver of contempt for him. No matter what litter he had come from he was a runt who should early have been put in a pail of water and had the lid clamped down.

When the men came again he had told Margaret that she was not to talk to them unless he was with her. Let them try to make trouble about it and he would deal with them. Racketing around in other people's lives all for the sake of a bundle of bloody government papers that probably were of no real importance at all. He knew the kind they were because his sort had always suffered from them before they learnt how to deal with them. They were like orphanage guardians, school inspectors, policemen, jumped-up bureaucrats in local offices . . . give them a little power and they used it, enjoying themselves. But not with him, or with Margaret. So long as she was his she would not be touched.

Outside the fox called again and was answered by the vixen. He turned over for sleep, moving his big body gently not to wake her, and kissed her cheek, his lips just brushing her warm skin.

\*     \*     \*     \*

Billy Ankers lay in bed, too. In a pub that evening he had briefly met Kerslake. He wasn't a bad type, Kerslake. But it didn't pay to get too close to any policeman. Liked his drop of drink all right but never over the line with it. Saw himself as going places, maybe. Well, good luck to him. He'd yet to hear of a copper who'd made a fortune at it. Bent or otherwise. For a time he'd wondered if Kerslake was after something from him. Nothing definite to go on, but he'd just had that idea. Well, he might not have wanted anything from him, but he'd given him something to think about. They'd chatted about local doings and then somehow things came round to the talk that was still to the front in most pubs and elsewhere . . . Maxie Dougall and Mrs Tucker. Big news in a small town like this. People had plenty of time on their hands to ferret about in the lives of others. Gossip was their daily bread.

He grinned to himself in the darkness. That Mrs Tucker. . . . She'd certainly come on. Taking old Maxie off on a holiday and now living with him over at Stonebridge. Bold as brass and her old man only a few weeks gone. Just casual like, he'd asked Kerslake if it was true and Kerslake had said it was, and added for good measure that it was nobody's business but theirs.

Tomorrow he'd do the letter for her. Brazen she might be. And why not? Leave a woman with her looks and figure neglected and it was asking for some man to make off with her. But she would have to pay for it. . . .

He'd draft the letter first in ink, get it just right, work everything out, and then all he had to do was to get his hands on a typewriter. Asking for it to use his own. The garage down the road shut at nine. The girl there used a portable. All he had to do was slip in the back way and borrow it. Take him an hour at the most and nobody to know the next morning.

Easy. He stared into the darkness . . . fragments of the letter beginning to shape in his mind. Then, as sleep took him, the heady thoughts of what he could do with a thousand pounds floated him away.

CHAPTER THIRTEEN

IT WAS RAINING hard, a steady, wind-driven downpour
which now and then lashed itself against the sitting-room
window. From where he sat Lassiter could see the pine trees
down by the river bridge, their green crests blurred by the
water-streaked window, swaying and swinging in the wind.
There were four people in the room, himself, Quint and Mrs
Tucker and the man Maxie Dougall. When she had shown
them in Dougall had been in the room. Nobody had suggested
that he either go or stay. A look between himself and Quint had
been enough to mark their lack of opposition. They wanted
her to talk, to be at ease. They could get more from her if she
were relaxed. So far Dougall had said nothing. Lassiter noticed
that although he was doing the talking Dougall watched Quint
most of the time. Maybe, thought Lassiter, he recognised
instinctively the real authority in the room. He was the quiet,
self-contained sort, and, he guessed, the man, too, would have
his own authority and power. If they started to push Margaret
Tucker, he would react at once. Love was possession and you
guarded your own prizes. He was glad that Quint had again
decided to leave it to him to handle Margaret Tucker first.

He said, "I know you may not see the point of all this at
first, Mrs Tucker—but the fact is that the Commander Tucker
we knew was a very different man from the one you knew.
And it was the man you knew who hid these papers—somewhere, we're sure, in or close to Lopcommon Barton. If you
would, we would like you to tell us something about this
man.'

Margaret said quietly, "I knew two men, too, Mr Lassiter. The man I married, and the man he became."

"Of course. But I don't think we need to go back right to the beginning. Let's start with the man he was when you first came to Lopcommon. Had things started to go wrong between you then?"

"No, not really. Though there were signs. He still came home quite often and we did things together. We had more of a social life, though that was not something he ever really encouraged. He was a member of the golf club but only for a short while. We had bridge friends and sometimes went to a race meeting or point-to-points, but not for long. He seemed content just to stay in or around the house."

"Doing what?"

"We gardened together. He liked that at first. But he went off it. I really don't know why. He was very good at it, patient and knowledgeable. In the end he left it all to me, and, of course, to the odd-job man we had up now and again."

"What did he do with himself then? Sit indoors and read, work . . . go for long walks?"

"Sometimes, yes. Most of the time, in the beginning, anyway, he used to work around the house."

"You mean he was a handyman?"

"Oh, very much so. I think most navy men are. He did all the repairs around the place and made things in his workshop. The drive gates at Lopcommon were made by him."

"He had a workshop?"

"Yes. It's the gardener's shed now."

"Did he make anything else? I mean, anything that you particularly remember, or something which clearly he was pleased about?"

She paused for a moment, searching her memory. Lassiter sensed that Quint would not stay silent for long.

Margaret said, "Well, I don't remember anything much that he was pleased about. The drive gates, yes. But mostly it was repairing locks, and electric light fittings. He did new draining boards for the sink and some cupboards I wanted. You know the kind of thing, painting and paper-hanging. All I know is that if there was anything that had to be done in the house . . . well, in those early days, he would do it. Then that went. He just wasn't interested any more—except for his naval things. When he finished with those . . . well, he let his workshop go and it was turned into a gardening shed. I came back one year from a holiday in Scotland and everything had gone."

Lassiter, deliberately giving Quint the few moments he wanted, said, "You went to Scotland without him?"

"Oh, yes. I used to go every year usually by myself when my aunt was alive. She was ninety-three when she died. Bernard came up for the first two or three years, but then . . . well, I went alone."

Quint said, "When you talk of naval things, what do you mean exactly, Mrs Tucker?"

"His ships. Little models of all the boats he'd served in, or ones he knew. He used to have them all around the study downstairs. Then one day, some years ago, he gave them all away. I think it was to some boys' club. In London, I believe he said."

And was there, Lassiter wondered, some symbolism in that?

Quint said, "All of them, Mrs Tucker?"

"Yes—except for the really special one. I told you about that. His first command. I brought it over here with me. A beautiful little model."

"How small?"

Margaret hesitated. "Oh . . . well about that long." She held her hands about two feet apart.

Quint said quickly, "I don't call that little."

Dougall stood up and spoke for the first time, "It's small—compared with the original. Smallness, Mr Quint, is relative."

Lassiter, smiling to himself, cut off any reply from Quint, and said, "Perhaps we might see it?"

Dougall looked at Margaret and said, "I'll get it, love."

231

When Dougall came back with the model, he handed it to Lassiter, and Lassiter, not without some pleasure, knew that it was Quint the man had marked, not him, as a possible threat to Margaret Tucker's peace of mind. The man was no fool, whatever else he might be.

He stood up and carried the model to the window light. It was beautifully made and he knew that Bernard would have got every detail right. The hull space was big enough to hold the papers. As he fingered the details of the deck fittings and the bridge structure, Margaret said, "You think that could be the hiding place?"

Lassiter, his fingers probing and teasing the model, said, "It could be a hiding place, yes." But, he felt, not one that Bernard would have chosen. Anyone searching the bedroom would have suspected it at once. Still, you never knew. . . . Anyway, it proved their point that Mrs Tucker carried information which they wanted and which only an unhurried, unfrightening session with her would bring out. Maybe they had already brought it out. . . . He put a little pressure sideways on the forward gun turret. It turned through an angle of forty-five degrees and Lassiter felt the deck and superstructure move. He turned, put the model on the table, and slid the whole of the upperworks of the frigate backwards. It moved like the lid of an old-fashioned pencil box, coming clean away from the hull. The hollow interior was empty.

Quint said to Margaret, "Did you know the top came off like that?"

Margaret hesitated. She knew she was going to look a fool, but there was nothing she could do about it.

She said, "Yes, I did. But until now it had completely gone from my mind. When Bernard first showed it to me he opened it like that. But it was years and years ago and . . . well, I've never thought about it since. I really had forgotten."

Quint said quietly, "Well, I can see that might happen. But please, Mrs Tucker, do try to remember everything you know when we ask a question. It may seem silly or unimportant

to you—but not to us." He smiled, reassuring her. "After all—
the papers could have been in the model, and we might never
have found them."

Lassiter gave Quint good marks for his restraint, but he
knew that it was not going to last. He slid the top of the
model back into position.

Margaret said, "I'm sorry."

Quint pulled a sheet of paper from his pocket and passed it
to her.

"That's the police list, Mrs Tucker, of all the articles found
on your husband after his death. You gave them a receipt.
Would you just check through it."

Margaret read through the list. Then she nodded and said,
"Yes, those are all the things. They're in his dressing table
drawer at Lopcommon."

"Not all, Mrs Tucker." There was a sharper note in Quint's
voice. "The gold wristwatch is not there. You remember
getting that back, don't you?"

"Yes, I do. In fact I——"

"In fact—you what?"

"I remember being puzzled by it. You see, as far as I knew,
Bernard never wore a wristwatch. He always wore a fob or
pocket watch."

"Yes, we know. He left that in his London flat. He wore the
wristwatch because it is a very special watch. It combines a
small tape recorder. He needed it for the conference he
attended before coming down to Lopcommon. The watch is
very important Mrs Tucker—for two reasons. It will contain
his comments and, maybe, other people's conversations during
the conference. And also—since he was conscious for some time
before he died—very possibly some last recording by him. If
he did record anything—and being the man he was I think he
would have—he would certainly have stated where he had
hidden the papers. He would have wanted us to know that,
and he knew that we would not overlook the watch. We'd
like to know where the watch is. Can you help us with that?"

233

"How can I? I left it in the drawer when I went away."

"And you haven't been to the house since?"

"No."

Quint was silent for a moment or two and then looked at Lassiter.

Lassiter, relieved that Quint was staying with the brief they had worked out, knowing how much the other would have liked to have gone hard in, said gently, "Mrs Tucker, and you Mr Dougall—we know all about your personal relationship. We're not interested in it, but I hope you will both see that if we're to do our job properly we can't entirely ignore it. Sometimes small, quite innocent actions can complicate serious affairs like this one. So I must ask you——"

"You don't have to," Dougall said. "If Margaret had given the watch to me as a present she would have said so. And so would I. I haven't got the watch, Mr Lassiter. It was in the house when Margaret left. Now you say it has gone. Then somebody has pinched it. Neither of us has anything to hide."

Lassiter said, "You're on the wrong tack, Mr Dougall. If Mrs Tucker had given the watch to you, Mr Quint and I know that she would have said so openly. The watch has been stolen. That is as far as it goes at the moment. I wanted to raise quite a different point. And it's a delicate one. So—" he paused, knowing that it needed only the wrong word or inflexion to rouse this man, "—let's start again, shall we? And this time with you. Are you entirely in Mrs Tucker's confidence, Mr Dougall?"

"Yes, of course."

"Has she told you about a consultation she fairly recently had with her doctor, Doctor Harrison?"

"Yes, she has."

Margaret said, "I told Maxie while we were away together. But I can't see what this could possibly have to do with Bernard's papers."

Quint said sharply, "Then let me put something to you,

234

Mrs Tucker. We can't afford to overlook any possibility even though . . ." he schooled his rising impatience, forcing his words to a slower tempo ". . . it may mean distressing you. You have had periods in the past when you did things and didn't remember you had done them unless there was some concrete evidence which you couldn't ignore."

"Yes, I have. I used to take things from shops without knowing it until afterwards. But not for a long time now."

"But you wouldn't have known you'd done anything unless you'd found the articles in your hand or your pockets afterwards?"

"No . . . I suppose not. . . ."

"Then I want you to consider this, Mrs Tucker. Relations are severely strained between you and your husband. He comes home for a weekend—the weekend on which you have decided to tell him you love another man and intend to leave him. But it's some time before you get a chance to tell him. He works all Sunday on his reports and papers. You know they are important. He has said so. When he's finished he goes up to his room and puts the papers away safely somewhere. He comes down for a drink with you. You tell him about Mr Dougall. There's an argument, a quarrel between you, and finally he storms out of the house. That's right?"

"Yes. . . ."

"Leaving you in a highly emotional state . . . mentally very agitated. Would you agree?"

"Yes."

"You want to be free to marry another man. He's denying you that—quite irrationally, it seems in the circumstances. I wouldn't find it difficult to believe that under this emotional stress you too might act irrationally. You do understand what I'm suggesting, don't you?"

"No, I don't, Mr Quint."

"You could have gone up to his room merely wanting to strike back at him, at anything of his. You could have seen the frigate model, picked it up to smash it, and then instead have

235

opened it, perhaps guessing that his precious papers might be in it. Or, perhaps, the top just came away a little as you held it. There could have been papers in it. You could have taken them, burnt them in the fire, or ripped them up and put them in the dustbin. Ten minutes later you could have come out of your blankness and not remembered a thing about it."

"Putting it like that, I suppose I could. But I didn't!"

"Of course she bloody well didn't!" Maxie Dougall went to Margaret, sat on the divan beside her, and put his arm around her. "What the hell are you two playing at? It's as crazy a thought as suggesting that she might have had a lapse of memory and gone out after him and pushed him over the rocks. Whatever Commander Tucker did with his papers it's nothing whatever to do with Margaret. Commander Tucker hid the papers somewhere safe . . . all right, in Lopcommon if you like. Then he went out and slipped over the edge of a path. If he was the kind of man you say he was he'll have recorded what he did with the papers. Any moon-faced yokel from the leafy lanes in this part of the world would know the answer you want is in that watch—and it's been pinched while the house was empty. I could name a dozen men in these parts who go for quiet walks looking for pickings. Not professionals, just opportunists who, spotting an empty house, try their luck and aren't too greedy and——"

"All right, Mr Dougall." Lassiter interrupted him and stood up. "Neither Mr Quint nor I want to distress Mrs Tucker. We apologise if we have done so. We may seem devious to you, but we're not." He smiled. "We're just hopelessly at sea over this. Quite frankly we wanted to put the suggestion to Mrs Tucker because we hoped it might start her memory working or bring out something, no matter how small——"

"Well, I don't like that kind of thing!" Maxie Dougall stood up. "Nobody has the right to play around with another human being like that. Margaret's had her fill of that already from Bernard Tucker."

Margaret said, "No matter what Maxie says—and I quite understand why he's angry—I want to help you, so if there is anything else you would like to ask me I'll try and answer."

Lassiter said, "That's very nice of you, Mrs Tucker. There's only one thing we want—those papers. Commander Tucker almost certainly hid them in the house, probably somewhere in or near his bedroom, and almost certainly in a hiding place he contrived himself. Perhaps you'd like to think quietly about that? Go back in your memory and if anything occurs to you— some small incident, some act, or some touchiness on his part that surprised you at the time—well, then we'd be glad to hear of it." He smiled. "After all, you did forget about the top of the ship model coming off. There may well be something else like that."

Outside, the wind and rain were roaring through the tall firs, and the river was beginning to run high and brown with spate water. As Kerslake drove the two men off Quint said to him, "When we get back Mr Lassiter will give you a description of a gold wristwatch which belonged to Commander Tucker. It was taken from his bedroom at Lopcommon some time after Mrs Tucker left here, but before we searched the house. Have the description circulated."

"Yes, sir."

When they reached the Empress Hotel Quint went in, but Lassiter stayed in the car to give Kerslake a description of the watch. As Kerslake finished writing in his note book and closed it he said, "Is finding this watch important? I mean as far as these papers are concerned?"

"It might be. Who knows." In his own mind Lassiter was sure that it was not. Bernard Tucker had given his ship models away. In a sense he had also given his wife away and, against his will, had given himself away to a service which he hated. Resentment had gone hand in hand with his own weakness. He had married his wife, not from love, but with the hope of escape. In his last few moments he was not the kind to do Warboys or the Department any favours.

As Lassiter moved to get out of the car, Kerslake said, "May I ask you a question, sir?"

"Why not? It's a free country—but I don't promise any answer."

"Well, sir, when you and Mr Quint first interviewed me you asked questions about a lot of local people."

"We did."

"Including William Ankers."

"That's right."

"You can choke me off if I step out of line—but I presume he was probably hired by Commander Tucker to watch Mrs Tucker."

"That's so. And I presume you just can't understand why we haven't made any approach to him?"

"Well, frankly, yes, sir."

Lassiter leaned back in his seat. For a moment or two he was disposed to say nothing which would in any way encourage Kerslake. He would be happier staying where he was in the long run. But he would never accept that.

He said, "You're thinking or hoping that one day you might get a chance to come into our sort of work. Right?"

"It's in my mind, sir."

"Then you'd better learn some first principles. If a State matter is highly secret or confidential you don't enlarge your enquiries any more than you have to—particularly with seedy types like Ankers who can't keep their mouths shut in pubs and other places. You don't do this—unless you decide that the gain may be worth it. What would we get from Ankers that would offset the rumours he would spread and which the press would pick up in fifteen minutes flat?" He grinned. "It's bad enough having to rely on the professional ethics of doctors and solicitors. A lot of them gossip, you know. And I've known a few policemen who were guilty, too. Satisfy you?"

"Yes, sir."

"Good. And take my advice. You stay down here, Kerslake. In the wet and windy West Country."

*        *        *        *

That afternoon Billy Ankers drove to Bristol and posted a letter to Mrs Margaret Tucker. He hesitated a moment or two before dropping the letter through the mouth of the post box, a hesitation which came from a doubt whether he had asked for enough money. After all a thousand pounds would be nothing to Mrs Tucker. Perhaps he should have asked for double that. In the end he let the letter drop, comforting himself with the thought that if this approach went smoothly there could always be—after a wise interval—another approach. He drove home through the heavy rain with the car heater turned full on, sucking gently at his pipe. Opportunity seldom knocked twice at any door. A man had to look after number one as best he could in this world, because for sure nobody else would bother to. Yes, if he worked it properly he could always come again . . . and again perhaps. Why not? A nice little pension for life. . . .

At six o'clock that evening Kerslake was with Quint and Lassiter in Quint's room at the Empress Hotel. On the table close to the drawn curtains of the windows lay the gold wristwatch. Lassiter lounged in a chair nursing a glass of whisky. Quint sat on the edge of his bed in his shirt sleeves, forefinger and thumb of his right hand pulling gently at his lower lip. Outside the rain drummed at the window. Kerslake, standing by the window, waited uneasily. From their expressions, for all he could tell, he might have done wrong in the eyes of these two men. If he had, then he could kiss any private hopes goodbye. If that were to be so . . . well, at least, it was better than having made no bid, no move to trap a chance that might never come again to take him into their world.

Quint said, "Why did you pick on Ankers?"

"Because he was to some extent already involved. He'd been

239

watching Mrs Tucker for her husband. I guessed that."

"And I confirmed it for him," said Lassiter.

"Also—although he's never been caught—we've always felt he had itching fingers. He's not over-greedy ever, and he's been careful. He would know Mrs Tucker was away. He could have gone snooping around out there. I thought it was worth a try. After lunch I checked at the garage where he keeps his car. It was out."

"So you broke into his place." It was no question from Quint; a flat statement offering nothing.

"No, sir. I called on him at his rooms. The door was open so I walked in and had a look around."

Lassiter said, "I've met that kind of door. Where was the watch?"

"At the back of the gas meter. He wouldn't have tried to get rid of it until any heat had died down."

Quint said, "So you walked out with it and left the door open so that when he came back he would think that somebody had turned the place over?"

"Yes, sir. I emptied a few drawers and made a bit of a mess. He won't think it was anything official. We get a good dozen robberies of a similar kind every week here. I thought you would . . . well, prefer it that way since there is such a large element of discretion attached to——"

"Quite." Quint interrupted him, and then looked at Lassiter. "What do you think?"

Lassiter shrugged his shoulders. "I think it saves a lot of time and trouble. The watch was found at Lopcommon by us at the back of a drawer or in some other convenient place into which it might have accidentally slipped."

Quint stood up. "All right, Kerslake. You didn't go to Ankers' rooms. You haven't been here this evening with us. You have never seen the watch. Is that clear?"

"Yes, sir."

"All right, you can go. Just report here at the usual time tomorrow morning."

240

"Yes, sir. Thank you. Goodnight."

When Kerslake had gone, Quint picked up the telephone and asked for a London number. As he waited for the call, he said, "He was lucky."

"Why not? We all have our share. He knew how to handle it, too. Just at the moment though he doesn't know whether he's been patted on the back or kicked up the bottom."

"Which do you think?"

"I think he's big enough to take either. Overall it makes no difference. He's now a name and a face you won't forget."

"Some time I'll think about it."

A few moments later Quint was talking to Warboys. His first words were no surprise to Lassiter.

"Good evening, sir. You'll be glad to know that I've found Commander Tucker's watch. . . ."

Lassiter sipped his drink, his eyes on the wristwatch. The tape in it needed a special machine for any playback. Warboys would come down with it, and Warboys would play it to himself first—alone. It could be that neither he nor Quint would ever hear any part of it. If that happened it would be no loss to him but he knew that it would hurt Quint. No matter; one thing he was certain about was that Bernard Tucker would never have wasted any of his last few seconds of life on telling them where the papers had been hidden. Bernard Tucker was the last man in the world to have stood on the threshold of eternity concerned only with the desire to tidy up the affairs of a professional career which had so surely destroyed his own private life. Virtues and talents he had undoubtedly had, but little real courage to make a success of his longing for escape. There was nothing he could say in the few minutes before dying which could ensure him redemption; certainly not gasping out details of the hiding place of a pile of papers in which he must have recognised the same sort of deviousness and human weakness which had marked his own life. The only thing to be said in his favour was that he had died at the right moment, leaving his wife free to nourish and enjoy love

241

and real companionship with a man for the first time in her life. He was beyond touching her now.

Quint put the telephone down and said, "Warboys is coming early tomorrow. The watch tape is not to be touched until he arrives."

Lassiter drained his glass and got up to go to his own room.

*         *         *         *

Margaret lay in bed listening to the rain and, over its steady pulse, the sound of the swollen river. In these days because of the extensive draining of fields and the lower moorland slopes, which in the past had soaked up the water and held it, sponge-like, to run off slowly, the storm water found its way quickly to the valleys and brought fast rising spates, short-lived, but often violent. She knew this from Maxie, who slept, snoring a little, at her side. She had learnt so many things from him, the presence and names and habits of birds and animals which had always been around her but which she had never noticed; the quick, mouse-like movement of a tree-creeper in the garden pines and the brief flirt of goldcrests in the fir tops. It was as though he had given her a new pair of eyes and ears, and more than that he had given back to her, or made her rediscover, so much of herself which she had thought was gone for ever. To love and be loved, to regard and be regarded, to laugh with him and at herself, and to take a joy in the growing store of small jokes and intimacies with which their life was now threaded was like finding a treasure, long hidden and forgotten, and now suddenly restored.

She lay there and thought of the two men who had visited her. Lassiter she liked, but the other, Quint, reminded her at times of Bernard. Maxie didn't like Quint either; Maxie who had come as near to losing his temper as she had ever known when they had upset her, though she hadn't been as upset as Maxie had imagined. They had a job to do and needed her help. She'd been a fool not to remember about the top of the

242

frigate coming off—but it really had gone right from her mind. She lay back in the darkness, feeling the warmth of Maxie's back against her own, the room contained by the sound of the outside rain. Could she ever possibly have done that? Gone to the model and taken the papers? Burnt or destroyed them without ever knowing it?

She remembered Bernard taking her by the shoulders and shaking her, and the last words he had ever spoken to her, *Go on then! Live with this oaf! Sweat it out until you come to your senses. You stupid, silly bitch!* Bernard had said that, and pushed her away into her chair, her head hitting the top of the wooden frame. . . . What had she done after that? So far as she remembered she had just sat there, hearing him leave the house, reaching for her drink, numb and miserable, until life had come back to her and she had gone up to bed.

But it could have happened—just as it had happened in the town shops. She could have destroyed the papers. In that moment when he had pushed her away from him she had hated him, could have done anything. She turned over suddenly, put an arm around Maxie and held herself to him. He stirred in his sleep and mumbled something, and his movement and the blurred tones of his voice comforted her. She forced the thought away from her, shut her eyes and reached back in memory for other images. Bernard when he had first shown her the completed model: he'd been excited and pleased, boyish almost with a new toy. Those had been the days when she still hadn't realised what was happening to them. In those days, she recalled, when he worked about the house she would hear him whistling to himself. He always did that when he was concentrating on his handwork. He loved painting, smoothing the colour on some cabinet door with a brush, precise, exact, tolerating no bad workmanship. In Scotland on a visit together he had painted her aunt's little dinghy. She remembered her last visit to her aunt and the old lady saying 'It's time Bernard came again. The dinghy wants repainting. . . .' She had gone back to Bernard that time knowing that she would never see

243

her aunt alive again—realising, too, that she would never know Bernard again because he had moved out of the bedroom they had shared. He had taken over the guest room and bathroom, had repainted and papered it, and made it into his own private suite, rearranging it all to suit himself, and with not a word of explanation from him. She, knowledgeable at last, had been too proud to ask for a reason. And now he was dead, and all this fuss about papers and a wristwatch, a fuss which could only be far removed from her, from this new life with Maxie, because for her Bernard had been dead for many years. Slipping and falling to his death was not the moment of his going. He had been already long gone, unable to be touched by her or by any anger she might have had against him.

In the darkness she smiled suddenly to herself. It was odd about the wristwatch. Christmas would be with them in a few days and she had been undecided in her mind about the present she would give Maxie, narrowing the choice between a new pair of fieldglasses or a gold wristwatch. Nothing now would make her buy him a watch. That would have to wait . . . a watch which was really a tape recorder . . . she began to drift into sleep . . . that was just the kind of gadget Bernard would love . . . this new-to-her Bernard, a man like Quint and Lassiter . . . secret government work . . . and, right in the middle of an important affair, slipping accidentally to his death after quarrelling with her. . . . Lying out there in the rain . . . dear God, poor Bernard, knowing he had only a few minutes to live. If he had used the watch, what would he have said? Well, if they found it they would know. What would you say if you knew you were dying, leaving a life which had soured all happiness and a wife and marriage which had long been empty of love? Poor Bernard. She stirred as she felt tears lip the corners of her eyes.

Maxie moved in his sleep, turned and with a sleep-drugged sigh put his arm around her and drew her to him. She lay close to him, tears breaking across her cheek, as she remembered a naval officer walking up the lochside towards her, sunlight lacquering the pine and rowan growths of the shore cliffs and cloud shadows racing across the first purple of the new heather on the high tops.

*    *    *    *

Warboys arrived at six o'clock in the morning. Quint had booked a room for him at the Empress Hotel.

Raincoated, untired because he had been chauffeur-driven, he stood in his room and took the watch from Quint. On his bed lay his suitcase which contained the special playback machine for the watch tape. Holding the watch in the palm of his hand, he said, "Where did you find it?"

"Officially—there was a break in the back panel of the dressing-table drawer. It had slipped through and rested on a strut behind the drawer out of sight."

"Convenient. You can tell me the truth later." He rubbed his free hand across his chalk-white, pointed chin and went on, "I'll play it alone. I'll call you later."

"Yes, sir."

When Quint was gone Warboys took the playback machine from his case and carried it to the window table. He opened the back of the watch, took out the small tape cassette and fitted it to the machine which was battery operated. The tape had run through its full length because Bernard had not switched it off whenever he had last used it. There was no doubt in his mind when that had been. He pressed the rewind key and sat down and lit himself a cigarette. He waited, looking out of the window, strengthening but weak daylight creeping over the river, the rain which had marked the night beginning to thin. The tide was running in, creeping up the mud banks. An old gravel barge lay abandoned and rotting on the far shore, its bows plugged into the mud and rushes. He had seen more tides come and go than he wished to know, the tides of the sea and the estuaries and the tides in the unimportant lives of men who refused to acknowledge that unimportance. A small cloud of black-headed gulls in winter plumage hung over the water, dropping now and then to the surface to scavenge. Men did the same, he thought, but with less elegance and grace. Although he was untired by the long night drive, there was a weariness inside him which time would abate though never banish. *The devotion to something afar from the sphere of our sorrow.* He'd probably got it wrong. Bernard would have corrected him. A grief, while life persisted, never to be banished. . . . *And grief itself be mortal.* But before then a grief to be rebuked, a secret love to be cruelly wounded . . . or, more deadly, simply ignored—just the quiet low hiss of an empty tape the only requiem for an unbidden, unwelcome love.

The tape rewound, he switched it to playback and sat listening as almost at once Sir Harry Parks' voice came over. *Two reasons. The first few people can escape. I want the money. I've lived my life for a cause. I've a wife and grown-up children and grand-children. You can have a cause and a family, Commander, but the family suffers. The work you do takes from them, and you give little back. You have to neglect them. You become a stranger to them. . . .*

The recording went on, still with Sir Harry, and Warboys knew why Bernard had made it. It marked the genuineness of the old man's motives. Not their worthiness, but the clearance from deceit, from any trap being laid. This was the professional Bernard marking shrewdly the moments which had formed his decision to recommend the purchase of the documents.

Then as Sir Harry finished speaking—*A nice, quiet, kindly winter morning. I wish though that I'd never lived to see it*—Bernard's own voice came crowding after it, almost without pause, but the passage of time between the recordings was marked by the anguish and shock in his words. *Jesus Christ! Jesus, Jesus. . . .* And then silence for a while. Warboys, sitting there, was in the darkness of the night with him, lying broken on the rocks at the edge of the floodfilled brook, dying with him, knowing that if some miracle could have transformed time and chance that he would have taken Bernard's place and gladly died for him. And then the voice came again more controlled now, but the

246

shock alive in the heavy breathing and clearer still in the words
. . . *God in heaven . . . I would never have believed it. Never. . . .*
*That such a thing could happen.* . . . Bernard's voice grew precise
and deliberate, each word exhausting the slender store of his
wasting seconds of life.

Warboys listening, a lean hand cupped tightly against his
mouth as though to contain his own pain, knew that these
words were not for him alone, that these were for other ears and
would have to be heard, though there was nothing in them for
him except the plainness of a duty to perform, a vital obligation
never to wipe them from the tape unless he wished to add
another betrayal to the lasting one which he, himself, had
already made of Bernard. These words must stay and be heard.

When they were finished, there was for a moment or two
the sound of the empty tape moving, the faint noise of the
nearby brook, and then a long, choking groan, the fight for
breath, for the grace of a few more seconds. Bernard spoke
again for the last time, weakly—*Tell Warboys . . . that we wound*
*without willing it.*

The tape ran on and on without words and finally ended.
And of those last words there were two that carried all, said all
that Warboys would have wished unsaid. *Tell Warboys.* With
his last breath he had removed himself, refusing to speak
directly to him, calling him Warboys. *Tell Warboys.*

With a cold, numbed mind, working automatically, Warboys
erased the message to himself from the tape, and also the first
section of Sir Harry Parks' talk. He left only the middle section.
That, though there could be little personal comfort in it for
himself, was something he could do for Bernard even after
death, something which justice demanded he did.

He went into Quint's room and found Lassiter there, too.

He said, "Telephone Mrs Tucker. I want to go out and see
her later this morning. You can take me out there. You can
tell her we've found the watch and that there's a part of the
tape that concerns her. She must hear it." He paused, and
then added, "There was nothing on the tape which helps us

247

about the papers. Commander Tucker never mentioned them. No matter what else has to be done—they still have to be found. I expect them to be found. When we've dealt with Mrs Tucker I suggest you concentrate on them."

He turned and left the room.

CHAPTER FOURTEEN

MAXIE HAD GONE out after breakfast for his morning walk. Through the kitchen window where she was working Margaret could see the river at the bottom of the garden, bank high with racing flood water. The rain had stopped. She smiled to herself as she thought of Maxie, walking somewhere across the fields or through the valley woods. He was unused to having someone to look after him and always left her after breakfast because he knew that she would not let him help about the house. Soon, she thought, they would have to talk about his future. But it was a move that would have to come from him. She would do nothing which in any way touched his pride and his natural independence. When he did talk, she knew that she would accept anything which he proposed. From her love that would come easily. There were plenty of things he could find to do, but he would have to find whatever it was for himself, and then she would be with him, encouraging and helping. Once or twice he had talked about farming. That would suit him. He was good with his hands, practical, and already knew a lot about the work. One thing he would never be was an artist. He knew it and she knew it. She turned and looked at a painting of a mute swan done by him which she had—overriding all his protests—hung on the kitchen wall. The bird looked like some wooden, haughty dowager, frozen in a clumsy moment of affronted dignity. She chuckled to herself. No, Maxie would do something . . . something which would satisfy him as a man, and no matter what it was she would be wholeheartedly with him.

The telephone rang. It was Lassiter speaking from the Empress Hotel.

He said, "Good morning, Mrs Tucker."

"Good morning, Mr Lassiter, I'm glad you rang because there's something——"

"Just a moment, Mrs Tucker. If I may speak first. I wanted you to know that we've found Commander Tucker's watch. He made a recording before he died but said nothing about the hiding place of his papers. But that isn't the point at the moment. Part of the recording concerns you directly."

"What do you mean?"

"Well, I can't say more than that because I haven't heard it. The head of our department, a Mr Warboys, came down from London this morning and he's the only one who has listened to the tape. He'd like to know if it would be convenient for him to come out later this morning and see you?"

"Why, yes, of course."

"Good. He'll bring the tape to play to you."

"All right. I shall be here. But what is it? I mean is it a personal thing from Bernard to me?"

"I can't tell you what it is, Mrs Tucker, because I haven't heard the tape. All I know is that it is very important that you should hear it—otherwise Mr Warboys wouldn't be concerning himself with it. What was it, by the way, that you wanted to say to me just now?"

"Oh, that. . . . Oh, yes—well it was something I thought of in bed last night, just before I went to sleep. You know, about where the papers might be hidden. I don't imagine it really will be of any help, but you did say that any little thing I could remember——"

"Yes, I did. And you have remembered something?"

"Yes. The last time I went to Scotland, a few months before my aunt died, well, when I came back I found that Bernard had moved out from the bedroom we were sharing. He had taken over the guest bedroom and bathroom. Quite frankly, I realise now, that was the end of things between us. . . ."

She paused, the memory even now not an easy one to hold.

Lassiter said, "And what particular thing, as far as the papers are concerned, came into your mind, Mrs Tucker?" His voice was quiet, sympathetic.

"Well, he'd redecorated the bedroom and the bathroom. But what I was thinking—this was this morning, when I woke up and it came into my mind again—was about the bathroom door. The bathroom originally had a separate entrance from the landing, but he had blocked this door up and made another entrance directly from his bedroom so that it became a self-contained suite. So it would have been quite easy for him to have made some, well, hiding place, wouldn't it? To do with the new or the old door."

"It certainly would, Mrs Tucker. And thank you for thinking of it. It might be very important."

"And you'll be out later this morning?"

"Not me, Mrs Tucker. Mr Warboys and Mr Quint will come."

"I see. . . ."

Margaret, after Lassiter had said goodbye, put the telephone down. As she did so she heard the letter box flap rattle in the hall, and knew that the morning post had arrived.

There was only one letter. It was for her, the address typewritten. She took it into the kitchen and sat down at the table, dropping it in front of her, her mind still occupied with the telephone call. Bernard had used the tape recorder before he died. What could he or would he have said either to her or about her? Lying out there in the rain . . . dying, and probably still full of anger towards her . . . more than probably very angry because he was not a man to go from one mood to another quickly. She was suddenly full of a weakness of spirit which was almost physical at the simple thought of hearing his voice again. She would be taken back to that night. She could feel his hands on her now, pushing her away in contempt and anger, wounding her, rejecting her. What words would he have left for her?

She pushed the thought away from her. Dear God, she thought, they've got the watch and there was nothing she could do that could alter what Bernard had said. Let them find the papers and go away from her life altogether. She just wanted to be left alone in peace and love with Maxie . . . just left alone to begin to live in the tranquillity and the security of this new life here with Maxie, with all its promise for the future.

She picked up the letter and opened it. It was typewritten and carried no address or date. It read:

*Dear Madam,*

*I want you to be sensible and not frightened about this letter. I've got nothing against your good self, but have to think of number one, and we can arrange things between our good selves without any trouble. But don't think I'm not serious. I just want one thousand (£1000) pounds for keeping quiet about what I saw the night Commander Tucker died. This to be a once for all payment, absolutely, but don't think I wont make trouble if you try any tricks or mention any of this to somebody else. Just between us it all is—and arrangements to be told you by me for payment in another letter soon to your good self. Any nonsense and the police will know, so I rely on your complete complience.*

*The night of that Sunday Commander Tucker died I was for my own personal reasons up at Lopcommon Barton and saw him leave the house and your good self some time after also leaving it. (You was wearing a raincoat, and a beret sort of hat.) Briefly, to spare you the memory, I followed you and saw you, after hiding, step out of the bushes and push your late husband over the path edge. No more I will say, except that Commander Tucker was no friend of mine, and I think he got what he deserved which explains this letter. Also I don't blame you because I know about your little shop-lifting spells without knowing about it and reckon this was probably per the same.*

252

*So don't worry, £1000 is nothing to you and I wont bother you
again. But no tricks or else. A further letter to follow with instructions
and so on.*

*Yours respectfully,*
*A GENUINE WELLWISHER*

Margaret sat, holding the letter in her shaking hands,
staring at it, the black lines of type fogged by the sudden tears
in her eyes, her mind a chaos of swift, disjointed thoughts. Had
she gone out that night? Gone out, not knowing it, just as in
some shops. . . . Dear God, no, no, no!

But this man had seen her. He described her clothes. Bernard
going to his death over the path edge; Bernard lying there in
the night while she walked back, unknowing, and then waited
for him to return; Bernard knowing she had done it; Bernard
knowing why . . . knowing . . . and lying there as his life went.
Suddenly she remembered the recording watch. She saw him
lying there, knowing he was going to die. With that night's
anger in him still he would never have spared her.

She dropped the letter and leaned forward, holding her head
with her trembling hands, a storm of silent grief and anguish
shaking her body. . . . The men would come, would play the
tape to her. That was why they were coming. . . . Her whole
nature rebelled at the thought. That was something she could
never face. From out of the darkness Bernard, his brief love for
her soon dead, had reached back for her, denying her all
the freedom and love she had longed for from him and finally
discovered in another man; Bernard who had made her what
she was so that in the end, from deep within herself, un-
controlled, unknowing, she had found the strength and the
dark power to walk out into the night after him and destroy him.
Only a little while ago she had felt herself standing on the lip
of all happiness, watching Maxie slipping on his pilot coat
before leaving the house, going with him to the door and
kissing him as he went.

She looked up, her body shaking with the misery of silent

sobs, and saw the garden and the river beyond it. Slowly, against the turmoil in her, she felt and welcomed the broad warmth and comfort of an unseen, familiar hand cradle her temple and knew the beginning of a strange peace and a clear purpose.

She stood up and walked away from the table, leaving the letter and its envelope lying there.

\* \* \* \*

Maxie came down the side of the valley through a pine plantation and out on to the river bank. The flood was running high, almost to the level of the meadow. He stood for a moment or two looking downstream. Fifty yards away the spate was cascading over a weir, a chocolate-coloured frenzy of water. He watched, fascinated by the power of the flood. Tree trunks and old branches swept by in a ragged armada. A heron, flapping lazily up the valley, legs trailing, saw him and veered away. A flock of lapwings rose from the top of the meadow. He watched them and saw a handful of fieldfares with them break off into their own flight pattern. He turned away towards the house, picking his way along the muddy path.

The rain had gone, the sky was lightening. The sun would soon break through. And his own sun, he thought, had already broken through. He had what he wanted—though nothing hoped for and finally gained was ever the same as the image which had been long treasured. Still, he had no grumbles. All this business over Commander Tucker had been a surprise. But that would soon be done. Quint and Lassiter would find their stupid papers and clear off. The sooner the better. He wanted to be alone with Margaret, and wanted beyond that the coming of that still amorphous freedom whose definition, now that it was so unexpectedly and quickly within his reach, he could not yet bring himself to picture in definite terms. He only knew that it could not be complete until he was entirely

254

alone, and on his own. Fate had dropped everything into his hands so easily. Margaret had given him the house and willed all she owned to him. If he loved her it was only a form of pride in his physical and personal delight in her. He had trapped her like a bird, caged her, and treated her well. There was time and plenty ahead before he need consider his own true freedom. First of all he wanted her truly to himself. That would come when these men went. They would buy a farm, and after a few years of quiet establishment he would by some simple act of concealed ruthlessness, smooth, never to be questioned, truly become his own man.

A jack-snipe got up from a clump of sedges almost at his feet and he watched it zigzag in alarm up the river and disappear around the bend below the house. As he did so, he saw a blue patch riding down on the surface of the flood. For a moment or two he watched it, thinking it was an empty fertiliser sack picked up by the rising waters. Then the blueness was lifted by a swirling fall in the current and he caught a glimpse of a face, of fair hair and the flash of a half bare arm.

He stood on the bank, shocked as though a sudden blow had been dealt him; stood, watching the blueness, knowing that it was no drifting sack, knowing the blueness of Margaret's dress as she had sat opposite him at breakfast, knowing the fair hair which he had caressed that morning when he had drawn the firm length of her body to him. Reason abandoned him leaving only a sudden rage. He knew that he stood now watching another turn of Fate in his favour, a Fate that had already worked too busily and quickly for him, doling out its charity to him who had been born into charity, had lived on charity, and who hated charity because it had usurped the place of love and deeply sapped his self-respect. Here now it was making another offering to him as though without its bounty he by himself could achieve nothing.

Margaret, his wife to be, the woman who had already given him everything she had, came rolling down towards him, spun and twisted by the strong flood, not a woman but an object, an

255

empty blue sack, flotsam lifted and being carried away by the waters. Over his anger he heard an inner voice almost shout into his ears, *See, I'm doing it for you! You would never have found the courage, never have found the will in yourself to do it!*

He watched her go by and saw her face momentarily as her body rolled and one of her hands broke water as though in a gesture of farewell. The simple, random movement suddenly freed him from his anger, from all design, from everything except the swift birth of a new truth about himself. He stripped off his pilot jacket, kicked off his gum boots, and threw himself into the river to go after her.

*    *    *    *

Warboys stood by her bed. Outside Margaret could see the rise of a faint evening mist hanging about the trunks of the pine trees and faintly she could hear the sound of the still swollen river.

Warboys said, "Would you like me to pull the curtains and put the light on, Mrs Tucker?"

She shook her head. Maxie had left them together reluctantly against Warboys' request. She wanted him back, felt now in her weakness that she could never bear him far from her, felt, too, uncertain about this tall, grave man with his pale face and still, dark eyes. He was of Bernard's world from which nothing good had come to her.

Warboys said, "I was a friend of your husband's, a very close friend. He made a tape before he died, a tape in which he spoke personally first to you and then to me. The words he left for me I have wiped from the tape. My reason for doing so belongs to me. . . ."

He put out a hand towards the instrument which he had set on her bedside table and Margaret saw his eyes half-close for a moment as though he were shutting out pain, closing off some memory which haunted him.

She said, "I don't understand it, but I only know that I am

256

sorry for you . . . strangely, perhaps, more sorry than I am for myself and for all that has happened. . . ."

Warboys said, "Listen to the tape, Mrs Tucker. The words are for you." He switched on the machine and walked to the window and stood with his back to her as the tape began to play.

Margaret lay in the dying light of the December evening and suddenly, distantly, faintly distorted but unmistakably Bernard's, the voice inhabited the room with its opening anguish. . . .

*Jesus Christ! Jesus, Jesus. . . .*

There was a pause during which Margaret caught the sound of Bernard's breathing, heavy, fighting for the strength to go on speaking, and then came his next words, calmer, growing controlled against the distress of his body.

*God in heaven . . . I would never have believed it. Never. . . . That such a thing could happen. . . . I was coming along the path, a path I've known for years, and I . . . I slipped. . . . God help me, such a stupid, stupid thing to do. . . .*

Margaret shut her eyes. She saw Bernard lying out in the night, knowing he was dying, saw nothing but that as the tape ran silently for a while, and then Bernard began to speak again.

*Tell Margaret this—that in my own way, if only for a time, I loved her, could have wished it to have been more than it was but could find nothing . . . nothing in me worthy of all that was offered because my eyes looked for other things, things, too, which I gained and then found only worth despising. . . . I ask for no forgiveness, only perhaps some understanding. Tell her, I regret my anger this evening, that I wish her all the joy which she deserves and pray for it with all my heart in these last few minutes of my time . . . and that time too short for any hope of grace for me. . . . To be taken so stupidly like this after all the wartime days of danger. Fate knows how to belittle us all even in death when we merit it. . . .*

The tape ran silently on.

Warboys moved from the window and switched off the machine.

257

He said quietly, "There is no more, Mrs Tucker—except this. You have no reason for reproaching yourself or nursing stupid fears of what you might have done. We've seen the anonymous letter you received. It's a pack of lies. You will have no more trouble in that direction. Forget you ever received it."

He closed the lid of the machine and picked it up.

Margaret, her face turned from him, said, "It could have been all so different. Thank you for letting me hear it. . . . Poor Bernard. . . ."

Moving to the door Warboys said, "Shall I tell Mr Dougall to come up?"

"Please. . . ."

He went out, and she lay there, the memory of Bernard vividly in her mind, the memory of the man who in the last few minutes of his life had spoken to her with truth and affection.

The door opened and Maxie came into the room. He crossed to the bed and sitting on it raised her and, putting his arms around her, held her close, saying nothing, just holding her and stroking her hair as she pressed her face into his shoulder. After a while he held her away from him, kissed her gently on the lips, and then said, "We're going to have to look after you, girl, better than we have done till now. You're a rare one for getting the wrong notions in that head of yours. But there'll be no more of that not while I'm around and that'll be for all the seasons of our lives. . . ."

*       *       *       *

Quint watched Kerslake reading the letter. He was young, about the same age as he had been himself when Commander Tucker had given him his chance to join the department. The people at the top went, others moved up and there had to come the new hands to leaven the bottom of the pile. From them came just a few who had the skills to go with their ambition.

258

Kerslake handed the letter back to him and Quint said, "You know who wrote it?"

Kerslake nodded. "Ankers. Borrowed typewriter—could be traced."

Quint began to tear the letter into small pieces. Kerslake watched him pile the fragments into the ashtray on the table and set fire to them. Flame and a little smoke wreathed upwards, a tiny pyre.

Quint said, "There's no truth in it. Commander Tucker gave a full account of his accident on the tape. Mr Warboys wants no *official* action taken."

Kerslake smiled. "I understand, sir. I'll talk to him privately at the right moment. For the rest of his days if he's needed for anything he'll be on a string. Just pull it—and he'll dance for you."

Quint said quietly, "Would you like it to be for us?"

"Yes, sir."

Kerslake looked out of the window, at the evening sunlight on the tide-swollen river, at the traffic crawling across the old town bridge, at a familiar scene which he knew he would soon be leaving. He was well content.

\* \* \* \*

Lassiter handed the Parks' papers to Warboys, the roll of documents and letters tightly bound by three flat, strong rubber bands just as they had been left by Commander Tucker in their hiding place.

He said, "When Commander Tucker put in the new bathroom door from his bedroom he used three hinges. Between the top and the middle one he made a long cavity covered by the apparently continuous run of the face of the casing. The edges of this were masked each end by the hinge plates screwed to the door casing. Taking out the screws of the top and middle hinge—you could do it in a few moments with a coin—allowed a piece of casing to be pulled out like a slide. The back of the slide was covered with a layer of lead to muffle any hollow sound if tapped. It was a very nice piece of work. I'd already examined the door a few times before Mrs Tucker pin-pointed it. Bad mark to me, I'm afraid, sir."

Warboys nodded, scarcely hearing what Lassiter had said. He held the roll of papers in his hands. They might be used or they might not. He would hand them over and take his reward in due time . . . in due time. Time was now the enemy, arrayed and inexorably waiting, to be lived through until grief itself became mortal.

*    *    *    *

Outside, high in the pine trees by the river a pair of coal tits were calling to one another as the evening light went. Maxie, who had sat watching over Margaret until sleep had claimed her, stood by the bed. In the shadowed room, in this house by the river, he accepted with a firm, quiet peace of heart and mind that he owed an everlasting debt to that Fate against which he had known anger. Through it there had been revealed to him the reality of a love which he would honour and cherish for the rest of his days.